The Treasures of Saint Germain

(Matt Drake #14)

By

David Leadbeater

Copyright 2016 by David Leadbeater
ISBN: 978-1536903324

All rights reserved. No part of this publication may be reproduced, distributed, or transmitted in any form or by any means, including photocopying, recording, or other electronic or mechanical methods, without the prior written permission of the publisher/author except in the case of brief quotations embodied in critical reviews and certain other non-commercial uses permitted by copyright law.
All characters in this book are fictitious, and any resemblance to actual persons living or dead is purely coincidental.

This ebook is for your personal enjoyment only. This ebook may not be re-sold or given away to other people. If you would like to share this ebook with another person, please purchase any additional copy for each reader. If you're reading this book and did not purchase it, or it was not purchased for your use only, then please return it and purchase your own copy. Thank you for respecting the hard work of this author.

Thriller, adventure, action, mystery, suspense, archaeological, military, historical

Other Books by David Leadbeater:

The Matt Drake Series
The Bones of Odin (Matt Drake #1)
The Blood King Conspiracy (Matt Drake #2)
The Gates of hell (Matt Drake 3)
The Tomb of the Gods (Matt Drake #4)
Brothers in Arms (Matt Drake #5)
The Swords of Babylon (Matt Drake #6)
Blood Vengeance (Matt Drake #7)
Last Man Standing (Matt Drake #8)
The Plagues of Pandora (Matt Drake #9)
The Lost Kingdom (Matt Drake #10)
The Ghost Ships of Arizona (Matt Drake #11)
The Last Bazaar (Matt Drake #12)

The Alicia Myles Series
Aztec Gold (Alicia Myles #1)
Crusader's Gold (Alicia Myles #2)

The Torsten Dahl Thriller Series
Stand Your Ground (Dahl Thriller #1)

The Disavowed Series:
The Razor's Edge (Disavowed #1)
In Harm's Way (Disavowed #2)
Threat Level: Red (Disavowed #3)

The Chosen Few Series
Chosen (The Chosen Trilogy #1)
Guardians (The Chosen Tribology #2)

Short Stories
Walking with Ghosts (A short story)
A Whispering of Ghosts (A short story)

Connect with the author on Twitter: @dleadbeater2011
Visit the author's website: **www.davidleadbeater.com**

All helpful, genuine comments are welcome. I would love to hear from you.
davidleadbeater2011@hotmail.co.uk

DEDICATION

For Mum and Dad.

CHAPTER ONE

Coincidence didn't sit well with Tyler Webb. There was always a man—or a plan—behind even the most innocent-seeming flight of chance.

Take the French city of Versailles, for instance. Founded by the will of Louis XIV, it had been the capital of the Kingdom of France for the whole of Saint Germain's lifetime, then just a few short years after the Count's death, that particular honor had been bestowed upon Paris.

Take the gruesomely bloated and romanced legends that surrounded the immortals of Transylvania for example—and then consider that the Count was born and raised there. Take the endless sightings after his supposed death in 1784, right up to this very day . . .

Webb shivered involuntarily. The emotion was not physical, he knew, but it should be. Now reduced to a gutter rat, the once great leader of the Pythians, in his opinion the greatest shadow organization that had ever been formed, whilst finding many parts of his new life greatly odorous, delighted in a certain few. In fact they were so juicily magnificent that the entire collapse of his organization and previous life was almost worth it.

He stood amongst a gaggle of tourists, staring at the black gates of the Palace of Versailles, grateful for the cold day as it enabled him to use a scarf and hat to help conceal his features. It was getting late too, the slow creep of ink across the skies aiding those who skulked and crept and loitered everywhere.

Stalking was so much easier when you were a lowly civilian. But three times now, Webb had let it interfere with his ultimate quest. Each time the sensations grew, the payoff increased, and the obsession deepened. The dark shadows sang to him in a way they never had before. The molten thrill of lurking outside windows and doors, trailing victims from empty bus stops, hounding a lonesome figure down a dark alley even here in Versailles, was hotter now than at any other time in his life. Maybe he had more to lose. Maybe the ever-present danger to himself had lit a different inner fire. A laughing couple marched by, their happiness interrupting his reveries.

Should he?

The man looked wimpy, kind of bookish. No doubt the submissive in that relationship. The woman was loud, confident, athletic and vigorous. Webb liked the look of the challenge. He almost started to move, practically put one foot in front of the other, before remembering the crucial and time-dependent significance of his situation.

The scroll led you here. The first clue led you here. Despite everything that has happened you still have . . . contacts . . .

Webb had maintained just a few, mainly those who could facilitate his efforts, turn a tricky situation into a manageable one. Take the Palace of Versailles, for example. Only a man with clever and secretive means could sneak in there uninvited, at night, with a dark, clandestine purpose in mind. Webb surveyed the scene. Too many tourists, too much light. One shady character across the way who almost seemed to be studying him.

Webb shook off the paranoia. It wasn't good. It was what *he* did to others.

But still . . .

The already-thick miasma that surrounded his intrigues and schemes had recently thickened. Another party was in play, one Webb had not counted on. Chiefly, because he'd never heard of them and still didn't really understand their agenda. Webb shrugged. Those were the breaks, the twists and turns of lifelong dreams and maneuvers coming to fruition. You rolled with it or you lost.

Rather than branching off any of his Pythian dealings, Webb thought the new players were centered around the Saint Germain conspiracy and had been alerted to him purely because of his most recent investigations and breakthroughs. He had the same people who'd facilitated entry into the palace tonight looking into them and their plots. It wouldn't take too long and should prove to be an interesting new dossier of information when complete.

It was time to lose even the barest hint of a trail and enjoy a good hunt in the process. The couple had melted away, much to his chagrin, but he soon saw another acceptable candidate—a man and wife, probably locals—hurrying past the palace without even a glance, heads down, and carrying a heavy shopping bag between them. How quaint, Webb thought. How sweet. A shame he didn't have the time to utterly destroy all they held dear.

Webb slipped away quickly, careful to take note of faces, colors of clothing, backpacks and other stand-out items at all his peripherals so he could later double-check any that might stay with him. The man and wife hurried along, not speaking, and he followed in their wake. He took a while to move up close, made his presence felt, then pretended to dally so they pulled ahead. Already he could see the tell-tale signs in the woman, the half-glances backward, the increase in pace, the tense set to her shoulders.

A quick check of the time revealed he could take things a bit further, so he pushed ahead and made eye contact with the woman, unable to hide the smirk that creased his features. Her look of fear mingled with distaste excited him. He made a move toward them. The woman slowed, then took in her immediate surroundings so fast Webb worried her neck might snap.

Sadly, there were many others around so Webb melted into the background. No longer a threat. It was time to return to the palace, but then a familiar perverse craving pulled him up short.

Take it a little further.

He ran across the road, making a beeline for the woman and her daughter, grinning from ear to ear. She stopped and now her husband noticed, staring at Webb with narrow eyes. He reached into the waistband of his trousers, hoping they'd think he had a gun there but not really caring which way they took it. The man stepped in front of the woman, visibly trembling. Passersby stared at him with curiosity. Webb ran hard, straight up to him, and then slowed, leaning in.

"Be seeing you later," he whispered, then ran on.

Dark excitement and deep pleasure bubbled through him.

Score one to Webb, he thought.

And left them staring at his back.

Chuckling then, he slowed and blended back in with the tourist crowd as the gates to the palace once again came into view up ahead. In all his vicious diversions he now realized he'd failed to carry out the one task he'd set out to do. Lose any tail. He put it down to enthusiasm and moved on. In a previous life as leader of the Pythians he'd have dropped someone down a well for such insubordination.

Webb was different now. This new life had changed him. He blended with the other peasants and riff-raff without any sign of distaste, and was pleased to see how far he'd come in just a few weeks. Give him another month and he'd be riding the freakin' *bus*.

A chirp alerted him to a cellphone message. It was time to get serious. Webb saw many tourists were now drifting away, which made him more noticeable in the wide expanse before the main golden gates. Flat, paved ground stretched out in all directions, broken only by the low walls and railings that surrounded the great palace.

The French chateau was a magnificent structure, filling the horizon. Webb left the main gate behind and wandered around the perimeter for a while, moving purposely but carefully toward a predesignated spot. Now, his heart was pounding. Now, he would seek out and find the second clue on the road to St. Germain's greatest treasures.

So far the scroll he'd bought from Ramses had proven utterly invaluable.

Webb thought about the scroll as he moved in. The tattered mishmash of parchments had paid off; Leopold had spent decades searching for St. Germain, closely, jealously guarding every secret he'd found until dying in the 1940s. Webb wasn't entirely sure what had happened to the scroll after that and how it came to Ramses, and didn't care a jot. All he cared about was that it was now tucked safely inside his coat pocket, double-zipped and wrapped in plastic. Webb had already studied it at length, though had taken care not to get too far ahead. Some pleasures were worth savoring.

The Treasures of Saint Germain

The pages were in the order they had been written; and in the order Leopold had traveled whilst on his great quest. Each passage an insight into what had happened that very day, sometimes even written as the German walked and searched. Webb found he could get into the man's mind, feel his excitement just by reading a paragraph. Many musings, thoughts and random ideas littered the passages—it took some doing to pick the bones out of it.

Purpose? Or circumstance? Leopold must have been a lonely man, living with himself and his notes, his obsession. Webb wanted it all, but knew he had to progress at Leopold's pace, not his own.

The ciphers were the key.

CHAPTER TWO

Webb approached a small, insignificant gate: a staff or service entrance. A shifty looking man stood there, transferring his weight from foot to foot. His eyes locked with Webb's and the requirement was known.

"This way. Hurry."

Webb wanted nothing less. He enjoyed the straight talk. He followed in the man's wake, straight into the closing palace, searching the lengthening shadows all around for any signs of pursuit. Nothing. If someone else was there, they were good.

"We have to be quick," the man said in an English accent. "They don't start getting antsy for a half hour after the doors close, but then . . ." he left it hanging, such a terrible threat.

"Who are you?" the man asked as he led the way inside.

But Webb, never one to reveal too much, found he could speak no words as he stepped through the old king's palace. The sudden onslaught of all that gilded gold, the mirrored-surface floors, the painted masterpieces that adorned the walls, the high, open spaces all lavishly decorated with exquisite detail, touched with an expert's eye. Webb could have spent days in here, studying this stunning symbol of the ancient regime, deciding what he'd most like to destroy or purloin.

"They said to leave you alone," the Englishman now said. "But I'm not sure I can do that."

Webb finally acknowledged the vulgarity with legs, seeing not for the first time one of the downsides of setting out on one's own. Normally he'd have some thick-necked Neanderthal teach this slug its place—but Webb had never been a real fighter.

"Carry out your instructions to the letter," Webb said without emotion. "I assume they said they would release your son or daughter when I was done?"

"Wife." The man swallowed quickly, his face furrowed with anguish.

Webb slowed a little, enjoying the man's fear. "Don't worry,

The Treasures of Saint Germain

I'm sure they're taking very special care of your wife."

"What does that mean?"

"Do you have a picture?"

The man fished out a folded photograph, worry making him appear a decade older, shoulders hunched in submission. Webb saw a pretty brunette with wide eyes and an even wider smile.

"Ah," he said. "Yes. So long as she keeps them happy I'm sure she'll remain safe." He had absolutely no idea as to her fate, but loved to instil the dread and see the panic take hold.

He waved at the gleaming rooms ahead. "Maybe you should hurry."

"Yes, yes." The man took off as if his feet were on fire. Gilt, gleaming wood and sparkling chandeliers lashed by as Webb was spurred along to a comparatively small room somewhere in back. Webb knew this was the bedroom where Le Comte de Saint Germain had stayed on countless occasions whilst visiting and advising the King of France. It was here that Leopold had found a second clue, a cipher, and wrote about it in his scroll.

Only the finer details were left blank, ensuring any who came after would have to search with the same fervor as Leopold himself. Which suited Webb just fine.

At last, the man paused outside a room.

"Are you sure?" Webb made his voice threatening.

"Yes, sir. This is the room."

Webb nodded. "Wait outside. I'll need a fast getaway."

"Please . . . please don't dally too long, sir. They will see us on the cameras."

Webb shrugged as if it hardly mattered to him and then turned every ounce of his attention to the door that stood before him and the room beyond. Even as he stepped through, a sense of wonder overcame him, rescinding all else. Gilded walls vaulted up all around to join at the apex of a high ceiling. Pristine, emerald-green paper covered the walls which were also beautified by old masterpieces, by man-sized, gold-plated mirrors and by hanging drapes of rich, crimson-red. Webb stood in awe, imagining the times over two hundred years ago when the Count himself would have slept and deliberated and planned right here. The man's intrigues were legion.

Webb carefully removed the scroll from its plastic cover and leafed through the stiff, old pages. The thick leather embossed cover felt like a soft balm to his fingers, Leopold's errant scrawl a surprising comfort blanket. The first few pages were now done with, describing the hiding place of the first clue that he'd already found in Transylvania, and then offering a further hint as to the type of cipher Germain had used to encrypt messages to his subsequent hiding places.

Webb approached the very bed, the very footstool, the very chair Germain once sat in. He read aloud from the scroll, hearing a scuffle outside the door but ignoring it completely. The Englishman was too impatient. Maybe Webb would pay him a little visit . . .

He shut it down quickly. *Concentrate.* Leopold described his entry into the palace in the early 1920s, essentially the same route as Webb had taken and ending up in the same bedroom.

"*Take heed, questor,*" Webb intoned softly. "*This is no light journey. An end to everything you think you know is all that you will find. Hold nothing dear, for all fades away.*" Webb paused, thrilled.

"*Except you.*"

He moved deeper into the room, skirting the bed and approaching the back wall. He knew these words off by heart, knew what was coming.

The road to Germain's greatest achievement, and the paramount accomplishment throughout all of human history led past every one of his lesser but no less incredible triumphs. Transylvania had offered a clue into the early stages of his experiments with alchemy. The Palace of Versailles would hopefully further that exploration, revealing to Webb even more of the Count's secrets.

Alchemy was more of a tradition, attempted mostly in Europe and Egypt. It was aimed toward the purification and perfection of certain objects, and the potential creation of new, powerful talismans. Some say a few down the ages came to understand alchemy at all its levels—Germain at least was one of those people, believed to be able to manipulate metal and form elixirs, and even a universal solvent in his day. Webb believed the clue in the Palace of Versailles would reveal some of those, but was quickly disappointed.

For there, carved in the wood beneath the mattress of the single bed was merely another cipher, this one leading no doubt to a third clue. Of course, Webb had half expected that. Surely the secrets of alchemy and their disclosure required a lab.

Nevertheless, disappointment cowed his soul as the cipher was revealed. He compared it to the scroll and then took a quick photo. This was a Baconian cipher, designed by Sir Francis Bacon, another mysterious, revered and enigmatic figure from before Germain's time, but also a dabbler in the methodologies of science, disputing known facts.

It had been postulated that Germain and Bacon were the same person.

But Webb had no time for that now. Scuffles again sounded outside the room door and now a cry that sounded decidedly English in tone. *What on earth . . . ?*

Unless . . .

Quickly, he tucked the scroll away, safeguarded the phone with the photo of the cipher on it and searched the room. Of course, there was an interconnecting door, this one surprisingly obvious for such an old chateau. Oh, how the French used to love their intrigues and secret passageways. Germain must have loved those times.

Hold nothing dear, for all fades away.

Webb ran those words through his head as he approached the door, understanding their deeper meaning and what they stood for where Germain was concerned. As he reached for the handle, the door at the other end of the room crashed open.

The Englishman fell through, face bloodied.

Webb paused, startled, unused to seeing such sudden violence. A life of pampering never helped in these situations.

Someone pushed the Englishman into the room. *A thug*, Webb thought. But it was a thug he recognized. This was the group who'd been dogging him since Transylvania, the group he had people investigating.

Beset by a strange fear and confusion, he pulled hard at the door handle.

The Englishman tried to rise, but the thug and one of his colleagues kicked at his skull, sending him reeling, sprawling across the polished floor. The blood leaked faster now. Webb experienced an insight into the world he used to help create as the men kicked out again and the Englishman stopped moving.

Now they locked eyes with him.

"You stay right there," one said, a local judging by the accent.

"The group wants a word with you," another said, this man swarthier, possibly of eastern origin.

Webb wrenched the door open, thankful it wasn't locked, and ran through. He wasn't a fit man, never worked out, but he wasn't overweight either and had already told himself that if these men caught him his lifelong dream was over.

Adrenalin fired his heart and his limbs. Webb raced through another bedroom where the bed was separated from the rest of the room by a golden railing lined by footstools and then twisted back toward the outer corridor, pausing at the door before peeking out.

Coast clear. Only two pursuers then.

He sprinted, arms flapping, knees pumping. He would be no match for anything short of a fit school mom, he knew, but need galvanized him. The halls were clear, each sweeping expanse of magnificent architecture blurring past so fast he felt a little giddy, until the shout was barked out from behind.

"Don't make me run after you, homme."

Webb pushed it, already seeing the side door up ahead and knowing all he needed to take from this place was the cellphone in his pocket. Once clear, he'd accelerate the investigation and put an end to this annoying group once and for all.

How dare they?

For now he smashed against the outer door and raced into the night, a chill breeze cooling the sweat on his forehead, the distant chiming of bells giving the city a solitary air. Not what he needed right now. What he needed was a crowd, a busy road, a parade of shops. What he needed was not to be chased into the streets as his, so far, very careful avoidance of CCTV would then be rendered ineffectual. Many of them were so good these days they'd ping your face over to Interpol in a matter of seconds.

Webb heard the pursuit gaining ground. Despite the shadow-jamboree he managed to spy the outer gate, the same he'd been spirited through. He lengthened his stride, almost tripping in the process and tried to stop the endless flap of his arms. It wasn't easy with his heart threatening to burst through his chest. And no respite was upcoming. The palace sat amid a great expanse of flat courtyard, stretching far and wide. Webb chanced a glance over his shoulder.

Hurry!

He knew the way by heart. Out of the gate and hang a left, past the Orangerie toward the train station. He already knew where the scroll would take him to next. The scroll provided the places, the ciphers the exact locations; the locations themselves provided the ongoing and unraveling wonders of Saint Germain.

Webb wrenched the gate closed behind him, spitefully hoping it might catch one of his pursuers in the mouth. A dreamlike moment hit him then, when he saw the same man and wife, hand in hand, hurrying the other way across the street—the woman staring at him. A small smile broke out across her features when she saw the panic in his face and the two large brutes chasing him down.

Webb puffed hard and continued on. But he was fighting a losing battle. As the train station finally came up ahead, one of the chasers came close enough to snag his outer jacket. A vicious tug and he was spinning, falling, going down to one knee.

He overbalanced, not realizing but actually helping himself as a haymaker smashed through the empty space where he'd been. The brute grunted, slipping. Webb shuffled away on his knees, looking for a place to stand. The jeans of his knees were scraped raw, and possibly his skin, a new experience. A low wall gave him purchase and helped him stand, and then he stood there, panting hard, taking in deep lungfuls of air whilst he still could.

One of the men crouched low, hands on knees, also panting. "We . . . told you not to run. But you ran. Now . . . now we have to hurt you as well as take you to our leader."

Webb would have laughed if he'd been able. "What are you, aliens?"

The man looked surprised, then angry. He went to sucker-punch Webb in the gut, but Webb stepped back out of the way and the blow whistled by.

Both the thug and Webb looked surprised that he had managed to dodge.

"Stand still."

"Why? So you can hurt me?"

"So I can break your skinny ribs and use them as a toothpick, homme," the Frenchman growled. "Make me run, will you? We'll see . . ."

The dangerous bully moved in again. Webb saw no reason to stand around, spun and tried to make off. Smashed into the second man's chest. Grunted.

"Don't you know who I am?"

It slipped from his mouth before he could rein it in.

The swarthy man laughed. "Not yet. But we will soon."

"Why are you chasing me?"

"Are you stupid? I already said the group want to speak with you."

Which group? Webb opened his mouth to ask, then found it filled with a bunch of knuckles. The pain came a split second later, then the blood, and a decidedly loose feeling in one of his teeth. *I could have made Beau train me. I could have fought my way out of this.* He moaned in pain as another fist connected with the side of his head. The train station now seemed so far away.

"Let's get him back to the car."

They hefted Webb, each one taking an arm, ignoring the stares of passersby. Webb struggled weakly, but even the threat of another punch doused his ire. The cell remained in his pocket along with the picture of the Baconian cipher, but anyone worth their salt would soon find it.

"That's better," the Frenchman said as Webb quit his resisting. "Know your place, homme."

That infuriated Webb all the more, but again he was no fighter. Best to wait . . . wait for an opportunity.

"Hey! Stop right there!"

It came sooner than expected.

CHAPTER THREE

Two policeman came warily toward them, hands hovering over the holsters that contained their guns. On guard at the train station, they must have spotted the altercation and seen Webb being dragged away.

Both his captors turned instantly, the sight of the approaching cops fazing them not one bit. Several passersby stopped to watch and, as if Webb didn't know already, the street cams would have spotted them. What happened next shocked every onlooker, including Webb.

Taking things into madness, the two goons drew their own weapons and instantly opened fire. No warning. No aiming. Bullets glanced off the asphalt and perforated a parked car. The cops dived for cover, one lucky, the other not so much. A bullet slammed into the meat of his calf, leaving him prone on the ground.

The Frenchman lined him up with a vicious leer.

The second cop fired now, bullets whizzing past Webb. Both thugs backed away. The second cop was already on the radio, calling for backup. And it would arrive in a hurry, the French assuming this another terrorist incident. Webb was caught in two minds as he was manhandled: stay put or run? Luckily, he knew that he was a coward now. But would these men shoot him in the back?

Doubtful. This mysterious 'group' wanted to question him, not kill him. They wanted to know what he'd already discovered. And how.

Taking the biggest chance of his life, he pushed Frenchie and kicked out at Swarthy. Parked cars were everywhere, so he pulled free and ran for one, slipping round the front end. Grating shouts pursued him. He veered away from the cops, spying a side street that ran alongside the station. A bullet zinged past, probably a warning but Webb felt his insides turn to jelly. One more and he'd wet himself, he knew. Head down he continued. The next sound of gunfire was further away as the cops engaged, and already sirens were screaming through the night.

This was his chance.

If he made it fast he'd be on a train before they shut the stations down. The witnesses saw him as a victim, not a perpetrator. The authorities wouldn't be as fixated on him as they were on the others. One brisk look back revealed that the swarthy man still watched, tracking his progress, but appeared to be pinned down. Webb wanted to grin or give a childish wave, but didn't dare. Not yet. Only when he was guaranteed safety.

Sirens shrieked closer, beginning to light up the black vault above with their lurid blue flashes. Webb felt for the reassuring packet inside his jacket—the phone and the scroll, carefully wrapped. All was well then. His teeth hurt like hell and his mouth still bled, but he'd cry about that later. First he needed to get on that train.

Inside, the station buzzed with activity, almost everyone ignorant of the events outside. Webb hurried as best he could, still trying to avoid cameras but realizing that particular game was up for tonight. It would take a while for the recognition to hit the right people anyway, and by then . . .

Webb grinned, spotting the time of the next train out.

Seven minutes. Perfect.

Paris beckoned then, along with the scroll's third clue. The pure alchemy evidence should be next, the full reveal. Then that could only lead him to greater things.

Le Comte de Saint Germain unraveled.

More treasures. More ciphers. If he could decode the Baconian cipher, around at the time of Leopold and one of the cipher's associated with the mystery of Saint Germain, then he should be able to at least interpret all the others. All connected with the Count—the Shakespearian code, Merlin, Plato and Columbus. All doors stopped at Saint Germain.

Webb had gambled his life on this.

The fruits of that stake were already paying off.

CHAPTER FOUR

Matt Drake and Alicia Myles were alone, the recent events in New York over a week past, enjoying more than a little R & R.

Drake checked his watch. "It's getting on for six, love. We have to be at the office for six-thirty."

"Man like you should be able to ram it home three times before then."

Drake shook his head at her crudity. "Let's make it once and make it a good 'un."

Alicia sniffed haughtily.

Drake jumped atop her naked body. "Owt's better than nowt, buggerlugs."

He put Alicia's lack of further questioning down to his prowess, though in truth she probably understood the Yorkshire slang from being around him so long. He fixed the tall blonde firmly in his thoughts, allowing nothing else to interfere. It had taken them so long to get this far. She was all that mattered now and nothing else was guaranteed.

Nothing.

The bed groaned and so did Alicia. With a feisty shove she had him on his back and then took control for a while, allowing him to spin her over once more for the last few moments. The night outside was darkening as 6 p.m. passed. Raindrops pattered the draped windows, their rattling filling the small apartment. For a while, the two became lost in a different world; free, cheerful and soothing.

When they'd finished, Drake rolled over. "So how was it?"

Alicia rolled onto her side, studying him. "Meh."

"Oh, thanks. It takes two you know."

"A team you mean?"

"Well, not necessary a *whole—*"

"Good, 'cause I was gonna question that, since in my

experience . . ." she paused. "Actually no, I'll let that one hang."

Drake was glad she did. One never knew if the spirited southerner was joking or not.

"Speaking of hanging." She glanced down between his legs.

"Bloody hell, woman, give me a minute."

"Hey, you got yourself into this."

"Oh, did I?" He flashed back on Alicia's explosion during the ghost ships battle, the way she had chosen him to vent upon. "Haven't we always been 'in' this? Together."

"Bollocks. That's too deep for me."

She slapped his right thigh before leaping out of bed, laughing and pulling on some clothes. "C'mon, Drakey. Duty calls."

He grumbled about having just done his duty as he followed suit, keeping the attire purely civilian as this scheduled meeting at the office was routine, nothing urgent. Following the events of New York, the outing of Robert Price at the very least as a terrorist conspirator, the embarrassment of the CIA, and even harder lessons learned about the state of America's true defenses, the SPEAR team had a mountain of problems to sort through. Hayden was leading the charge, but the entire team was being called upon to pitch in.

"So long as they don't ask me to fix any furniture in whatever new office they give us," Alicia spoke his own worst nightmare, "I'm good. Y'know, I almost wish there was another crisis to get us outta the way."

"Dahl's little escapade wasn't enough?"

Alicia snorted. "Torsty's vacation? I just love the way he squirms every time I tease him about it."

"Tease? Alicia, you couldn't tease if your life depended on it. It comes across as more of a fully-fledged act of war."

Alicia shrugged. "Whatever."

Drake echoed her statement in Yorkshire fashion. "Be reet."

Both laughed, meeting eyes at the foot of the bed in the tiny room and never feeling safer, more content. For a second neither of them moved, happy to let the moment stretch out and mature. It was a rare event for any of the SPEAR team to be able to experience a true moment of pure relaxation. Drake thought that finally, he'd found the person who might help him find those moments more often.

"We ready?"

"Hell yeah." Alicia eyed the bed. "Round three?"

"Later perhaps."

"Perhaps, eh? We really do have to work on your vocabulary."

The couple exited the apartment and the complex close to the Pentagon, heading into work, and not a cloud marred the horizon. Drake saw the great calm now that the rain had stopped and felt it in his emotions too.

The problem was, what came next?

Smyth looked up as Lauren walked through the door. The expression on her face was breezy, innocent, but he knew where she'd been.

"Traffic bad?"

Lauren struggled with an answer. He wondered if she'd lie to him. "It was okay."

"Thought you'd have been back an hour ago. You remember we have to be at work for half-six?"

"Yeah, but we can still make it."

Smyth grunted, giving nothing away. "It would have been easier—"

She rounded on him. "Say it. Why don't you just say it?"

He gave her the familiar tetchy grimace. "Thought a girl from New York would have held out longer."

"And what exactly is that supposed to mean?" There was an underlying danger in her voice, something he only understood when he re-examined his words and considered her past.

"Your secret," he said quickly. "I only meant your secret."

She looked like she had a thousand secrets to keep, probably because she did. "That is one broad statement."

Smyth grunted again, testy. "You know what I mean. You know *exactly* what I mean. Dancing around it only makes it harder."

"I don't dance around anything, Smyth. Like you said—I'm from New York."

"What do you see in him?"

There it was. Laid out on the line, grated, drawn from Smyth's raw throat like a length of taut barbed wire.

Lauren toned down her quick, caustic attitude when it came to Smyth, he knew. She'd had a tough upbringing, a hard life, and had once told him she found it hard to engage fully with the opposite sex because she'd seen it in all its forms of degradation. He saw the struggle to stay civil on her face.

"He's trying to help us."

"No. He's a freakin' terrorist, caught red-handed. And now he's trying every trick in the book to stay out of super-max."

"He was coerced. In any case, he's changed."

"Nicholas Bell is a Pythian," Smyth threw at her. "Nothing's changed."

"You don't know how he's been helping."

"I don't *want* to know. I don't care."

Lauren threw her hands up in exasperation. "And there you have it. It's just *you*. Anger before reservation. Guilt before question. Stop being such a negative asshole all the time."

Smyth flinched. "So now I'm the asshole, huh?"

"Don't expect an apology."

Smyth didn't. Lauren found it almost impossible to say sorry even when she was blatantly wrong.

"You spent time with this guy before. Only one night, but yeah, you managed to get close. That didn't stop him colluding with the enemy, Lauren."

"Once you're in it's hard to get out." She alluded to her own past.

"What's this? You trying to identify with him?"

"Of course not. But I see what he's doing. Smyth," she licked her lips. "He's helping us track Webb through their network of old contacts. Thanks to him we know Webb visited Romania recently. His giving us every name, every number. This is information you can't find *anywhere,* because it only exists in someone's head and doesn't have to be given up!"

Smyth watched her face as she broke off, trying to rein it all in. Saw the emotions there, the deeper feelings, and grew scared.

More than scared. Lauren was being manipulated and didn't know it. Bell was using her, and Smyth hated the terrorist all the more for it. How could he stop Nicholas Bell now?

Lauren indicated the time. "We're gonna be late."

He didn't care, but picked up his jacket and followed her out of the room. Usually, through years of training he was easily able to compartmentalize.

Not this time. He just couldn't shake the feeling that Nicholas Bell had to be stopped. Permanently.

Torsten Dahl made the journey to work swiftly and alone, still smarting from his recent 'discussion' with Johanna. Since the very recent reality checks in their lives they had been trying to make a better go of it, to work something out. At first, after the Barbados hell appeared to change them forever, the rocky road had smoothed out, given them an easy passage, safe havens opening up all around. But even in the short time since, pitfalls had started to reopen, past problems rearing their obnoxious heads. On the positive side his kids seemed to have shrugged the horrors of that day off, with only an occasional reference bringing back the nightmares. Oh, and Julia never wanted to see a beach again. At least for the next three weeks.

Dahl flicked his ID through a couple of card readers and then stopped abruptly as his name was called. Well, shouted actually. No—*screeched*.

"Torsten! Torsten! Hold up!"

He sighed. He was the only person assigned to look out for her and without him, she wouldn't be able to gain admittance to the building.

Not the worst possible outcome, he thought.

Kenzie slipped through the gates, the only comforting sight in his opinion the lack of the customary katana. Offensive and dangerous, the ex-Mossad antiquities smuggler had developed a soft spot for him, and never failed to remind him of it.

"So you're still here," he said gloomily.

"Helping you people has its perks," she said. "And also keeps me under the radar of several notorious kingpins who may or may not be on the lookout for me."

"Not to mention the hope that the US government gives you a pass on older crimes," he said.

"Yeah, and I wish they'd, how do you say: get their asses in gear?"

Dahl saw no reason to remind her yet again that he wasn't American, or English or any other of the nationalities she kept coming up with. Together, they started down the corridor, side by side.

"You given Mrs. Dahl the hoof yet?"

Dahl rounded on her. "That's none of your business. And, Kenzie, stop trying to get under my skin."

"Where would you like me to get?"

He tried not to see her long black hair and lithe body, the promise in her eyes.

She grinned. "I won't be around for long, you know. Best take advantage while I'm agreeable."

"Why? 'Cause you're gonna be trying to kill me in a month or two?"

Kenzie shrugged, not ruling it out. "Sides change, my English friend. As do allegiances. Every day sometimes. Just ask the Americans. Oh, and speaking of side changers..."

Dahl glanced up as she nodded. Mai Kitano and Beauregard Alain were heading up the corridor, also side by side. He found it a little odd at first that they'd arrived together, then realized Kenzie and he must appear the same way. He nodded at Beau and smiled at Mai.

"Heard anything from Grace?"

The Japanese woman smiled softly. "All the normal, natural, content and typical things that one might expect from a teenager."

Dahl returned the smile. "I'm happy for her."

The group carried on, treading the halls with care, at least two of them more than a little wary of the signs of heavy security that were positioned all around. A few moments passed in silence and then Beau spoke up.

"Do you think they, ah, found us a new headquarters?"

Kenzie studied him with a critical eye. "Who knows? So where's the bodysuit, my friend? I much prefer the bodysuit. Makes things . . . easy on the eye."

"They prefer I dress normal in the five-starred building."

"I bet they do." Kenzie laughed and even Mai smiled.

Dahl followed Beau's thread. "I hope they have. This constant security tires me."

"You guys do have a bad track record for HQs," Kenzie pointed out, having been apprised of most of the SPEAR team's history by now.

"Point taken. But the new Secretary of Defense may well move us out of here."

Mai looked back. "See anyone else arrive?"

"Ah, no, sorry. They may already be here."

"They?"

Dahl grimaced. "I thought you meant Drake and—"

"There are ten people on our team." Mai threw Kenzie an appraising glance. "Well, nine for sure."

Dahl stayed silent, regretting his lapse. Seemed like no matter what he did he constantly upset the opposite sex these days.

"So, Mai, you're staying for good this time then?" Kenzie loved the conflict.

"I might be persuaded to take a week's leave just to drop you off where you belong."

"Really? And where do you think I belong?"

"Some kinda hellhole. Atoning for all those you've directly or indirectly caused harm."

"And I guess you never hurt anyone, eh?"

Mai gritted her teeth. Dahl could hear the grind. "Be careful, Kenzie," the Japanese woman hissed.

"Oh, my. Did I say something wrong?"

A guard they recognized stood up ahead. Dahl engaged him in a little chit-chat as the others stood in a twitchy silence. It occurred to him again that maybe they should get rid of Kenzie as soon as possible, the thief appeared to present no more than a wart on the skin that held the team together.

Best not to explain it that way though.

The door to their office stood open just ahead, inviting, welcoming, but through the gap Dahl could see nothing—only a deep patch of darkness. Shrugging off his own worries he wondered what might await them within.

Nevertheless, he walked straight through.

CHAPTER FIVE

Hayden and Kinimaka had been sat alone, awaiting the team's arrival since around 5:30 p.m. They kept the office dark and quiet, equipment switched off or dimmed down low, so they could sit side-by-side on a desk and talk.

Hayden swung her legs back and forth. "I'm trying to be totally honest here, Mano. We're not unsteady. We're not facing obstacles. We're fucking fucked."

The Hawaiian looked morose. "Because I didn't want you to torture a guy?"

"That was weeks ago. And he deserved it. But it's not that. It's deeper." Hayden couldn't bring herself to fully explain the problem—it involved her view that Kinimaka hadn't been man enough to take things all the way—and not just on that occasion—and how that demeaned him in her eyes. The same thing had happened with Ben Blake. *Shit,* she thought. *Poor Ben. I hope you're happy, my friend, wherever you are.*

"I love you," Mano said simply, maybe a bit desperately. "I worry about you. All the time."

Hayden felt faraway. "Did you ever consider our future? I mean—look at our lives. Do you think there's a beautiful wedding day for us? A Hawaiian honeymoon? Do you think we'll end up at Disneyland with our kids?"

Kinimaka's face went a little soft. "Why not?"

Hayden now saw the gulf that stretched between them. "We won't change."

"Everything changes."

"Then change it now. All of it. You. The whole SPEAR team. No one's irreplaceable. Let's disband and go private."

Kinimaka breathed deeply in surprise. "You want to disband?"

"I put my career first, no matter what," she said. "And I need strong people by my side to lean on."

"This team works," Kinimaka said. "You know it does."

"Then it would work anywhere."

"Wait." Kinimaka held up a hand. "Just wait. I thought we were talking about us."

Hayden swung her legs faster. "Shit, Mano, we are. I'm full-on, remember? You're cautious."

"Out of the two of us, who's been shot the most?"

"Oh, hold my ribs before they crack from laughing."

The Hawaiian stopped all movement as the desk gave an alarming creak beneath him. Hayden felt a lightening in her chest; his clumsiness and fear of it had always been one of his most endearing features to her. He spoke whilst staring at the floor.

"If you love me, don't let go."

"There's more to it than—"

"No. It doesn't matter whether it's between adults or if it's your kids. There are always tough moments, moments you want to take flight. But don't. Fight it. Don't run away from those you love."

Hayden hadn't expected that from Mano. Despite her mind, which was already made up, she took pause. She held back the words that hovered on the tip of her tongue and took a long breath.

"Do you have any suggestions?" she said instead. Lame but workable.

"Shit, no." Mano laughed.

Hayden saw shadows crossing the doorway and the unmistakable figure of Torsten Dahl passing through. It was time to put the game face on. Time to go to work. She wondered for a further moment if she should go easier on Mano and propose they simply take a break, but then remembered his words and their long history and the way he'd once made her feel.

Another chance. We're worth that.

Kinimaka jumped down from the desk, almost toppling her as the enormous weight shifted. Dahl smiled at the unintended antics.

"You two," he said. "You're a fine comedy couple."

Hayden didn't smile at all. That was what she was afraid of.

CHAPTER SIX

Drake winced a little when he realized Alicia and he were about to enter the office last. That sent every pair of eyes twitching in their direction, and wasn't helped when, as he opened his mouth to say hi, Alicia nipped him painfully on the ass.

The greeting squeaked out in a strangled cry.

Mai's face was unreadable; Beau's an illustration in resigned acceptance. Dahl looked over as tolerantly as he might indulge his children.

"You made it then."

"Good to see you, Matt," Hayden said.

"Big session was it?" Kenzie slipped in, upsetting four people at once, not quite a record for her.

Drake addressed the greetings in turn. "Dahl. Any more vacation plans we need to clear our schedule for? Hayden, 'ow do? Kenzie, go fuck a doorknob. And why the hell are you still here?" He smiled at the almost unnoticed Yorgi, sat in a corner.

"No prison can hold me." She shrugged.

"Be nice to test that."

"How are you, Matt?" Mai asked nicely.

"Am fair t'middlin'," he answered, then added, "That's Yorkshire for 'ok'."

"I know."

Alicia stepped around him. "What? Am I friggin' invisible?"

"We can wish," Kenzie said.

Alicia rounded on her. "With you, bitch, there's no *we*. Only *I*. Don't think you'll ever fit with this team."

"Still sore 'cause I kissed ya? Or just sore?"

Alicia clenched her fists, but Hayden had already seen it coming and jumped off the table. Her words doused all the rising tempers.

"The new Secretary of Defense is about to be announced."

"Already?" Dahl said. "That's great."

"The President's office says they'll be up to speed in a couple of days."

"We don't have a great track record where secretaries are concerned," Smyth said gloomily. "Probably best to keep him at arm's length."

Drake saw a fleeting expression of hurt twist Hayden's face and wished there was a way to turn Smyth off sometimes, knowing how close she had been to Jonathan Gates, the man who'd originally had vision enough to create and support the SPEAR team. That made him think of other people they had lost along the way. Ben. Sam and Jo. Romero. Kennedy Moore. And Komodo.

Just to name the first few.

He saw the same distant looks in several of his colleagues' eyes, including Dahl's, and wondered if it was always a soldier's lot to keep departed loved ones alive by remembering them, day after day, night after night, year upon year. If so, that was fine and right.

The best we can all hope for is that somebody remembers us when we're gone.

Mortality concerned everyone. It was hard to believe the world would just carry on after you died, people living their lives, dawn breaking, the same trees and the same buildings standing uncaring, the same worries and fears and sheer delights being visited upon a new generation.

Alicia put a hand on his arm, perhaps guessing where he was. And her own motto stood forward in his thoughts once more: *One life, live it.*

He broke the introspective silence. "He have any plans for us?"

Hayden flicked a switch that turned the screens and all communications on. "I don't know. But new officials usually change it up, so expect him to come up with something you least expect."

"I hope that's not a bloody omen," Dahl said.

Kinimaka walked carefully over to the coffee machine. "I'm pretty sure it will be, brah."

"Shit," Smyth vented. "You should know better by now."

Hayden calmed them with a steady cough. "All right. Quit it, boys. Let's all get a little focus here."

"On what?" Lauren piped up. "You called us all in here for this? Nothing's happening."

"Hooker's got a point," Kenzie said.

Now Smyth sized up the Israeli. "You wanna push that a little further?"

Lauren clicked her fingers. "I can fight my own battles, Smyth."

Alicia picked up on that. "You still call him Smyth, eh? Dude, do you even *have* a first name?"

"When we're alone we don't talk overmuch," Lauren said.

"Same for most soldiers," Yorgi reflected.

Hayden finally managed to get herself heard over the chit-chat. "Updates!" she yelled. "As you know we're kept informed of what's going on in the world. Now, let's start with Syria . . ."

As Hayden ran through the various new incidents around the globe, none of which were deemed serious enough for SPEAR to get involved with, Drake wondered if their patched, rag-tag crew was starting to fray. Was fatigue setting in? Did they all need to go and do something different for half a year?

Kinimaka came around with coffees, a bold Kona blend which Drake knew would keep him awake later but it was so bloody nice. Also, it was both hard and dangerous sleeping with a frolicsome Alicia bouncing around your groin. He'd slept in war zones that worried him less.

Dahl wandered over to him. "If I were you two I'd be a bit more discreet. The dynamic here is shaky enough as it is."

Alicia frowned. "And yet I'm always there, aren't I? Pulling you out of the sea after you couldn't handle a little nuclear explosion. Flying to Barbados to join your busman's holiday? What's next—babysitting?"

Dahl looked horrified, as intended, and Drake let out a good chuckle. "Personally I'd love to see Alicia babysit your kids," he said seriously. "Imagine the aftermath."

Dahl shuddered. "Fine. I'll shut up."

"Good idea."

Hayden cocked her head as an internal line started to ring. It wasn't surprising that someone knew the team were here late, evaluating. They did work for the government after all.

Hayden flicked a button. "Yeah?"

"Hey. Interpol's flagged up something you guys might be interested in. I'm sending it over to your inbox now."

Hayden thanked the tech and tapped at a nearby screen. She threw the information up onto a large screen with a flick of her wrist, enjoying the standard Pentagon technology. What appeared to be an official email sat, scanned, virus-tested and cleared, ready to be opened. Drake noticed the sender's name.

"Armand Argento," he said. "Remember him? Good guy. Good agent. He was Aaron Trent's inside man at Interpol."

"The Disavowed crew?" Beau said. "I remember them too from Niagara Falls, though never had the pleasure of . . . bumping into them." He gurgled, clearly remembering the skirmish where he'd inflicted several bruises upon the SPEAR team. "I know Argento too, from some European travels. A smart guy."

Hayden opened the message, taking time to digest the information. "All right. It seems they sighted Tyler Webb." She spoke the name as if she'd gotten a bad taste in her mouth. "But it's over a week old. In Transylvania." She shook her head.

Nobody spoke out with the expected flurry of bad jokes; instead focusing on Argento's text and further information.

"Nothing concrete. Just a sighting by a local cop," Hayden went on. "Reported too late to act upon. They believe he may have been visiting the local castles in the area."

"It's all guesswork. There are many castles in the vicinity, not to mention hundreds of homes, churches, villages . . ." she tailed off.

The team were all processing the email simultaneously.

"But then much later in Versailles," Dahl said.

"When?" Alicia asked quickly.

"Just six hours ago."

"The world's most wanted man," Smyth grumped. "And the

French let him slip through their hands."

"As did the Americans," Beau said. "And most other countries."

"He hasn't slipped away yet," Hayden continued to read. "They backtracked and say Webb boarded a Paris-bound train a few hours ago. It seems he was being chased through Versailles, at least, which is probably why he broke cover."

"And it was not just a random robbery," Yorgi pointed out. "Shots were fired, cops injured."

"But they were *defending* Webb?" Dahl's voice was laced with incredulity. "Why?"

"One thing's for sure," Smyth growled. "We won't make the same mistake with Webb that we made with Nicholas Bell. This one ain't comin' back alive."

"We will need to identify the chasers," Dahl said.

"And why Webb has popped up in Versailles."

"They backtracked his movements to a break in at the palace." Another observation, this one from Mai. "Webb's on the trail of something."

"That's why he let the Pythian organization destroy itself and then wither away," Drake said. "His obsession with this Saint Germain character."

"It must be a heck of a treasure," Alicia said, "to so readily relinquish his entire privileged life for. What prize could be worth all that?"

"We have been lax," Kinimaka said. "We should have been researching. But I guess that was Karin's forte."

"Not long now," Drake put in. "She'll be back."

"The big question is . . ." Dahl added softly. "It seems by the wording at the end there, that Interpol are inviting us over?"

"Appears so," Hayden replied. "So they can take on board our recent dealings with the world's most wanted man. And Argento knows us."

She made a call. "Wheels up in thirty. I'll call Argento and then the State Department. Make your preparations. We should arrive in Paris by 4 a.m., local."

The team took a common, deep gulp of air. This was how it

always began. Planning for the new job, calling relatives to give them the news, not even time to slip back and grab a hug. Their lives were about to change once more, for better or worse.

Drake wished they could leave all the uncertainties and discontentment at the door, but this team had changed. Whether it was for the better was about to be determined.

CHAPTER SEVEN

The Baconian cipher was a relatively simple cryptogram, but one that could still be tricky without respect and concentration. Webb had given it both, and figured out a location for the next clue on the train to Paris. The address was particularly interesting. Not a museum or church or palace this time, but a residence of sorts. Maybe this time he'd become one of the few individuals throughout history to be privileged enough to stand in one of the Count's many laboratories. Maybe certain alchemical secrets would be revealed.

Webb had found his excitement rising. He'd better quell it before giddiness took hold and made him careless. No doubt the authorities would eventually track him from Versailles to Paris— that was unavoidable thanks to the gun-toting goons back in Versailles, but once he left Gare du Nord, Tyler Webb would wholly and completely vanish once again.

When the train slowed and the famous station loomed closer, lit up in the dark and recognizable to Webb, he had risen out of his seat and readied to disembark, face down. Every little helped, of course. Quickly then, he'd escaped the station, breathing a sigh of relief at the lack of police presence and knowledge that he hadn't yet been recognized on CCTV. Time passed, and he melted away, using his stalking skills to avoid cameras, busy areas and tourist hot spots where surveillance would be at its highest. The residence sat exactly where he expected it to be, so he'd made a fast reccie, then paid cash to sit in a hotel room not too far away.

Waiting for the night.

Webb now had other problems, bigger complications. Never in his decades of research had he come cross a group that might already be on the path to Saint Germain, or perhaps guarding it. But that appeared to be the case. Investigations had revealed that the group dogging his footsteps were secretive, largely unidentified and unfamiliar. Webb reasoned that they must be Saint Germain nuts, purists, keeping their criminal ardor only for the Count, otherwise they'd be red-flagged by now and easier to research. Of course, he hadn't embarked upon this trip unprepared—he had contingencies upon contingencies. Ways of escape and backup plans and worse, much worse, if it seemed somebody might be about to catch him. *The years of meticulous planning will pay off.*

Chase me all you like, he thought. *I have so many ways prepared.*

The room was tiny, comprising of a single bed with a coffee-stained top sheet, a wardrobe with enough room for two T-shirts and a shower that might just be large enough for a dog. Webb thought of the grand hotel rooms he'd stayed in, the sumptuous suites and world-class service. Oh, to fall so low in the name of the Count. The fever burned bright within him. Twenty four hours had passed since he came here and he hadn't even embarked upon the dark prowl. But as he looked out the window, plenty of candidates showed their true colors.

It didn't matter though. With the lab almost certainly discovered all else could wait. The problem remained though . . . this so-called *group*. Would they be observing the lab?

Of course. If they had seen him at the castle and the palace, they'd obviously be at every stage. But how did they know about these places without access to the scroll? Was there another tributary in existence that led to the vast pool of mystery surrounding Saint Germain? Or was it something else . . . ?

Webb made dire instant coffee and sat again, patient as the sun lowered across the skies. Enquiries were still ongoing but, so far, the group appeared to be well funded protectors of Saint Germain's greatest treasures. Probably wanted them all for themselves. *Assholes.* But they wouldn't stop him now. Nobody would. Webb remembered the attentions of Hayden Jaye and her mountainous boyfriend, of Matt Drake and his vulgar girlfriend, and of the highly capable Beauregard Alain. It wouldn't take them long to jump on the trail. Webb had lingered thus far, enjoying the freedoms and joys of the quest, but could afford to do so no longer.

To the end.

The sun sank lower. Webb could see the Eiffel Tower if he leaned at an awkward angle across his grime-spattered window. The Champs-Elysees was within walking distance. More information had trickled down to his tablet now regarding the organization he now thought of as "the group". It seemed there were several societies or bodies or cults around the world who believed in the existence of beings called Ascended Masters. Webb had yet to be informed of the exact meaning, but this group believed Saint Germain was a member of that ultra-exclusive set. As he waited, though, and perused the new information, time ran out.

Darkness fell.

Not at all deterred by the events in Versailles or his almost-certain public reveal to the authorities, he collected everything he would need to break into the residence and search for what he was sure would still be there. The ironic thing was, the group's presence so far only confirmed and strengthened his resolve. It showed he was on the right track, from reading the scroll to deciphering the codes and clues.

Thank you, *group*.

Webb exited the room, taking all his belongings and not expecting to return. The street outside was quiet and dark, and he turned in the direction of the Champs Élysées, knowing his route and not too concerned yet about concealed eyes. The building in question had been transformed many times during the last two hundred and fifty years but was currently a vacation rental home, upper scale, set around a small courtyard filled with trees, benches and a paved, meandering path. It took Webb eight minutes to walk there.

Approaching wasn't easy; there were no easy ways to reach the front door and the side entrances bordered on a well-lit side road. Webb sauntered at first, then sped up past the green area. The blueprint in his head should lead him straight to the area of the house in which Germain's lab was located, well below ground level, his major concern that someone had tampered with it in the last few centuries.

Of course, that seemed less likely now with the radical group involved at every step—hopefully there would have been people of influence observing the changes to Germain's residences down the years and discreetly ensuring certain areas were left untouched. He guessed this could probably be achieved in any number of ways—from sticky red tape and planning control to downright bullying, discrediting and ruination. Maybe they even went further.

Not by luck but through diligent and constant investigation, Webb's small network had learned where the service entrance was. Service entrances were notoriously left unlocked, for several reasons from frequent smoker's breaks to keeping delivery schedules at any time of the day so as not to annoy the residents. When Webb tried the door, however, it was locked, showing how fickle his life had become and how everything could turn on a mote of luck. Of course, more in-depth preparations had been made. Some service staff could quite easily be paid off.

Webb waited, standing in the shadows. The feeling of unease that trickled across the breadth of his shoulders was an alien one, and rather thrilling. It almost felt as though he might be a little vulnerable. Webb worried only for the scroll, and was relieved when a faint click came and the door inched open.

"Oui?"

Webb played the game and spoke a password.

The door opened and Webb entered, making sure it closed and locked behind him. Then he waved the dubious looking man away and followed the outline in his head. Corridors branched off this way and that, and Webb got the impression that only about a third of the vacation home was in use, as he switched from side to side and walked carefully toward his first destination: An old set of stairs built against a far wall.

Down these he spiraled, stopping once to listen to the house and hearing no suspicious movements. He licked his lips, feeling the dryness there, and tried to quell his rapidly beating heart. The wooden bannister was rough under his fingers. Reaching a level below ground he found the walls peeling, the floor rough and a peculiar odor hanging around. A great deterrent to the curious.

Moving forward, he flicked on a small torch, illuminating the way ahead. No need to stop and investigate the slightly ajar rooms down here, they would be full of junk, unwanted items and newspapers for the most part.

The next significant movement he made involved a dusty, dirty chimney breast and a heavy trapdoor set in the floor to the left of it. Webb fell to his knees and used a couple of tools to dig around the trapdoor, found the thick metal ring that lifted it, and tugged. It took some effort, but eventually the door came grating upward, spilling debris all over his knees. Webb rose and dusted off, then shone the torch below.

A rickety set of timber steps led below, cobweb-covered and thick with dust. No footprints anywhere. Webb felt elated to see that nobody had been down this way in decades, or longer.

"Wait."

He forced himself to take a breath, pay attention to the house. This would be no quick getaway. He needed valuable information from this, the third clue. The building remained silent all around as if it sat with bated breath, waiting to see what would happen.

Webb took the first step, then descended below ground, deciding to leave the trapdoor open. No way did he want to risk being trapped below ground. The steps were evenly spaced and eventually he came to a rocky floor. Now, the hard bit. Four overlarge, pitch-black rooms sat down here.

Webb broke out a bigger torch—a flashlight now. At length, he found that the third room had been partitioned—a strong plasterboard wall effectively cut it in half. Webb attacked the plasterboard with gusto, coughing as the dust swirled, and began to choke. He ripped off a chunk with his bare hands, seeing himself as an aggressive conqueror destroying everything that stood in his way. He threw plasterboard portions to the corners of the room, and stamped on others. He stood amidst the churning powder, a god.

The enlarged hole revealed all he sought. One of the labs set up by the Count himself; one of the labs built to further his investigations and delvings into alchemy.

Webb entered, finally humbled.

*

Seeking the true secret of alchemy, delving into the deep enigma that surrounded its very name, had always been the quintessential goal for a certain kind of treasure hunter—namely those in search of the Philosopher's Stone. Webb didn't see himself that way, naturally; he wanted everything that Germain pioneered. A way to turn base metals into noble ones. A way to fashion gold. An alternative to accepted science.

Using a heady and complex mix of lab techniques, terminology, theory, experimental method and a firm belief in the power of the four elements, the Count was also guided by magic, mythology and religion. A dangerous mix then, unsurprising that its very practice set the hands of kings and priests trembling and native pitchforks a-twitching.

Webb trod the hallowed floor as gently as he might sneak upon an unsuspecting victim, biting his bottom lip to hold in the excitement. A waist-high wooden bench dominated the room, stretching almost wall to wall, and upon this sat various items; a flotsam and jetsam accumulation that was potentially centuries old. Webb skirted the table, spying a cupboard in a far corner and a stack of boxes in another.

On the table sat an array of beakers, a cylindrical shaped vessel Webb knew to be a boiling glass, a flask, a funnel, a measunder, a meabul and a medicine glass. Vials lay everywhere and he also spotted a mortar vessel and crucible with some kind of ancient, furred mush inside. A spirit lamp sat at one end, a vial claw and stand at the other. Webb had found at least one set of Saint Germain's sacred alchemical tools. The path of his future was now set.

The book that lay half open on the table revealed the first alchemical formula. Without reading Webb knew part of the recipe would be missing. Real alchemists thought if the one who followed wanted to aspire to greatness he would be able to fill in the missing piece himself. Masonic symbols stared back at him, and words for base metals, other formulas.

The path of the *seed* of the metal.
I see it now.

First—*distillation*. Separate the sanctified metal from the crude; the blessed essence from the basic crust. Next, *digestion*. When it becomes a black glutinous matter and attains purity. And then it is drunk, or molded or poured into vials for further manipulation.

The perfect seed, Webb thought. *Fit for proliferation.*

The use of water, air, earth and fire in conjunction with salt, mercury, sulfur and other elements was paramount and divinely sound. *A medieval chemical science?* So it had been said, but Webb believed differently. *Speculative?* Not anymore. He touched the dusty leaves of the book, reverently, as a priest might touch the hand of the greatest martyr. Oh, if only things had gone differently and he could linger here. Linger for days, weeks. The agony of being forced to forge ahead tore ragged strips from his soul.

But in this room somewhere was written the type of cipher to use on the next part of the scroll. Webb had to locate it quickly in case he was interrupted. The many secrets of alchemy were in plain sight; the cipher would not be. Shaking off his humble reverence, Webb took out the scroll and read the last clue once again in conjunction with the Baconian cipher. It pointed him toward the open book itself, the tome Webb least wanted to tamper with. Inside here . . .

Inside here is . . . everything.

He took a deep breath and let it out slowly. No time to double check, no time to dally. The hallowed shouldn't be besmirched, however, so Webb slipped on gloves and took his time turning the pages. Inside, they were unsullied, the symbols and words leaping up at him like playful children, demanding attention. He fought against considering them, at last finding the page he sought.

The next clue in the scroll would be decoded using the Shakespearian Cipher. Made sense, of course. Many down the years had unearthed facts proving Sir Francis Bacon had actually written the Shakespearian works. And Sir Francis Bacon was Saint Germain. Depended how far you bought into the histories. Webb knew from this new group that if you followed them blindly all the way to the nth degree you'd end up believing the Count was an Ascended Master and still alive to this very day.

He shook it off, already seeing the next clue in the text. In addition to alchemy, Germain had been a master of languages too, and the key to that discipline lay in another European city the Count had visited—only by resolving that clue would he learn how to find the next.

Another day, another trip.

Webb had done all he could in this lab, on this day. He assumed all would remain in place until he found a way to return. It was well concealed, even with the wall busted. He would take this to the very end, earn the greatest reward and then take all of Saint Germain's treasures to a place only he deemed worthy, to own for the rest of his very long life.

Webb smiled in the dark, then headed for the door.

CHAPTER EIGHT

Outside again, and it seemed an age since he'd seen the same darkness, smelled the same air. Paris had changed considerably; the entire world was smaller, less significant. Webb, questing alone, had solved age-old mysteries.

Not that he'd doubted himself.

Out here, the air should be his to manipulate, the earth a possession he might control. *One day.* A patch of lamplight pooled off to the right, and Webb shied away. He left the Parisian vacation home and checked the time, surprised to find it was only around 9 p.m. He'd imagined he'd been down there half the night. And that was a shame, because tourists still littered the streets with their cameras, food bags and backpacks, and Webb wanted them all to himself.

Everything changed a moment later.

From out of the shadows and through the solitary lake of light they came, six this time and all with faces as hard as forged steel. Webb took off fast, bruised muscles from a few days ago flaring up as if in warning. Heavy boots thundered after him. Not a word was spoken though, and that sent a bolt of fear through Webb's very soul. They would wipe him from the face of the earth tonight, if they could.

He raced head down, and aimed toward the only people he could see, but in the direction of the famous Champs Élysées. The crowds roamed there twenty-four-seven it seemed, and offered Webb his best chance of melting away. A car crossed his path, almost silent in the night, a freakin' electric mutant that he never heard. Webb's heart leapt in surprise, his awareness increasing exponentially. He followed the car as best he could, hopeful the owner would slow, but of course, on this occasion, he had no luck.

Dark windows lined the street and several rows of topped

trees. A small group of tourists stared, watching the action, one even starting to take the cap of his big Nikon. Webb veered toward them with an idea in mind, then sprinted past only to hear shouts from behind as the cameraman was assaulted. *Good.* The goons thought he'd taken a snap and were now wasting precious time teaching him a lesson.

He glanced back. No such luck. Only one goon had remained back there, the others were closer still. He saw garbage cans lined up ahead, ready for recycling day, and toppled them in his wake. Leaves, branches and vegetation spilled over the road, the big bins getting in the way of one pursuer and sending him headlong and face-first into the road.

Webb then experienced some more misfortune, landing badly as he crossed a standard curb and turning his ankle. He went down. The goons were on him in eight seconds as he struggled to his knees.

" 'Old 'im," one said in British accent.

"No," Webb said. "Not now. I'm too close. I—"

A fist slammed off the side of his head, sending spots dancing all across his eye line.

"Shut the hell up."

Webb hung his head, making himself heavy. His ankle throbbed. "Please."

They shook him violently and the spots kept on dancing.

"Gun," one of them said menacingly.

"I have money," Webb tried. "More than you can imagine. Shit, a month ago you were all probably working for *me*."

"Shut yer gob."

"Who do you work for now?"

"Our employer doesn't like violence," another man said. "So he employs others who do. That's us." A jab to the ear. "Get the picture now?"

"Yeah, but I could double your pay."

"You got the wedge on ya?"

"No. It's—"

"Then stop wastin' my time. I'm already knackered from the run and gobsmacked you even got this far. Now stop all yer kerfuffle and die."

Webb understood little of it, but got the general idea. He cast around for anything he could use, but the mercs were covering him well, all angles spoken for. This time he had no way out. This time Tyler Webb's lifelong dream was really going to sputter to a stop.

Webb was down to the desperate measures he'd hoped never to have to call upon.

A small incendiary device, almost like a firecracker or vigorous sparkler, might make these hardened men laugh in the battlefield, but one shoved inside their clothing was no lightweight matter. Webb had palmed one from his small backpack earlier and now thrust it inside the Englishman's jacket. The reaction was instant, flames singeing and scorching, and the man jumped back with a screech, smashing at his own chest.

Everyone stared.

Except Webb.

Pushing from his heels and with every ounce of strength, he broke through the shocked men just as flames burst through the man's jacket. These men didn't know whether to stop and help their leader or give chase. This then, was why the Pythian mercenary force never conquered the world.

Webb saw it all first-hand now and ran hard for the end of the road. A man stayed with him, though, sending a fist to the ribs which, on the run, gave Webb heart palpitations. He veered away, saw a man walking a small dog, picked up the sniveling mutt and hurled it straight at his looming attacker. Mayhem surrounded him. The dog walker complained loudly, the dog itself snarled satisfactorily, and Webb broke away.

Free. Now don't—

A gunshot blasted from behind, the bullet slicing across his left thigh. Webb squealed, the pain temporarily washing all else away, the terror blinding him. The dog walker screeched too, then fell into him as he turned to run, tiny mutt forgotten.

Webb staggered, holding up both hands. He looked down, expecting ragged flesh, protruding bone, but saw only a thin tear in his jeans, and thus an even thinner tear in his flesh.

I got shot.

And lived! The leg was already badly wounded of course. Webb had twisted an ankle. Maybe fate was giving him a chance. Feeling like the world's most heroic soldier, he limped away toward the Champs Élysées, now close enough to smell the exhaust fumes and see the endless droves milling around.

A chancy look back. The fire still blazed, though the man now lay prone on the ground. A shotgun aimed at Webb. Briefly he wondered if he might be able to dodge a bullet, rating his chances a little better than fifty-fifty. Best not to wager on that and his newfound prowess yet, though. He snaked between parked cars. The next shot blew out a windscreen, then another thunked into the door skin. Webb scrambled on, knees ablaze now too.

Tourists stared at him, cameras twitching. He ignored them, skirting their mindless groups. Some laughed, some looked concerned. Others ate out of fast-food bags or stood staring at buildings, probably imagining what it might have been like hundreds of years ago. Actually, Saint Germain may have done the very same thing in this neighborhood, considering what it had been like in the sixteenth or fifteenth century perhaps, and wondering if he might find the answer to the meaning of life. Cars honked their horns, taxis sped by, safe in their imagined immunity to all things bad. These people had heard the noise, probably couldn't get their tiny little minds around the fact that, yes, it was actually a gunshot!

Once on the Champs Élysées, he headed unerringly toward the throngs and the wider spaces, toward the Place de la Concorde.

The place of many executions.

Webb would never stop running, nor searching. Here he was, finding new depths to himself and new abilities.

It was then he saw her to his left; his favorite victim.

CHAPTER NINE

Drake pounded down the Champs Élysées, the team running with him, spread out to all sides. Interpol agents and French police dashed along too, the group making quite a sight as they rushed headlong up the wide, tree-lined road. Tourists made way for them and when they didn't, the team leapt over the front ends of cars or jogged right over the top. The world's most wanted man had been spotted up ahead, and pieces of him were required.

It had started as a phone call, filtering through to the pocket-sized ops center Hayden had arranged to be set up. Webb was sighted somewhere near the Eiffel Tower, reports streamed in. Forces had been mobilized; Interpol in charge but allowing the SPEAR team almost full reign due to their reputation and work on the Pythian case so far.

Argento slapped down half a dozen complaints by jumped up, pompous officials so full of themselves and their own importance that they couldn't tolerate help from outside forces, and others who just couldn't see that foreign forces could and should work in tandem. These men, these arrogant pricks, would rather Webb escaped than have their pride walked upon.

The Eiffel Tower sighting was a gaffe. Alicia ended up taking the man they thought was Webb down with a tackle worthy of Jonah Lomu, after deciding the French police were a bunch of "pastry-eating pussies standing around and waiting for the worst to happen". The man bounced—three times—before rolling onto his back with a look of utter shock on his face. Right then, they knew they'd made a mistake. Alicia picked him up, brushed him off none too gently, and then walked away, not noticing as his legs wobbled, gave way, and sent him pouring back down to the floor.

She eyed Drake and Dahl. "You know it was the right thing to do. Could have ended this shit right there."

Drake glanced over at the weeping huddle of a man. "I guess he got lucky you went soft on him."

"Never gonna happen, Drakey. Not whilst there's filth and cowards out on our streets, hurting civilians because they think they have some kind of right to."

"You and me both," Dahl agreed, his recent vacation highlights no doubt surfacing.

Hayden rounded them all up. "Another sighting, now along the Champs," she said. "This one accompanied by gunfire."

"Sounds more credible," Mai said. "And we really need to leave this place behind. Fast."

Drake saw the recovering figure waving to the assembled authorities.

"How far is the Champs?"

"A fast run," Beau said. "I know this place. Just follow."

"Gladly." Kenzie fixed her gaze on the seat of his tight-fitting trousers and jogged into line. Drake settled alongside Smyth, noting that the soldier seemed even more irritable than normal these days.

"Don't worry," he said. "We'll get him this time. No more Pythians. No more stalking."

Smyth's return was revealing, at first incomprehension and then a blank nod. "Sure, man. Sure."

Beau led them directly to the famous street and its brightly lit byways. As if in greeting, gunshots rang out ahead and the entire force burst in that direction, flowing along the road beside crawling cars, dodging excited tourists and mingling locals, using benches and verges, car roofs and the sides of statues, anything to thread through the throng and get ahead. A motorcyclist veered and then stalled in front of Alicia and Mai, but the pair picked him up by the front and back wheels and tossed him aside. Another insistent weaver found his bicycle lifted and deposited in a nearby tree by a growling Torsten Dahl and decided to remain there for a while, amidst the branches.

More shots ahead, and the force poured the speed on to the very limit. Mai inched ahead, surprisingly followed by Kenzie and then the Swede. Drake slipped back, panting slightly.

"Quit with the bacon sandwiches," Dahl exhaled at him out of the corner of his mouth.

"Meatballs and muesli," Drake wheezed back. "Is that what you think I need?"

"Anything would help."

"Maybe . . . maybe I'll try a holiday. Oh no, wait . . ."

Dahl ignored the jibe as Beau slid past them all, giving the impression he was bouncing from place to place, the soles of his feet barely touching earth, the panther-like gait eating up the distance.

"A bloody real-life Tigger," Drake moaned, not for the first time wondering where the Frenchman found so much speed, poise and energy.

"And a Yorkshire Winnie the Pooh," Dahl chuckled back at him.

"Fuck off, Dopey."

They saw the running figure ahead at the same time.

"Bloody hell!" Drake shouted. "He's right there."

Beau was already arrowing in on Webb, determined to close the man down. From a side street came a flood of men, clad in black and making a very poor attempt at concealing nasty looking weapons.

The French police went ballistic, screaming at the new arrivals to desist or die. Interpol agents swerved to and fro, caught in two minds, but seemingly unworried about the threat to themselves. Drake and the SPEAR team had only their major goal in mind.

Hayden leapt over a fallen civilian, whilst Kinimaka bent down to help the man up. Mai matched Beau for speed. Alicia's lips were in constant motion, but Drake couldn't hear the words. Probably for the best. Smyth ran beside Lauren and Yorgi, though Drake could tell he was holding back. Nobody looked comfortable. Kenzie fairly galloped along ahead of Dahl, grinning wildly as if this place, on this night, was exactly where she wanted to be.

A car zoomed ahead of Beau, cutting him off. Tyler Webb ran

on, limping, a wild look back confirming his identity. Drake closed the gap. They were almost abreast of the chasing mercs, and had to decide how to handle them. Hayden was expected to shout out the orders and didn't disappoint.

"Drake, Dahl, Alicia, Smyth—take 'em out. The rest on Webb!"

Drake immediately pivoted, aimed and sighted a handgun. Mercs scattered, seeing the attention switch. One remained standing, tracking Webb. Smyth fired first, spinning the man around with two bursts and spraying the nearby trees red. Drake rolled past a slow-moving car, its wheels crunching a few meters from his head. Then quickly up, two-short bursts, and another move. Mercs dived for better cover.

"Who the hell are we fighting?" Dahl asked.

"Not a friggin' clue, mate."

Hayden lowered her head and increased her speed, pushing harder than she'd known she could. More than anyone in the team, she had reason to take Webb down. She had reason to take him down as hard as she possibly could.

Good job Kinimaka isn't around.

Knowing the big Hawaiian was back helping the civilian when the man who'd sneaked around, filmed and tried to terrorize them in their own homes was a hundred meters away, took a storm-cloud to Hayden's already thundery outlook and made a volatile tempest out of it. She was close to becoming her own woman again: solitary, self-contained, intense. Already, she'd tried that new mantle on in her head and liked how it felt. The writing, as they said, was well and truly on the wall.

Webb scuttled gamely up ahead, listing from side to side and clearly drawing each consecutive breath as a scream through tortured lungs. The man was unfit, but he wasn't giving up. Hayden saw Beau lock on to a running merc like a heat-seeking missile and veer away to head him off.

That left just her and Mai at the front of the remaining pack, with Kenzie gesturing in confusion.

"Are we taking this man down? Or not?"

Hayden surged ahead.

"For good."

CHAPTER TEN

Ever since the stalking began, Hayden had known she would come face to face and on equal terms with her shadow. Seeing him now, exhausted, panting and bloody, his face slack, made her wonder how on earth he'd ever gotten so far under her skin. But that didn't matter now.

What mattered was what happened next.

Webb stared, a mini-shockwave trembling though his features. "Hayden Jaye."

"You have two choices. Come with me now or go straight to Hell." She shrugged, holding her weapon angled at his feet. "Either way, I'm good with it."

"I'm unarmed," he said. "And I must say . . . it's good to see you again."

"Straight down then."

She lined his skull up between her sights.

Kinimaka let out a yell from behind, far away. His words didn't matter. Webb looked aghast, an expression that warmed her heart. Even Kenzie gaped though, and that single expression was what gave Hayden cause to hold back.

"Witnesses," the Israeli was saying. "What are you thinking?"

I don't care, was on Hayden's lips. Her hand trembled, her finger quivering. One shot, one blast and it would all be over. No more chances for this destroyer of lives, no long reprieve. Just freedom, for everyone he had ever touched.

Webb flinched as her finger spasmed. The bullet flashed past his skull amidst a terrible, impenetrable silence.

"Well look at that," he quaked. "I dodged it."

Hayden jumped in, but a heavy hand on her shoulder jerked her backwards. She knew that hand, and then the voice that accompanied it:

"You're out of control. Stand down. I'll handle it."

Kinimaka stepped past her and approached Webb. Hayden, beyond surprised, made no move but to wonder if the Hawaiian was right. It had to be said that if she hadn't wasted those moments contemplating killing him she'd already have the man in cuffs.

Out of control? I don't think so.

She pushed up alongside Kinimaka, making no comment. Webb watched them both, a slight smirk on his face.

"I remember the last time we met as a threesome," the Pythian leader said. "You both looked a little different then."

Just a few meters separated them. The Champs Élysées still surged with a vital, fluid life all around them; those running from gunshots, those curious and those who hadn't heard anything. Onlookers inched forward, excitement in their faces. Sirens screamed somewhere distant, coming closer. The night was alive. Journalists and cameraman were trying to climb trees for a better vantage point. Police cars tried to slice through the already heavy traffic.

Hayden attempted to relax. No way could Webb outrun them now. To the right Drake and the others traded gunfire with the remaining mercs, only about four of them now. Interpol and French police tried to flank the mercs. A Frenchman was down and an Interpol cop lay bleeding, medics giving aid. She ignored the man-mountain at her side and gestured fiercely at Webb.

"On your knees."

"As much as I do like the concept and potential outcome of that idea, Miss Jaye, do you really think I don't have a few last-chance scenarios planned?" Webb asked them, entirely too confident for Hayden's liking.

Then thunder swept the streets.

The helicopters were already approaching.

CHAPTER ELEVEN

Seeing two enormous black birds swooping over the Champs Élysées, Hayden screamed out a warning. Kinimaka bellowed too and mayhem seized the entire area with an unshakeable chokehold. Sharp bursts erupted, adding panic to the mix. Hayden instinctively hit the ground, Kinimaka falling like a building at her side.

Right where he always was.

The thunder approached. The Hawaiian's arm draped her shoulders but she shrugged it off, listening hard. Those small bursts sure as hell weren't gunshots. Over the tumult she heard Drake's unmistakable accent.

"It's all a trick, love! Webb's off down t' road!"

Understanding little but the urgency of the words, Hayden rose and took in the scene. The choppers approached, as loud as monsters, but the incendiaries they were dropping were not much more potent than fireworks. This was all that Webb could muster then, now that he had become a fallen king. Birds guided by desperate men, paid-off and almost certainly about to spend the rest of their lives behind bars. For what?

Something only Webb's resources could provide no doubt.

Hayden watched the choppers, already disappearing. Nobody fired, the local authorities were digging out radios to help track them. Hayden looked around for Webb, but already knew what she would find.

Nothing. Nothing at all.

"Bastard has more lives than Jon Snow." She looked over to Drake's position. "You go help them, Mano. I'll search for Webb."

"Are you sure?"

Hayden stalked off, hunting the hunter.

*

Drake estimated the exact moment the creeping Interpol agents would catch the mercs' attention and then let lose an entire clip, winging two men and sending the others scurrying. Dahl broke cover with Mai and ran hard. Alicia lined a lurker up as he prepared to take one of the agents out, and fired her weapon just a second or two before he did.

"They're running," Drake observed.

"Let Torsty and the Sprite have 'em. That's grunt work."

Drake laughed, still surveying every angle and wondering if Webb or the mysterious mercenaries had anything else planned. Maybe Hayden should have winged him, but Webb looked like he'd already been shot. It certainly wasn't hard to disappear into the crowd along the Champs Élysées, especially when three-quarters of it were panicking. That left them with just a couple of alternatives.

Where did Webb come from? And who are the mercs?

"Hey love, fancy a bit of interrogation?"

Alicia eyed him. "Is that some kinda Northern pastime, or something?"

Drake hung his head. "Whoa, that north-south divide. It never gets old."

"So you mean the mercs?"

"Yep, that's what I mean."

" 'Cause, to be honest I'm happy either way."

"What else is new?"

Cautiously they approached the area round where the mercs had made their stand. Some were dead, others bleeding, watched over by several none-too-concerned local cops. Dahl had already hooked his arms under one man and was pulling him into a sitting position. Yorgi and Lauren walked up and hovered around the fringes, not getting involved but always listening, always watching.

"Are you likely to talk?" the Swede asked in cultured tones. "Or would you like me to introduce you to some of my friends?"

The man, a blue-eyed, bearded individual with an old scar across his forehead, rested his back against a low wall, breathing heavily. Drake saw he'd been shot in the stomach, but wasn't in too much imminent danger.

Apart from the obvious.

Alicia knelt down so that her eyes were level with the merc's. "You gonna talk, or am I about to get some close-up target practice in?" She held her weapon across her knees, casual style.

The merc winced, making a show of being torn between loyalties, then caved. "You ain't about to like what I'm gonna say," he drawled in an American accent. "Joined this crew just a few weeks ago. Extra insurance, they said. Didn't firkin help much." He shook his head sadly.

"Keep talking," Alicia growled.

"Wish I'd never bothered. But the money; it was good. Firkin good. Could'a taken a year off, maybe two." He paused as a pair of eyes bored into his own, those eyes owned by a fellow mercenary clearly more invested in his client than he was. Dahl dragged the man out of the way.

"Guess I should keep it shut," the merc muttered.

"Don't worry, they're gonna get theirs," Drake told him. "This is your chance to get less."

The merc looked dismally at the floor. "I can't remember the last good decision I made," he said. "The job was easy. Watch a palace, watch a house. Report back. Report on the foot traffic, guys who appeared to be interested in certain areas or items. Watch real close. My brother did it. Then I did it. Became a family thing." He tried to guffaw then sobered and continued. "We were using field glasses, walk-bys, crooked guards and cleaners, food companies, mobile listening devices, photography. We pretended to be tourists . . ." he tailed off. "Every trick in the book they had."

Drake joined Alicia at his level. "Who is *they?* And to do *what?*"

"They've been on it for years." The merc seemed surprised. "Easy money. Some of these local mercs forgot how to pull a firkin trigger they got so cozy. But then—" he blinked "—something happened."

Drake looked up. The team were gathering around, the Interpol agents also listening. Traffic had ground to a halt up and down the road and a man was shouting through a bullhorn.

"This guy, this *Webb,* appeared from nowhere. Got their panties in a bunch up at Transylvania he did; scared more of Webb muscling into what they consider their territories than ole Vlad the Impaler, they were." He guffawed, then coughed and grimaced in pain, holding his stomach. "Then . . . then Versailles happened, and that's when the hens really started destroying the henhouse. Webb again. Some head honcho went off the rails in panic, faster'n a Fourth of July firecracker . . . called doom down on that poor bastard's head."

Alicia rocked on her heels. "I wouldn't describe Webb as a poor bastard."

"Whatever, dude.

"But do go on," Dahl encouraged.

"Versailles changed the game. Suddenly they were all on alert, taking calls and disappearing to make quiet calls. Favors here and there too. The big boss man called us long-distance like, every hour. More guns, more ammo. And dude, I don't even know what we were guarding."

Alicia slapped him across the face. "Call me dude again, I dare ya."

"Umm, sorry. I call everyone du . . . that. But like I said—I don't know what we were guarding."

"Any of those guys know?" Drake jerked his head at the other mercs.

"Dunno. Maybe. Try Milner there. He's a veteran. We were told to watch for Webb and take him out. Before that though, orders were to find an old book inside his jacket. They said we should get that too."

Drake watched Dahl stride off to chat with Milner. "Your boss then, mate? Who is he?"

"Ah, I don't know much, dude. It's some kinda organization, or group. Low key. But, shit, they're firkin fanatics. Pure, radical freaks. I know they have good lives, wealthy lives. They're privileged, and I mean like *gods.* But this one thing with Webb seemed to set them off."

"Names?" Drake asked. "Anything? Addresses? Nicknames? Phone numbers?"

"I got nothing. But I could list all the places we were tasked to guard."

"That's a start."

The merc broke out into another fit of coughing, making Alicia shuffle back. Drake waved to a nearby medic.

"Make sure he lives."

Alicia tucked her gun away. "Doesn't matter who we follow," she observed. "Webb and these assholes won't be far apart."

"True. But we'll soon know what Webb visited in Paris. And then we'll know why. Next time, the good guys will be a step ahead."

Alicia squinted. "Good guys? Did I miss something?"

"You don't think we're good?"

"I guess we have our moments."

Mai walked up then, and Dahl returned. The looks on their faces said the other mercs hadn't talked. Kenzie hovered at the fringes, eyeing proceedings, as Hayden garnered as much information as she could from the local cops and Interpol.

"So where did Webb come from?" Mai asked.

Hayden reeled off an address. "It's a ten-minute walk from here."

The team gathered, checking weapons and ammo, staring at the dark street from where Webb and the mercs had previously come.

"Any more of his friends down there?" Smyth asked, referring to the chatty, despondent merc.

"Says their team was eight strong. Could be some went back to keep watch or—"

"Or destroy the place," Alicia said. "Let's move."

CHAPTER TWELVE

"So what the hell is all this crap?"

Alicia kicked at a chipped table leg, clearly bored. Drake studied the underground room which looked like it hadn't been visited in decades before tonight. Alicia kicked again and moved the table, wood dragging across the concrete floor and plumes of dust taking to the air. The small room felt cramped and the team looked stressed out—they had taken precious time finding this place and now every moment of it appeared to be a waste.

Kenzie flicked through the old book, fingers leaving prints in the grime. Kinimaka almost dropped a glass vial in his efforts to read its label. Smyth leaned glumly in a far corner, waiting for someone to tell him what to do. Mai said she felt a little exposed and wandered out of the room, to a few baffled looks. Drake knew she just wanted to be useful, and since there was nothing she could do down there she decided to guard the perimeter. Smyth went with her, and then Beau too. Not a bad border guard.

"So what do we have here?" Hayden asked the obvious rhetorical question. "Let's put it all together."

"It would take weeks to sort through," Yorgi said.

"Liquids." Kinimaka pointed at a stuffed shelf. "Potions maybe? Medicine? I'm not sure."

"A book." Kenzie slammed it down. "Full of masonic symbols and spidery, smudged handwriting. Old stick drawings."

"Chemical paraphernalia." Dahl pointed out a burner, test tubes and several other items.

"So many containers you could sink a ship." Alicia indicated the haphazard clutter of shapes.

"Tells us very little," Hayden said. "But this is all we have to go on, guys. We can't rely on facial rec the next time. This was our best chance to find Webb when we knew he was here. The man's a ghost again."

"There's nothing obvious," Drake said. "A map would be nice. Or a set of clues."

"Not exactly a treasure trove," Dahl said. "More a collection of grunge. C'mon, Drake. I'm sure there's a Yorkie expression for it."

"I'd just call it a shithole," Drake remarked.

"All right." Hayden looked like she agreed with the overall consensus. "Only the experts can root through all this—"

"Crap," Alicia added in helpful fashion.

"Yeah, that. What else can we do?"

"Head back up top," Kenzie said. "Give me my katana and one of those uncooperative mercs. I'll make him sing like Shakira in concert."

"Would we have to pay five hundred for a family ticket?" Dahl wondered.

"Probably, yeah." Kenzie stalked out of the room.

The team made their way out into the night once more, despondent and a little desperate by now. What appeared to be their best lead had quickly vanished almost as fast as their prime suspect. An Interpol agent saw Hayden and came over, gesturing with a cellphone.

"Take this please."

"Sure. Who . . . oh, hi Armand."

Drake listened to her one-sided conversation with Argento, the gist being that they needed more information and by any means. Argento had an awful lot riding on this, as did his superiors.

Including the SPEAR team's involvement.

Hayden nodded at Kenzie. "Choose your man."

The Israeli looked surprised and pleased. "Really?"

"They tried to kill us and the French cops. They fired randomly across a busy street. I'd choose the leader, but it's your call."

Drake watched as Kenzie considered her first real directive as part of the team. With a snarl she hauled the leader to his feet and dragged him by the collar nearer the shadows that surrounded the house. No sounds emerged, no screams or muffled thuds, but something was going on in there. Drake could see a constant shift of the darkness.

He heard Kinimaka's whisper, "You gave her the job you wanted."

And Hayden's reply, "Leave it, Mano."

Kenzie returned, an injured look on her face. "I honestly believe they don't know anything." The merc crawled along at her side, unable to stand.

Smyth surged forward, muttering angrily. Clearly, the soldier had had enough of waiting in the wings. His victim struck out, but Smyth subdued him with a simple punch. A broken rib and jaw soon followed, the soldier's anger getting the best of him.

As Kinimaka leapt in to pull him away an aggrieved voice shouted, "Dubai! They're in Dubai, but that's all I know!"

Smyth paused and so did Kinimaka. The soldier stepped away. Lauren caught his shoulder.

"What was that?" she hissed. "You scared me."

Smyth turned away.

"Now you're scaring me more."

"Interesting," Smyth said. "That I scare you more than a Pythian terrorist."

"Oh, give it a rest. And hey, you'd better not have hurt him before we left."

Smyth looked like he wished otherwise.

"You'd better not hurt him, Smyth."

"And how could I do that?" Smyth rumbled. "He's in lockdown."

Lauren clammed up, staring up at the skies.

Drake was busy wondering if he'd heard correctly and nodded at Yorgi. "He said Dubai, right?"

The Russian widened his eyes. "Oh, dah. I heard that too."

"That just makes everything weirder," Dahl stated. "Dubai? I mean how do you connect that with . . . this?"

"Guys, we have to focus," Hayden urged them all. "Right now, Webb is in the wind and we're nowhere."

"He's getting desperate though," Beau said quietly. "Webb. The man I guarded and worked for all those months would not make mistakes like this unless . . ."

"What?" Smyth cut in quickly.

"He is nearing the end. Anxious. Webb is almost at his ultimate goal."

"And, I'd like to point out," Hayden said. "That's something else we're practically clueless about."

"Chemistry. Versailles palace. Transylvania. What's the connection?" Dahl shrugged.

Hayden brandished the cellphone. "Let's head out," she said. "There's nothing more here for us to do. Get some rest guys, because when this all plays out I've a feeling we're gonna need it."

Argento came through the old fashioned way. He called Hayden and she called the team together, and they traipsed down from their hastily acquired rooms to a cold, empty conference room. They all sat about the dusty table, staring at the bare floor and shivering, watching the windows grow brighter as dawn began to rise.

"You mentioned he'd get desperate." Hayden nodded at Beau. "You were right. Webb is now on the trail of something else, another part of the quest. The guy's injured, hounded by whoever those mercs are working for, and now hunted by us. Not to mention half of Europe."

Beau nodded. "He has no choice."

"He also knows the Dubai-run group will be waiting for him at every stop," Drake pointed out. "I hope he's a sniveling bloody wreck."

"Not Webb," Beau said. "He truly believes he is owed something. The man will assume he's able to dodge bullets until this is over."

Hayden laid her cellphone on the table and hit the speaker. "Go, Armand."

The Italian Interpol agent let loose in characteristic fashion. "So, this Webb, he is running around like a boy chasing a mouse, yes? He seems to be following a trail, a map maybe, who knows? But until Versailles he kept it all very quiet, on the *down-low* as you Americans say."

Hayden nodded agreeably. Drake stared at Alicia and then at Dahl, eyes wide and lips about to start flapping. Then the Swede chuckled. "Now," he said. "Now you see what it's like."

Argento's word-storm never abated. "So he's back on the map, this Tyler Webb. Most wanted scum-sucker in the world, you say. I say there's worse, but it matters little. Ever heard of the cannibal cult of Peru? No, well, never mind. Interpol knows all. You will catch up. Webb is no longer sneaking, he is in full-tilt, fully-exposed, pressurized mode, hounded everywhere. He needs every ounce of assistance, every last morsel of help he can muster. Clearly, he still has money, influence, a network of sorts." Argento paused to draw breath before he died of asphyxiation.

The team realized they'd been holding theirs too and gulped air.

"And thanks to your pet Pythian—Nicholas Bell—we now have names, contacts, locations and files for all of them."

Drake couldn't help glance over toward Smyth and Lauren, conscious of their differences. The soldier sat tight-faced, eyes fixed dead ahead whilst the New Yorker made a point of shifting in her seat to stare right at him.

"Don't say it," Smyth mouthed.

"What? That I told you so?"

"Yeah, that."

But Argento was forging ahead. "Everything's monitored. Everything. Webb recently used fake IDs to buy a flight to Barcelona. We can't intercept that because he only made contact *after* he landed to arrange something else, something very worrying for Interpol. We have no facial recs so he's now hiding successfully. My friends, you have to get to Barcelona. Fast."

"Why?" Hayden asked. "What's so worrying?"

"He bought tickets and arranged to meet a contact at the Camp Nou tomorrow night. And knowing Tyler Webb, the distractions he arranges . . . well, that could be catastrophic. He has no sense of morality."

Alicia was looking blank, and so was Mai. But Drake sat bolt upright. "The *Camp Nou?* As in the football stadium? Oh shit, is there a match planned?"

"Yes, *mi amico*. A big one. The stadium—it will be full."

Drake was already on his feet. The rest followed as Hayden headed for the door, Argento's voice urging them on like incessant machine gun fire. The pictures he painted were truly shattering.

CHAPTER THIRTEEN

The jet hummed along, thousands of miles above the earth. Darkness pressed all around, a dense cloak enfolding all the simmering secrets that traveled within.

Drake found himself seated around a table with Alicia, Mai and Beau and hours to kill. After eating they sat back and took advantage of the night flight, dozing and day-dreaming. Drake asked Mai about Grace's welfare, and the ex-Ninja inquired as to Karin. Drake found himself floundering; Karin had been out of touch for weeks and a gentle enquiry had told him she'd almost finished training and was on some kind of special mission. Unhappy, but unable to learn more, he'd swallowed a bitter bullet—it was one thing pulling strings to practically force an unexpected recruit into a unit, it was quite another to then keep track of that recruit.

He told Mai as such.

"It will be hard for her," she said. "But necessary, I think, if she is to stay with this team."

After Komodo's death she could have gone many ways. Drake was pleased she had taken this unexpected route, after losing everything she loved to war. The young woman had buried too many people for this stage of her life.

"She's a fighter," Alicia added. "My kinda girl."

"Do not tell me you've kissed her as well," Beau queried, only half-joking

Alicia shrugged. "Not that I can remember. But who knows? Some of the older things clattering around my mind are a little woozy."

"Does that include Drake?" Dahl put in with a guffaw from across the aisle.

Drake narrowed his eyes. "You just keep on cozying up to your new bird, mate. You two look real happy over there."

Dahl looked a little embarrassed, pulling away from Kenzie.

Drake gamely tried to include Beau in their conversation. "So, how did you meet Michael?"

"Crouch?" The Frenchman waved it away. "It is a long story. And not for idle chit-chat. I worked for Crouch and you by infiltrating the Pythians, yes, but the initial decision was not made lightly—" he paused "—or wilfully."

Drake allowed his eyes to widen. "Bollocks. And here's me thinking you're a good guy."

"No, my friend. Are there any left?"

"I'd like to think so."

Beau settled back. "I see none. You think Crouch is all good? You ask him one day how he influenced my help."

Drake found it hard to gauge just how upset Beau was over Alicia. Common sense told him the two had been merely passing time; but intuition said more. *How did it all become so complicated? Everyone happy on the outside, or at least accepting, but what are they all really thinking?*

Mai put it out there. "Sleep, I think, is probably best for now."

Avoid it. Ignore it. Let it heal before you touch it. Drake could think of nothing better.

Hayden and Kinimaka sat at the back of the plane, rows and rows of empty seats between them and the others, ostensibly to plan out their movements in Barcelona.

In truth, mountains were moving.

Hayden twisted her blond hair into a short bob, wrapped herself in an overlarge jacket, and drew her knees up. Kinimaka was droning on about Webb and his clear mortality, and his inability now to stalk them for pleasure.

"It's over, Mano." The words were out before she measured them fully. "We need a break."

The Hawaiian stopped in mid-flow, his face so full of surprise that she hung her head.

"Don't tell me you didn't know it was coming."

"I thought we were concentrating on the mission."

"Then I guess you were wrong."

Kinimaka coughed. "You sat all the way back here just to tell me we're taking a break?"

"Well, maybe, I didn't want the entire team part of our intimate discussions."

Kinimaka let out a long breath.

Alicia grunted. "You should lower your voice then."

Hayden gripped the sides of her seat. "What do you want from me, Mano? We've been over it a dozen times. It's too hard to be together so we should both see how we fare apart."

"This all started when I wouldn't let you torture Ramses, right?"

"Stop dramatizing it."

"Or was it before that?"

"A few times," Hayden admitted. "I thought you could have stepped up a bit quicker."

"I've always been at your side. Through everything."

"I know. That's not what I mean."

"Yeah, yeah," Kinimaka agreed and shifted in his seat. "Y'know, there's no 'taking a break', Hay. No month-long breathers or time-outs. You bail now, you bail for good. We're done."

It wasn't him, Hayden knew, but the man was hurting. She'd carved a wound and exposed it, dug deeper and analyzed it. The future held . . . what? More fighting, more hardship.

"Maybe it's better that way," she said, not even sure if she believed it. "Maybe."

He used the seat in front to hang onto as he maneuvered himself out of the seat next to her and walked down the length of the plane. Silence followed their conversation, broken only by the buzz of the plane.

Smyth watched Kinimaka take a new seat and then turned to Lauren. "You wanna end up like those two?"

Lauren spread her hands. "Do you even know what we are now? Right this minute?"

"We fight enough battles," Smyth said. "Without fighting them between us too."

"Ya got that right. So why try?"

"You know why. Look at your new boyfriend."

Lauren pinched the bridge of her nose, exasperated. "Is the

child in you your leader, Smyth?"

"I see Nicholas Bell as a terrorist trying to save his ass. You see him as someone trying to turn his life around whilst helping out the good guys. I remember you meeting him in that room, dressed as Nightshade. Who's right?"

Lauren gestured, the New York swagger clear. "Well, I am. Obvious."

Smyth stayed quiet, the annoyance clear on his face.

Kenzie leaned into Dahl, no doubt trying to make him feel uncomfortable. "All these problems, eh? Bet you're so glad to be married."

The Swede tried not to wince, then stared at Kenzie to see if she was taking the proverbial. Hard to tell. She was ex-Mossad and well trained. He elected to stay neutral.

"We all have our problems, Bridget."

"Oh, calling me by my first name. That spells doom."

"No. *You* spell doom."

"Do you think? After everything I've been through—you think I'm damaged beyond repair?"

Shit, Dahl didn't know and really didn't want to get too in depth with her as the plane perceptibly began to descend toward Barcelona. He stared hard at the seatback before him. "Everyone gets damaged. It's how you heal and move on that counts."

"I regret ever trusting my superiors," she said. "I regret later choosing an unlawful life. I regret—" she shrugged "—an awful lot. Doesn't mean I don't have hopes."

He met her gaze. "What hopes?"

"Simple ones, for now. Like living and staying free and helping new friends out." She laughed.

Dahl measured the flippant remarks and still believed he'd initially been right about her. In Kenzie was the soul of a tortured, betrayed individual struggling to overcome something good and true and right. She hid it well, but the Israeli cared for more than just revenge and ancient artefacts.

"I think you're on the way to redemption then," he said with an equally offhand laugh, but held her gaze to make sure his words appeared as heartfelt as they were.

I hope for you.
Sounded corny, somehow wrong. But it felt right.
Dahl watched the runway appear below. Barcelona's night-blanket was giving way to a pre-dawn drizzle. Somewhere down there terrorists might be planning an event just so they could enable Tyler Webb to slip away once more. An event potentially as large as anything they'd yet seen. The road to hell was open and they all walked its ruthless, terrible byways.

Not this time, Dahl thought. *We're a step ahead of you this time.*

He hoped.

CHAPTER FOURTEEN

As they landed and started to disembark, Hayden took a call.

"Argento," she said before pressing the button.

"I have taken some time to seek out more information on this mysterious group," he said in a voice loaded with high-spirited Italian reverberations. "They are extremists, fanatics, cracked in the head."

"My kinda talk." Drake grinned.

"Terrorists," Hayden agreed. "And about to take an interest in Barcelona."

"No, not terrorists," Argento discharged faster than a cheap battery. "Fanatics yes, but *only* interested in the welfare of one thing. One agenda. Le Comte de Saint Germain."

Hayden paused on the edge of the runway, just realizing that Kinimaka had been left to fetch her gear. *Shit.*

Drake crowded in. "Saint Germain you say? I *knew* it would be all about that guy. Just knew. I'm sure I mentioned it."

Dahl shook his head. "Not that I recall, mate."

"How would you know? Barbados was trying to kill you."

"Well, not the island. Just some of the people."

"No hard feelings then, eh?"

But the irrepressible Argento was already forging ahead. "So, we are still continuing our investigations. These people, this *cult*, is based in Dubai. The figureheads I mean, and it's unsure if these figureheads are just that, named people, or if they are involved in the day to day running of the . . ." He paused. "I was going to say cult. Shall we call it a cult?"

"They're worse than social deviants," Hayden said. "At least. Let's call them a cult."

Argento started to crackle as they entered the airport building. Drake took in the endless panes of ceiling-high glass, the austere corridors and frowning guards. *Must be another* airport in another country then. But at least it wasn't drizzling in here. A clock told him it was 10 a.m., still plenty of time to get this thing sorted before kick-off time. He noted that Lauren walked along at his side and smiled.

"You okay?"

"I don't know," she said quickly. "I'm beginning to wonder why I'm here, you know? My skillset ain't exactly crucial."

Drake shrugged. "You're a part of the team. Like all of us. Doesn't matter when you step up so long as you do when the time comes."

"I guess."

"So Webb's gonna be at the Nou Camp, meeting a contact," Drake went on. "Maybe we can use you there."

Lauren arched an eyebrow. "Oh yeah?"

Drake laughed. "I'm not hinting. Just saying 'you never know'."

Lauren joined him in laughter as they walked down more endless corridors, bypassing the normal route taken by millions of tourists and locals.

"Don't matter what happens here," Smyth put in. "Webb has some way of staying ahead. Bastard always knows where to go next and then vanishes on us. Here, now, is where we put him down for good."

"That's the idea," Drake said a bit caustically. Smyth seemed to have that effect.

Hayden turned her head to talk as she walked. "If the cult hangs out in Dubai, guys, somebody's going to have to pay them a visit."

"Shit," Drake said. "Don't send the Swede. He has a bad track record with tourist destinations."

"Piss off, Yorkie."

"I was thinking a strong team," Hayden said. "In case we get chance to take them out."

Drake agreed. "Great idea. Gonna be hard to get it past the local cops though."

"We do not exactly need the help," Mai said almost inaudibly.

"Ooh," Alicia yelped. "Clandestine mission. We haven't done one of those in . . . umm, ages."

"Speak for yourself, bitch." Kenzie grinned.

Drake turned on her. "You had better not have been getting up to anything during your downtime in DC, Kenzie."

"Depends what you mean *exactly*, lover." The Israeli smirked.

Drake let it go, conscious that Kenzie loved to see the hackles raised and wedges driven between friends. She was a bad fit for the team, but Dahl saw something in her and, despite his misgivings, Drake trusted the Swede's judgment. He nodded at Hayden.

"We'll sort Webb first," he said. "Then Dubai."

"Agreed."

"We're here to liaise with the cops now though, right?" Kinimaka asked.

Hayden appeared to catch a sigh. "Yes, Mano."

Barcelona flashed past as they were escorted from the airport to a local station, all courtesy of Argento's planning, the most impressive sight being the incredible Sagrada Familia, the Roman Catholic church which began construction in 1882 and remains unfinished to this very day. Drake remembered once being told about this place with a couple of friends over coffee, but the place itself defied all description.

Dahl put everyone's thoughts into one succinct sentence. "Half-true stories and deep secrets for a future generation."

Ahead, the traffic forced them to a crawl and then they were leaving the flow, parking up and being shown where to go. Drake kept an eye out, as did they all, conscious that Webb had retained at least one influential thread of his organization, one that very much included expert surveillance.

Inside, they took up positions and watched over operations. The cops did their jobs well; this was fast becoming the command post for their surveillance operation and the place to watch as hundreds of monitors started coming to life. A tall, white-haired man with jutting teeth orchestrated it all like a conductor, positioning cameras and swiveling mounts, parking up mobile cams and jumping onto local feeds. As much coverage as was possible, and then more.

Hours passed and lunch arrived. Weariness from inaction

stole over the team. Streets, roads, alleyways, gates and parking areas were scrutinized with blanket coverage. Bus disembarkation points were subject to a flurry of high-powered lenses. Drake and the others started to turn content gazes upon one another. They would get their man.

Then the crowds started arriving, bodies packed so tightly together they had to walk in rhythm, vehicles gridlocked and buses dropping passengers off in any free space they could find. As the gate time approached, the task for the authorities became harder and harder. Local colors helped blend body with body; and caps, face-paint, even balaclavas and hoodies added to the problem. The facial recognition software ticked away, identifying known criminals, hooligans, gang members and other unsavory types, but nothing stood out in relation to Tyler Webb or terrorist groups.

Drake watched the men work; they knew their jobs well and constantly pointed out familiar faces or zoomed in on new ones. Pickpockets were identified, photographed for file and radioed down to the foot patrols. Troublemakers were blown up on cameras so powerful Drake could count the chin stubble. A hunted thief was spotted, and a man recently escaped from prison. Members of supposedly friendly intelligence agencies, including the CIA. Hayden flushed with embarrassment at that one, but ultimately spread her hands. They had rooted out the worst of the bad seeds there, but some agencies would never tell all.

"We watch them all," the buck-toothed man said. "We have to. But the resources are stretched every time."

"I get it," Drake said. "For every ten 'friendly' agents you spend time on, one terrorist could just slip by."

"Yes, sir."

"An hour until kick off." Hayden pointed at the clock. "We should go to our positions."

"Check comms," the surveillance team-leader said.

They did.

"Be ready and familiarize yourselves with our grid system. You should know every point, so that when we call out a position you can converge immediately, as one unit."

"Your men too," Smyth rasped.

"They will do as they are trained to do," the leader said a little cryptically.

Hayden signaled and the team moved out, their position only a few minutes' walk from the famous Camp Nou stadium. For Drake—a one-time soccer fan and now an idle follower—the sight was a little underwhelming at first. The same as many modern, similar stadiums, the curving painted concrete walls and advertising spoke only of the moneymen, the surrounding streets merely the same. A hubbub of noise, laughter and shouting filled the streets, a riot of color bounded before his gaze. Men, women and children sauntered, queued and darted without apparent purpose. Crowds huddled to discuss team sheets and recent performances, upcoming player transfers and new arrivals. Rival fans called out in friendly fashion, at least for now.

Drake threaded through the pack with his team around him, heading for an obscure side door built into the concrete wall. A keypad was spotted and a six-digit PIN entered, and then they were inside the huge arena, treading hallowed halls where no fan or soccer player ever walked. Nevertheless a deep rolling thunder of sound could already be heard, spreading through the very foundations of the stadium and echoing through every wall. The chants of the faithful, the songs of all the dedicated believers. Drake imagined the players gathering now and wondered if they could hear it in their changing rooms—something incredibly uplifting for the home team and entirely intimidating for the visitors.

"How many does this place hold?" he asked.

"Over ninety nine thousand," Dahl said immediately. "Largest in Europe."

Drake slowed as they approached a door that led out into the stadium itself. They all took a breath, ready for the onslaught of noise and light, the eruption of passion.

"We ready?" Hayden asked.

"Occasion doesn't choose dates," Mai said. "This is an occasion, and we have to make it happen."

Drake smiled across at her. "We always do, love. Always do."

CHAPTER FIFTEEN

The enormity of their task was immediately clear. Drake hadn't been to a soccer match in many years and some of the others had never encountered a stadium like this in their lives. It wasn't only the vast scope of the seating, the infinite curve of the walls, the bobbing, matching colors—it was also the sheer swell of noise that assaulted the senses like a battlement full of Gatling guns. Hayden hesitated under vocal fire and Drake took her by the arm.

"Focus," he said. "We're only here for show. The real work's being done by the surveillance units."

Endless rows of seating bowed away in two directions, some rows blue and some purple. The walkways in between tiers were what Drake was looking for and he pointed them out to the team.

"Our way of getting around," he said. "But it's gonna be hard reaching Webb without being seen."

They walked the narrow path between levels, scanning faces in the crowd as far back as they could. One thing soon became clear.

"We have to split up," Dahl said. "We're no good all stuck together like this."

The team went in separate directions, climbing the stands and switching back, staying in contact through their comms. Drake watched the swell of the crowd, ignored the chanting and the antics from the stands and tried to focus on faces. Kick-off time was approaching and a sense of rising excitement amplified the already churning atmosphere. The field down and to his right lay bright green and seemingly flawless, soon to be picked out by floodlights. Faces bobbed and grinned in all directions, many of them Spanish, which helped immensely as he sought the American in their midst.

Several times, he spotted potential suspects, but each was

discounted after closer study. Both Mai and Alicia transmitted over the comms that they'd marked a candidate but facial rec was quickly carried out and the man omitted. Hayden told them all to recheck their own phones where she'd sent a picture of Webb to help their inundated senses maintain a center of attention.

Many thousands passed inspection. Alicia and Mai were both among the crowd, Smyth approaching those whose backs were turned and spinning them around whilst Yorgi looked on. Dahl shouldered his way through groups and lifted the caps of those who unwittingly hid their faces. Mostly surprise greeted him with the odd angry word.

Eventually Hayden, Smyth and Kenzie ended up back at the CCTV HQ, hating the onslaught of overwhelming noise and thinking they might be able to do better behind a TV screen. Drake remained in the thick of it, not once staying still.

"Bet I clock 'im before you do, Ikea boy."

"If by that you mean catch sight of the critter then I very much doubt it. I'm taller, younger and overall the better bet."

"You're on."

"Guys," Hayden drawled. "I think the cameras are better than your eyes."

"Then you're on too."

"Maybe we could form teams," Alicia put in a little slyly. "Me and Drake, and Dahl and Kenzie."

The Swede bit hard. "You wear your insinuations well, lady."

"Maybe." Mai spoke carefully. "But Drake and I work so much better together."

Drake winced, sensing a coming battle. Mai was not a woman to give up anything easily, let alone something that spanned decades. He guessed the only reason she held herself back was because she'd left so suddenly and with no guarantee of return. It must have hit her very hard.

His feet quickened, his senses hyper-alert. It came as a surprise to see the crowd on their feet and he realized the game had kicked off; he'd been fully in the zone. Floodlights blazed and the players stalked their positions as they tested out the opposition. Drake couldn't see an empty space, but now all the faces were turned toward him.

Alicia called in a possible spot that proved fruitless. So did Beau. The whole quadrangle that entangled them became a slowly contracting noose. Where would it all end? He stopped, watching an American standing silent and unmoved amidst a gaggle of noisy human geese, hopeful but knowing full well it wasn't Webb.

Then Dahl broke the radio silence. "I believe I have him."

Hayden shot a comment back, and then Drake was waiting, no sarcasm now but hopeful that somebody had spotted their prey. A timer was ticking somewhere, for something, they just didn't know what. Was it to cover Webb's escape? Or something worse? And where had the cult positioned themselves?

Hayden's voice slashed across the airwaves. "That's him! Go get 'im, Torsten!"

Drake moved fast. He knew exactly where Dahl was and wanted to back the big Swede up.

Dahl blinked, almost shocked that the affirmative had come back. That really was Tyler Webb then, standing near the back row of a tier, in the middle of the aisle, next to a woman wearing the Barcelona colors. Fans gave voice to their feelings all around the two as they bent their heads together and talked.

"Two marks," Dahl said, moving carefully and seemingly without aim. "The woman beside him appears to be his contact."

"Running her now," Hayden came back. "If she knows Webb well enough to meet like this she can't be good. Watch out."

"Yes, Mom."

Dahl inched ever closer, affected by the knowledge that Webb knew him by sight and just one, tiny uplifting of those eyes would . . .

There.

Webb spotted him, locking on and spitting out a curse word. The woman bolted without even a glance; clearly expecting the worse from the get-go. Dahl saw her scarper to the left, pushing fans aside, and Webb started to move to the right. Bodies moved aside or were pushed hard and windmilled their arms as they staggered. Dahl had no option but to chase after Webb, dashing down the closest aisle and dealing out the same treatment to the row of fans gathered there.

He trampled feet, kicked shins and elbowed stomachs, knocking one larger man who saw him coming, over the back of his chair. The man had decided to challenge the Mad Swede. Not the best idea at any time, but even less so when Dahl was chasing one of the world's most wanted men.

Dahl shouted into his neck mic. "He's running. Converge!"

Webb reached the aisle first and dashed up the steps that separated tiers. Dahl danced around a pregnant woman, lost ground, then hit the steps himself on one knee, leapt up and ran hard. Webb jumped into another row, causing havoc.

"Someone chase down that woman!" Hayden cried.

"On it," Alicia answered, and Mai also called an affirmative.

Dahl leapt up another row, now only one away from the fleeing Webb and half a dozen seats behind. He called out for the man to halt, to no avail. It was all a distraction procedure anyway. Webb stumbled, but caught himself on a chair arm and practically jumped into a seated man's lap. Dahl shouldered past a thick group, and lost sight of the American for one moment.

"Best hurry," Kinimaka came over the airwaves. "We don't know this man's exit strategy."

"One thing's for sure, it won't be discreet," Smyth said.

Dahl tried to leap over the back of an empty chair, missed and went sprawling, but immediately picked himself up. The scrapes didn't matter; the bruises routine. "Where are the Spanish cops?" he asked.

"Right with you now. They're cutting Webb off at the pass."

Dahl glanced ahead and saw cops racing for the next set of stairs in time to intercept Webb. The Pythian made a desperate leap, landing just three or four steps ahead; Dahl joined the cops in the chase, now turning more heads than the household names that occupied the pitch.

People roared in encouragement.

Dahl bowed slightly as he ran. Best to acknowledge praise when one received it. Webb led the pack, running for the upper stands. Already people were leaning over the barriers up there to get a better view of what was happening. Dahl passed two slow-moving cops and then one more as the man slipped to a tumult of applause.

Pitiless, these soccer fans. Pitiless. And where the hell is Beau? The Frenchman's usually lightning quick.

The Swede looked for a way to head Webb off, but the stadium was uniformly laid out and offered no short cuts. "Where are you?" He keyed the neck mic.

"Coming in from your right," Drake shouted and then he was there as Dahl swept around a sharp bend, the Yorkshireman using his shoulder to reduce speed.

"Just behind you," Smyth said.

"And me," said Yorgi.

"I am, of course, ahead," Beau said, the slippery tones extremely smug. "And waiting for Webb."

And now Dahl saw the Frenchman. Somehow he'd gotten above Webb, probably vaulted from seatback to railing and over vendors, knowing him, and was crouched on top of a barrier waiting for Webb to race into range.

Dahl slowed and readied.

"The last of the Pythians is about to go down," Drake said.

CHAPTER SIXTEEN

Beau sprang. Webb didn't see him coming, but certainly felt the impact, letting out a grunt and a half-scream before collapsing to the floor. Beau bounced off the Pythian's stomach and landed on two feet, as fleet as a cat and more deadly. Drake and Dahl slowed even more, coming up to a struggling Webb. Hayden's hesitant but hopeful voice filled his ears.

"Did you get the bastard?"

Drake paused, cautious. Webb was already upright, glaring at Beau as if he might have the power to melt the man with eye lasers. Luckily for him, he was unscathed.

"You betrayed me, Beauregard Alain. Protected my back long enough to thrust a knife into it. You were never a believer."

"In chaos and death and the accumulation of supreme power? No, I will never believe in that. These days, I believe only in myself."

"Then you are weak. Just like the rest of them."

"Hey, pal," Drake called out. "You're the one who's about to go weak. At the knees when I break your bloody nose."

"Get in line," Kinimaka growled.

Webb turned to stare at them, the whole scene now peculiarly still. The crowd still roared and the fans cheered or jeered depending on who had the ball and the state of play or the referee's decision. But a small sphere enveloped them—the sphere of absolute focus.

"Do you think I would do all this with no backup plan? Ladies and gentlemen—" the madman spread his hands "—I have, and they're *limitless*."

There it was then. Drake held his breath, conscious that this monster could cook up the most terrible of brews. Yorgi suddenly had eyes everywhere.

"She's run off," Dahl said. "Your woman friend. Gone."

"You will never stop me. Never kill me," Webb said with a smile. "Do you know why?"

Drake stood prepared. "Because death's too good for you," he said with a surety.

"Because I am the next ascendant. I will find the elixir. And *I* will not only join the Master—I will assume his position!"

The cops moved in slowly. Dahl chuckled. "I know one position you're going to be assuming, old boy. Just as soon as we get you into general population."

But Webb flung his hands into the air, a black device in one hand, and pressed a red button.

"Let them fly!" he screamed. "Let them fly now!"

Drake froze, ready for anything, the first image he had of the new threat was a sparkling rush from above. Flashing edges of light caught his eyes, which were drawn to the skies.

People in the crowd were letting loose small drones, not many but enough to scare the security and some of the crowd. Drake took immediate shelter behind the concrete wall at his side, but the drones just hovered there, menacing.

Panic swept the area.

Drake knew how this went. Everyone who'd seen the cops chasing a man now saw the drones and assumed the worst could be happening. These drones were tiny, though, too small to hold any real threat, but nobody really knew that. *How had Webb pulled this off?*

No matter. They'd come to that eventually. Right now . . . He cast around for Webb.

"Where . . . ?" Dahl surveyed the area.

Now they saw Beau, presumably in pursuit of Webb, leaping from railing to railing, but the crowd were starting to get in his way. Some were already clogging the aisles, others sheltering there. In another moment the drones all dived and spun in the air and then made their way back to their owners, eight in total.

No danger. Just threat. This was what Webb had been reduced to, but the madman still made good use of implied terror.

Somewhere above, at the Nou Camp's top level, Webb raced up the stairs, heading for an exit. Hayden jumped on the comms, filling Drake's ears with American expletives. Drake cut across her.

"Do you have eyes on him?"

"Yeah, but go. Just go!"

Drake took off fast, jumping two or three steps at a time, trying to pick his way through a confused, milling crowd. His urgency seemed to upset them even more and some followed in his wake, making it harder for Smyth and Dahl behind. Beau slipped up ahead, distracted by an anxious couple tugging at his arm, and trying to calm them.

"Slow down, people." The voice drowned out Hayden and surprised Drake.

"Argento? What—"

"You're inside a full capacity Nou Camp stadium. I don't have to tell you what will happen if panic fills that place. Now slow down and act as if all is well."

"Armand!" Hayden cried.

"I understand your frustration, but Webb is one man. And this is his get-out plan. One hundred thousand souls are packed into that stadium. Think smarter. Use the CCTV, Hayden, and catch him outside."

Despite everything, Drake agreed with the Italian. With a conscious effort and fighting every instinct in his body, he slackened the pace and smiled around into concerned faces.

"All okay, folks," Dahl called out. "Just a pickpocket."

Drake shook his head. "You're worse than a daily rag for finessing the bloody facts. As if they're gonna believe you."

Dahl shrugged. "They want to, that's what counts, mate."

Drake saw it in their faces. None of them wanted to miss the match, this highlight of their week or, for some, their year; none of them wanted to walk away from the global atmosphere. Their own optimism bred new belief that someone had played a malicious prank.

"You'll be okay," Drake said to a dithering couple. "Take your seats."

He believed it. Webb had shown his new and apparently only recourse—contacts who couldn't or wouldn't cause mayhem on a large scale. At least for now. Maybe it was Webb's way of staying below the radar. Or maybe he had so few collaborators left this was all they could whip together.

Still, they seemed effective.

Drake reached the top of the steps, thankful that the crowd appeared to be settling. Thank God that the cult had held off. Perhaps *they* were waiting for Webb outside. Drake passed his thoughts along.

They pushed through a door and then switched right along an open area, looking for some stairs. Eateries stood to their right, causing Kinimaka to give vent to a groan of longing.

As he ran, Drake caught sight of familiar faces running straight at them, chasing a fleet figure. "Hey!"

"Quit fucking goggling and stop that roadrunner bitch!" Alicia's mild tones caressed his ear drums.

"All right, all right. Calm down."

Drake saw the woman who Webb had been meeting with race toward him, as fast as anyone he'd ever seen. Mai and Alicia were chasing hard but dropping back, no match for the quick runner.

"Ha." Drake couldn't help himself. "You two stop to get your nails done?"

Dahl also planted himself in the way. "I see it's a good job I'm here. As usual."

The woman didn't slow; face untroubled as she saw the obstacles in her path.

"Er, excuse me, love—" Drake began as the gap closed fast.

Dahl braced himself. The woman had her long blond hair wrapped into a vicious bob which slapped both sides of her face as she ran. The trainers were vivid green, Asics, and brand new. The outfit was tight, made for running, the Barcelona shirt now gone, and the small baseball cap barely hanging on. Drake saw only one way to go and moved forward himself, not believing she would actually tackle the two of them but preparing for the chance.

The woman skidded in, dropping low and kicking out at

Drake's knees. The polished floor was a perfect surface for her, almost as if she'd planned for it. He skipped left, avoiding a broken shin or knee, and tried to tackle her about the waist. The position was awkward. She sailed past.

Dahl waded in too, but the woman angled her body so that the mad Swede toppled over her. He hit the floor hard, groaning. Kinimaka positioned himself at the end of her slide, reaching out with open arms. The woman skipped left, then right, gave him a wide berth and prepared to take off again. In fact, Yorgi was the only one capable of matching her with his buildering skills and knowledge of parkour, but what he gained in movement he lacked in fighting ability. The woman met him head on—literally—and gave him a bloody nose.

Drake scrambled toward her, using the floor for purchase. "Shit, did you see—?"

"Slipperier than a Frenchman covered in baby oil," Alicia agreed. "And nothing solid to hang on to her with. Shit, you two are bloody useless."

Drake dived for the woman, a headlong plunge, just as she jinked right and scurried for the stairs. His outstretched fingers brushed her ankles, but she evaded him, leaving him sprawling and staring at the well-polished floor.

"Bollocks."

"You were saying?" Mai panted as she skipped over him. "About nails?"

Drake rose, but Dahl cut him off, managing to barge the woman at the exact moment she turned on the speed. Her momentum changed and she staggered headlong, reaching to keep her balance. Then she spun, drove a hand under Dahl's neck and another into his groin, left him shuddering and shocked, moaning on the spot.

"That was close," Kinimaka said.

"Get the f-feeling she held back," Dahl said.

"Good job you were here though," Alicia mocked. "To slow her with your balls."

At the top of the stairs now their quarry chanced a look back. Mai was almost upon her, Alicia a step away. Drake and Dahl scrambled up and Kinimaka lumbered alongside. The flight down to the next level wasn't long. Mai slowed slightly and reached out.

Alicia barged past her. "Pull your big girl panties up, Sprite. This bitch goes all the way down."

The Englishwoman barged hard into their quarry, smashing her against the handrail and forcing out a scream. Without pause the woman rebounded past Alicia, saw a gap, and leapt four stairs straight into it, landing like a cat and with perfect poise.

"Talk about a freakin' cat burglar," Kinimaka said.

Drake had never seen anyone so 'on it', except perhaps for Beau. This woman had mad evasion skills and was embarrassing the team. What had Webb required of her? Alicia was fuming, almost angry enough to take her shoe off and throw it at the escapee.

Dahl then stepped around them all. "Let's stop pussyfooting around, shall we?"

The Swede reached out, ripped a metal trashcan from its moorings, held it aloft and dropped it over the railing, timed perfectly to land on the fleeing woman's head. She never saw it coming, but the impact was a loud, resounding clang. The force of the heavy object sent her into a slump and a slither down the rest of the staircase.

Now, finally, she stopped moving.

"Shit, Torsty, we didn't want to kill the bitch," Alicia growled.

"She'll be okay," Dahl said. "See, she's twitching."

"Let's hope she can still speak."

Drake hurried toward her, then reached out tentatively. The woman was well and truly out cold. He keyed his mic.

"We have the woman. Beau's on his own though, chasing Webb."

"Seriously?" Hayden came back. "It took five of you to take her down?"

"She was one thorny little snag," Alicia said.

"Beau?" Hayden said. "You there?"

"Lowest level," the Frenchman said. "I have eyes on Webb. Thought he'd evaded me but I got lucky. Come fast, he's about to run again."

"Still in the chase, guys," Hayden said. "Stay on it. Take Tyler Webb down."

"And stay alert out there," Kinimaka added. "We haven't heard from this cult yet and I get the feeling we're about to."

CHAPTER SEVENTEEN

Tyler Webb was finding that the last few days of running had started to give him a new lease of life. Ignore the cramps and the pain, the shin splints, the knee jabs and the black spots dancing wildly before your eyes, and it really wasn't too bad. Overcome the agony, and he felt he could probably run forever. Outrun an Olympian. Take on one of those new-fangled mud sports.

In any case, I can shake off Drake and his cronies.

Not that he wanted to shake off *all* of them. Hayden Jaye—she still had possibilities which he longed to be in a position to explore. Maybe later. Maybe after.

For now, Webb escaped the stadium with only Beauregard close enough to worry about. *Only Beauregard.* Bit of a contradiction there; he knew the Frenchman's capabilities. Almost on a par with his own. Little to choose between them. But still, he'd best evade a fight. He laughed out loud.

Webb raced past security men too engrossed in their Bluetooth comms to see him coming. He'd stashed a gun outside the ground earlier, and now felt retrieving it might help slow the pursuit. He headed that way via the big gates, seeing the Frenchman coming closer but more interested in what Sabrina the thief had told him.

She was the best of her kind, a midnight prowler without reputation, rival or equal. The world's greatest thief that nobody had ever heard of. And mostly, that fact soothed her. Occasionally it infuriated her.

Webb didn't know her well or call on her often, but the huge retainer he'd deposited in her account every month paid for a short window of loyalty. This was it. The woman—named Sabrina Balboni as far as he knew—was a tall, lithe woman with a fiery Italian heart, moves that made The Flash look sluggish and a temper that could overpower volcanoes. Though appearing blond, she had jet black hair and jet black eyes. Webb had called upon her because the next few steps of his quest were beyond most people—even him. They required entry to some complex places.

The last clue in Paris had been so wondrous, revealing the arts of ancient alchemy to his awestruck eyes and providing pointers to the next stage of his quest, here in Barcelona. The thing that rankled was that Drake and co. had found it after him, and were now no doubt scratching their heads over the discoveries. But never mind, he was still way ahead of them and counting down toward the culmination of all he had ever sought.

The great treasure of Saint Germain.

Webb was roughly snatched out of his dreamworld and catapulted back to the present as Beauregard caught him up. Too desperate to be shocked, Webb barged through the gates and outside the ground, spied a gaggle of tourists and onlookers, and plowed straight into them. Screams sounded as Webb put on a high-pitched dramatic voice.

"He has a *gunnnnnn!*"

Beau was slowed and Webb accelerated. Something realistic and regular inside told him he stood no proper chance against the Frenchman, so he quickly sought an alternative. Red hot flashes sped from the soles of his feet to his hips as he almost toppled. This running around would be the death of him.

Traffic was heavy and he fancied that Beau might be able to outrun a pushbike, so Webb settled on something else. The motorbike rider was sat astride his red and silver machine, studying a map at the side of the road when Webb barged him aside without warning. The man flew, the bike crashed to the floor.

Webb glanced back and saw Beau breaching the gang of onlookers and locking on to him so fast he might be giving off a halo, or something similar. He struggled with the bike, ignoring the moans of the man who looked like he'd broken an arm in the crash. Webb kicked him in the stomach. That helped untangle the idiot and felt rather good. Webb hefted on the handlebars, hauled the heavy lump upright. The keys were there, the engine just ready for ignition. Webb concentrated on getting it started and then squeezed the throttle. Beauregard couldn't be too far behind; no time to waste.

He accelerated hard, felt a hand brushing his ribs and an icy flash of fear. *No! Not now!* The front wheel rose as he twisted the throttle wide open, engine roaring. Beau had no choice but to fall away. Webb arrowed it between two slow moving cars, not caring about a woman trying to pass through, laughing as he almost clipped her shoulders with the raised front wheel. The meek passed in his wake, as they should. He was a whirlwind, born to rule and destined to become their absolute master. They would live and die like weeds before him, unless he chose to cut them down first.

The bike leveled out. Webb swung it past front and rear fenders, in between vehicles, scratching metal where the gap was tight and not caring. A car-free but pedestrian-filled crosswalk provided a chance to open her up again, and to laugh as the weak and the fearful scattered like terrified sheep. No way could Beau or the Drake crew live with this. Webb was a god amongst men yet again, heading for . . .

He paused the self-acclaim in his head. *Crap, where am I heading? Is this the right?*

Sabrina had done her research previously, and then told him the location of the place he sought—a deep-rooted, long-standing college that Germain had frequented in his heyday. More important, and led by the clue he discovered, Webb had told Sabrina of the library inside the college, which he sought.

Germain had used this library almost as his own resource room, studying there for days at a time and allowing none within to join him as he worked. Webb had previously known of the library since it was listed as one of the many European haunts the Count frequented, but until now knew nothing of its underlying importance.

The Count had been seen at so many places, his movements so well documented by local dignitaries and kings and queens, it was hard to pick them apart. Sabrina had pinpointed the place and told Webb how to reach it—the doors to use and windows to avoid, passages to use and places through which to creep. He'd thought about making her come along, but remembered she might have the guile to see his brilliance and attempt to steal all his glory. Still, if all went as planned he would need her impeccable services at least once more.

Webb read road signs and tried to make sense of them. The college was at least a half hour from here, but the traffic was so thick it steered even him in but a single direction. He considered cutting across several lanes of traffic, but thought he might end up with something broken. Behind, he saw figures approaching, more than one, and felt just a small niggle of despair.

Tenacious bastards. Why couldn't they have died at Niagara Falls? Or Tokyo or Arizona? Didn't they have anything else to do? All he asked for was a nice, quiet life, enjoying the freedom to destroy others. It was his gift, a birthright. Briefly, he wondered if he could talk to them about it. Explain. Surely . . .

Reality kicked in again as a horn sounded. Webb glared at its owner, then tried to memorize the license plate for later amusements. He shot by, seeing the instruments of his downfall fast approaching. Gaining hard. Nowhere to go. Webb joined another stream of traffic that appeared to be moving faster, leaned over the front of the bike and urged it on. He could hear them shouting now, urging him to stop.

Wait . . .

To his right came more hunters, these ones terrifyingly familiar. Aboard motorcycles and toting guns they swerved and veered and plowed toward him. Back at the Camp Nou he'd been expecting the *group*, it was why he'd chosen the crowded venue— more bodies to put between himself and the guns—but out here, in the crawling traffic, he was intensely vulnerable.

Webb gunned the motor, firing forward. Black shapes darted across from the side and shots started to ring out. Pedestrians stared in disbelief, then scattered. The stupid sounded their horns at the passing bikes. Others cracked open their doors and raced for cover, adding to the traffic jam that already clogged Barcelona's streets.

Webb hunkered down as far as he could, guiding the bike with vigorous abandon and trusting to his inbred, godlike ability to survive. As if by magic the answer emerged from the haze of light ahead.

Webb opened the throttle, taking the bike up onto the sidewalk.

CHAPTER EIGHTEEN

Drake saw Webb steal the motorbike and Beau's last lunge to try to stop him. The Frenchman fell short and hit the road; Webb roared away.

Drake cursed. "Shit, Webb has more lives than Mario on freeplay."

Yorgi nodded. "Beau is not on his game today."

"Webb's clever," Kinimaka admitted. "We know that."

"Stop blabbing," Hayden said. "And help chase him down."

They chased their prey down, reckless through the traffic, skirting cars and avoiding pushbikes and pizza delivery cycles. Drake found the delivery guys and the locals the worst, all darting in and out of spaces to gain half a car's length and making everybody else's lives that much harder. He bounced off a Prius, came back off a 4x4's tall tire and darted past a dangerously weaving motorcycle. Pedestrians slowed him down; Alicia and Mai finding a quicker route along the sidewalk. Dahl picked the weaving motorcycle up, complete with rider, and placed it out of the way, facing the wrong direction. Kinimaka stumbled against a white Range Rover, pulling an apologetic face at the shocked driver. They caught up to Beau as the Frenchman slowed for them.

"Bit slow there, mate," Drake observed breezily. "Unlike you."

"He was lucky."

Ahead, Webb drove recklessly, arrogantly. It was Hayden who noticed the new team coming in from the left, weapons as visible as their helmets, bikes all a uniform pitch black, intentions as clear as their intended quarry.

"Heads up!"

But Drake and Dahl had already seen them and were angling their runs accordingly. Drake wrenched a pizza storage box off the back of a bike and threw it at the first rider. It smashed into the man's arm, exploding, sending plastic and pizza everywhere. The bike wobbled, crashed against a car before righting itself and shooting off again.

Drake targeted the next before he could bring his gun to bear. The bike zoomed past just a few inches away and the Yorkshireman yanked on an arm. Both bike and man went skidding through the traffic, ending up piled against the wheel of a Nissan pickup. Dahl collided with his man like a charging rhino, both of them crashing to the floor and scraping along for several feet. The difference was that Dahl took the man's gun and rendered him unconscious before then stealing his bike and gunning the throttle.

"Hop on," he said to Drake.

"I'll catch the next one," Drake replied.

The third to pass their position received a flying kick to the ribs that sent his gun zipping away, and even his helmet clattering down the street. Drake hefted the bike, its wheels spinning, and righted it before motoring hard after the Swede. Kinimaka and Smyth were mopping up behind, giving the front runners freedom to close the gap.

Drake and Dahl chased the six remaining bikers as they pursued Webb through the crowded streets of Barcelona. Alicia and Mai hammered along the sidewalk, keeping pace several meters to the right. Webb bounced his own machine up onto the opposite sidewalk, his own intentions unclear. Drake saw a crowd ahead of him and no easy way through. He angled the bike over, slipped through several quickly disappearing gaps, and came up behind one of the cult's rear-guard.

"Oy!"

The helmet turned, the gun swiveling too. Drake accelerated up the other side, clipping the curb but hanging on, and then kicked out at his adversary. The bike wobbled, the man shaking wildly but holding on, and then leaned back, decelerating.

The gun now poked toward Drake.

Quickly, he yanked on the steering and smashed his own bike against his adversary's. This time the man took flight, crumpling as he landed, and yelling out in pain. Another gun skittered away.

Drake tracked Webb as best he could, confident the man would have to return to the road any second. Then he could . . .

Just then the ex-Pythian hauled so hard on the brakes that the back tire lifted and came around ninety degrees. Webb leapt into space, leaving the bike to crash into the floor. Drake slowed and left his bike at the curb, then saw Dahl up ahead battling with a rider so close they were practically sat on each other's seats. The Swede managed to lug the cultist over and left the bike to tumble, then dropped a shoulder and threw the other man hard onto the hood of a nearby car whilst still seated. Metal crumpled, bones broke. Dahl carried his bike out of the way and then deposited it against a lamppost.

"Marking your territory?" Drake had kept half an eye to make sure Dahl was okay and the other on Webb as the man headed for a building almost covered in flashing lights, advertisements and flickering billboards.

"Don't men still piss on lampposts up in Yorkshire?"

"Oh aye, lad, they do. The women too."

"Lovely."

Drake saw a rider up ahead, black clad, trying to steer his way through a crush of bodies. He stood little chance and fell to the floor, but a wave of his gun sent dozens of people running. Drake saw Webb enter a rotating door ahead and finally saw where the man was headed.

And why.

The Barcelona International Motor Show.

It's gonna be so crowded in there you couldn't find a giant wearing an octopus hat. Webb's next backup. Another chance to slip away. But wait . . . maybe not. Could Webb finally have made a mistake?

The football match would divert thousands for its duration. Drake ran flat out to try to keep eyes on Webb. The flashing lights, rather than grab his attention, annoyed the hell out of him and made him look away. Droves roved outside the entrance, discussing the cars or the city or the match, or a multitude of alternate entertainments. Drake pushed through the doors and flashed a temporary ID badge at the guard.

Don't stop me . . . don't stop me . . . I don't want to cause any incidents—

Then Dahl was behind him. "Are we in? Or do I have to plant him with the hydrangeas over there?"

Drake winced, eyes still locked on Webb but only seconds away from losing the madman. The guard stared at Drake and then Dahl, catching sight of their cuts and bruises.

"Come on, man," Dahl said. "We're in pursuit of an international terrorist who just entered your friggin' showroom."

The guard took another look at their badges and then ushered them through, calling on security. Drake hurried along the same route he'd seen Webb take. "You know it's a motor show, right? Not a car showroom."

The pair didn't wait, but rushed through the acceptably slender throng, grateful now for the gargantuan event not too far away. Kenzie and Smyth caught them up and then Hayden, who reported the rest were just behind.

"Any sign of the gunmen?" Dahl asked her.

Hayden shook her head. "No, and that's not a good sign. They will be seeking a different entry point, that's all. And then . . ." She exhaled with a worried look. "It could be bad in here. I've already alerted the locals."

"There!" Drake cried.

"What? Webb? The cultists?" Dahl stared over in anticipation.

"No. It's the new Ferrari F12 TDF. See the new side vents and enhanced wheel arches? The—"

"Fucksake, Drake." Alicia sauntered up on his left. "I know cars are the greatest love of your life, but. . ."

Hayden paused as the crowds again became overwhelming. The vast hall was filled with splendor and gold and glitter at every turn; manufacturers showing off their latest offerings and draping them with striking colors, banks of lighting and half-dressed models. People gathered at the best vantage points, taking their photos and discussing the finer points of what was on offer. From German to Italian, English to Japanese, the whole gamut parked their wares on rotating turntables and invited special guests to cross the red-rope barriers and sip champagne whilst trying to look cool and extremely wealthy. The walkways between such brands as Lamborghini and Porsche were full to capacity, whilst the paths between less extravagant brands were much more navigable. Hayden switched the group past the Toyota offering and Drake quickly followed.

Webb was ahead, two stands away, the man and his backpack standing out from the milling crowd as he pushed through. The first gunshots echoed terribly inside the motor show, blasts resounding around the high ceiling. Immediately, Drake saw the running gunmen coming down an aisle that crisscrossed Webb's, their guns aimed straight at him. He jumped over a rope barrier and ran among a display of Mitsubishis, bullets marring the metal all around him. Lights shattered and exhibition stands blew apart. More shots ripped the excited ambiance to shreds.

Drake drew his gun now, having no qualms about taking the shooters out for good. He ran fast and stooped, Glock held low. Webb's head popped up briefly amongst the Mitsubishis, followed by a volley of lead and several smashed windscreens. A tower of paper cups flew through the air. A bottle of champagne exploded along with a pile of brochures, the whole collective shooting up and showering the area.

Drake saw people ducking and diving, and fired at the first running gunman. He flew sideways, colliding with a temporary display and smashing it to pieces, streaks of red blood marring the exclusive designs. The team spread all around him. Dahl leapt up two revolving platforms to gain the dizzy heights of a Peugeot stand and crouched behind a silver car. Alarm bells resounded, clearing the public out. The crowds that once stared at and admired the shining vehicles now streamed for the red exit signs.

Dahl fired his weapon from atop the stand and another cultist went down. More followed though, swiveling and firing up at the Swede. Drake saw him duck behind a wheel, and lay down some cover fire.

Hayden was crouched low, keying her comms system. "Webb's heading for the rear exits. Anyone there?"

Only the local cops answered, not sounding entirely sure.

Drake crept closer to the running men. The team all opened fire now, causing their enemy to scatter, duck and hide behind vehicles and metal stanchions. Dahl crept down the other side of the Peugeot stand, moving on all fours. Alicia popped up and fired at Drake's side, keeping the enemy hemmed in.

"Move closer," Hayden said. "I count eight remaining. Speed wins the day here, guys."

Drake wondered if that was an intentional double entendre.

Lauren was the only one to remain behind as the rest of the team stole ever closer to their enemies' positions. Two cultists tried to bolt after Webb, but Smyth and Kinimaka made short work of their mad dash. Webb himself appeared to remain cautious, keeping his progress steady and watchful, not risking anything but aiming inexorably for the rear of the enormous hall.

Drake changed the clip in his Glock. Gleaming lights shone down from floating ceilings above their heads, designed for the cars but picking out the firefight in every detail. The cultists had chosen to take cover among a shining spectacle of highly polished Jaguars, an SUV and a blue sports car now fully peppered with holes. Drake groaned as bullets flew overhead, hitting displays behind them with the flags of Italian marques.

"This is not good," he said.

Alicia knew him. "You mean for the event or the bloody cars?"

Drake gave her a 'duh' glare.

"Such beautiful bodywork and machinery being destroyed," Drake said.

"Shall we concentrate on the terrorists?" Mai asked.

Argento's voice filled the comms, strikingly high-pitched and different. "It is important that you protect the Alfa Romeo brand. Do you hear? Highly important. It is our great heritage, our undying passion, our—"

A flurry of gunfire shut him up. The cultists were well dug in now, the Jaguars listing badly, a bullet-strewn pair of vertical light-stands rising above them. A small fire had started to the right of the stage. Another man rose to take a pot shot at Webb, and Drake missed his forehead by an eighth of an inch.

Hayden cursed. "They're helping him *escape*."

The team evaluated, gauged distances, gaps and lines of cover. Then Torsten Dahl made a positive sound. "Just give me a minute," he said. "And I'll save the day."

Drake started to say: "Oh, yeah, very droll—" but then the Swede was moving and the team scrambled to give him shelter. Their bullets tore apart front wings and all remaining panes of glass, burst tires and shattered rear lights. Drake managed to sever the cords of a hanging light which smashed down among their enemies.

Dahl bounded down a few steps and onto the floor, an eager guard dog, switched over to the right, and approached an adjacent podium. It took Drake only a moment to figure out what was about to happen.

"Oh, shit. Get ready—"

Dahl broke apart a two-meter-wide stand dedicated to the unveiling of a new style of alloy rim. The heavy, eight-spoked rims crashed to the ground hard, but Dahl reached down and took one under each arm. As the cultists looked over to assess the threat, Drake, Mai and Alicia rose firing, racing up the steps of the Peugeot stand to get a clearer line of fire. Cultists collapsed, groaning. Three aimed at Dahl and another charged the Swede.

Dahl spun fast then let go. An enormous, incredibly heavy rim arced through the air and hit the running man chest-on, its force crushing everything it touched. The second rim then went flying, smashing into the cultists' main position, glancing off a head and a shoulder, causing total mayhem. Guns went flying. Heads smashed metal or each other. Dahl picked up a final rim and hurled it before anyone thought to move.

Drake, Mai and Alicia ran down the steps, still firing hard. Blood began to seep under the chassis of the ragged looking Jaguars.

The third rim came down like a descending meteor, denting a bright red wing and then deflecting onto a skulking, black-clad chest. The lurker let out a screech, but was afforded no mercy as a running Smyth finished him off. Dahl flexed his muscles to give them a little relief and then drew his own gun, flanking Drake.

"I think we now have your new online ID," Drake mouthed. "Rim Tosser."

"I was The Beach Runner last week."

"Oh aye, but I think this one suits you better."

The two men crept to the front of the Jaguars.

"Better than Office Bike, I suppose."

"Hey, that's Alicia's."

"Fuck off, you two."

They sobered as the scene unfolded. The cultists were lying dead or dying, some with guns still clasped in their hands and still attempting to point them at the SPEAR team.

"Really?" Alicia said. "Even now? You people must be off your heads."

"They belong to a cult," Mai said. "Which is everything to them. They would rather die than betray its secrets."

Drake remembered Mai had been sold into her own hell, not exactly a cult, but something close. He felt a pang of sorrow at moving on from their relationship so quickly. Had he done the right thing?

That's me alright, he thought. *Having to choose between two of the most dangerous women in the world. What could possibly go wrong?*

Hayden shouted over the airwaves: "I'm not so sure these men are actual cultists, guys. More like hired mercs."

Kenzie put a hand on Dahl's shoulder. "You okay, Torst? I think you owe Jaguar a new car."

Mai and Beau passed among the downed men, disarming and restraining for the cops. Another shot rang out then and Drake looked to the rear of the hall.

"Still some out there chasing Webb."

Hayden panted over the comms. "We're in pursuit. Webb's close to freedom."

"Not today." Dahl clenched his fists and mock-glared at Drake. "Maybe this time you could even help."

CHAPTER NINETEEN

Drake ran again, ignoring the aches and pains and bruises of battle. Experience helped him scan the plethora of hiding places from nearby to far ahead, and he noted only three remaining adversaries.

And Webb, the figure vague and approaching the auto show's back doors, where metal overhangs, wide stanchions and high ceiling walkways cast everything into indistinct shadow.

"Bloody 'ell!"

Drake saw Hayden and Kinimaka, and sprinted along the aisles. The pair had halted alongside half a dozen motor show models, trying to instil some kind of calm among the women. It didn't help when one of the cultists turned to take a pot shot. Alicia fired back amid the screams, scaring her enemy into flight.

They ran on, the bright lights glimmering and making them sweat, the shiny vehicles and vivid colors a pure assault on the senses, the remaining pockets of hidden civilians a heavy deterrent to engaging the cultists. They kept low, less threatening. Hayden climbed a podium belonging to Aston Martin to keep an eye on Webb.

Drake then saw the answer. Some of the cars at these shows were so unique, so secret, their success reliant on hype and expectation, that they were exhibited just a few short hours before being whisked away to private showings. Especially in the early evening prior to the show's closing, cars were rolled and then driven out the back. Drake saw one such car at the side of the hall now, having been abandoned by the manufacturer's representatives when the gunfight broke out.

Chiron, he thought.

Screaming for attention it drew him to the left as the others carried on. Drake keyed the comms.

"Two minutes."

Now praying the firefight would have made even the most dedicated technician abscond without a second thought, Drake approached the outlandish car and reached down for the door handle. Glad to see it was at least open, he let the door swing wide and took a look inside. Unable to help himself, he took that extra second to revel in the utter luxuriousness of it all, the flawless interior art.

No keys dangled from any ignition, sending his heart sinking until he spied the butt end of a curved object protruding from under the steering wheel. Jumping in, Drake knew the starting procedure for this car's predecessor and tried the same technique.

Demons roared from the back end, the tailpipes spewing forth hellfire and madness. Drake felt his face crack into a crazy grin, engaged drive, and set the hypercar into motion. Feeling more nerves than he ever did in battle, he guided the car around the back end of the auto show, passing between metal stanchions that loomed threateningly close. As he cleared the two pillars he got a look ahead.

Webb stood before a red-marked exit door, looking over at him as if drawn by the incredible thunder spitting from the car. Three enemies loomed close behind, their guns not pointed at Webb but being forced to protect their own backs. Alicia, Mai, Dahl and Smyth bore down upon them like avenging demons, straight at the readied barrels of three weapons.

Drake floored the accelerator, letting out a yelp and a cheer at the instant turn of speed. The beast pounced, burning rubber, slewing slightly as it ate up the distance between it and the cultists. Unable to ignore the impending threat, they turned.

The car plowed into them. One flew over the low hood, taking flight as his arms and legs pinwheeled faster than a skier falling down the seventy-meter slope. Another rebounded, the thump bone-jarring, the sudden stop and reverse momentum mind-blowing. The third somehow landed hard on the hood, denting it enough to make Drake wince as the two shared a look through the sparkling windscreen.

"Get. Off. My. Car," Drake mouthed.

The man's eyes bulged as Dahl grabbed his ankles, pulled him clear and swung him across the floor. He skidded further than expected, the high gloss complementing the slide, ending up far enough away to shake his head and then start reaching for his gun. Mai finished him off with a single shot, then rolled her eyes at Dahl.

Drake flung open the door, now opposite the exit Tyler Webb had used only a minute ago. The chatter through his comms tripled, excited voices exuding information at a rapid rate. He joined Alicia and Smyth at the door.

"Thought you'd fucked off 'ome," Alicia greeted him.

Drake wrenched the door open. "And choose between you and the car?"

Smyth shouldered through the gap, ignoring them both, game face on. Drake followed, knowing the soldier expected instantaneous backup. Surprisingly, they emerged into another hall, this one much smaller though nonetheless high and spacious, and filled with trailers, vans and every mode of car transportation, either en-masse and cheap, or private and overpriced. Offices bordered the building, with gantries and metal bridges spanning the gap. Drake stopped in the face of uncountable obstacles.

"We're gonna need a bigger—"

Hayden joined them. "How many exits?" She spoke into the throat mic.

Drake heard the reply. "Eight, plus three double doors."

"You have people on them?"

"We're . . . trying."

Drake shook his head. "Split up," he said, without much hope. "We may get lucky."

Alicia hadn't the spirit left to summon up a double entendre.

"So that's it?" Smyth growled. "Webb gets away. Damn it!"

"Not yet," Dahl said, ever the optimist. "Not bloody yet."

But outside the skies were blacker than a killer's heart, the streets as helpful as a call center. Webb could have gone a dozen different ways, and then a dozen more. Drake took a breath and waved at his colleagues.

"We're not done yet. Webb's here for a reason, and it wasn't to watch football or ogle high-end brands. He's not finished here yet, and we still have a good lead."

"What?" Smyth rasped.

"The woman."

CHAPTER TWENTY

With Mai and Smyth double-checking their perimeter, the SPEAR team strode back around the side of the arena toward the front doors. Conversation was passed, the most significant part of which for Drake, was a comment made by Beauregard.

"The cultists' men, they are slow. Lacking, due to years of watching and no action. Perhaps they are complacent, but have now become aware that they will have to step it up."

"These are mercenaries," Hayden said. "Not true cultists."

"That is exactly what I mean," Beau told her. "That their *bosses* are slow, lacking. Inactive. They will have to improve and amplify their skills if they are to achieve their own goals."

Hayden nodded slowly. "You could be right. Idleness breeds complacency. They can't remain idle."

"One more reason for a trip to Dubai," Drake appended.

Upon returning to the front entrances, Drake began to wish they hadn't. The unsure masses had congregated and milled around whilst being told what to do. The clamor drowned out all conversation. Hayden waved them all back again.

"Argento." She tapped the comms. "Where are we?"

"No facials. Webb has gone. The dead terrorists are simply that at the moment. No identification. On a much brighter note our new female friend just started to sing higher and longer than Pavarotti. She—"

Hayden smiled grimly, taking in the team. "We'll be there soon, Armand. Good job."

"Of course, of course. I am merely magnificent."

"Now." Hayden breathed out a ragged sigh and glanced around, her hair framed by a huge white Motor Show sign. "Where the hell can we find a car?"

*

Despite the proximity of innumerable vehicles it took thirty minutes for their transport to turn up. By that time the team was chomping at the bit and bordering on irritable. With no further information forthcoming, Webb's trail was growing colder by the minute. Beat cops and informants failed to find anything on the street. CCTV cameras came up blank, even the covert ones.

And Europe was a big continent. So many places to disappear.

A minibus packed them all in, with Dahl taking the wheel. Ironically, as he set off, the streets of Barcelona became much easier to navigate as people left the area or turned in for the night.

Alicia wiggled her elbows into Yorgi's ribs. "Whoa, it's a good job you're smaller than a woman, Yogi. And stop friggin' wriggling, 'less you want me to headlock ya."

Drake turned partway around. "Don't let her bully you, mate. Give her as good back."

"Webb came to Barcelona for a reason," Hayden was saying. "Are we to believe it was just for her?"

"She had skills," Dahl said. "Took a major weapon to take her down."

"A blunt instrument." Drake thought about the litter bin and then glanced over at the Swede. "*And* a major tool."

"Weapon," the Swede amended.

"Y'know, I'm not convinced—"

"Still," Hayden interrupted. "If the woman's so important— who is she?"

"Just wait," Kinimaka said. "And we'll find out."

"Maybe not Barcelona." Mai always thought outside the box. "Maybe Spain."

"To recap then," Hayden said. "We have fanatics dedicated to preserving the secrets of Saint Germain, and Tyler Webb journeying from Transylvania to Versailles to Barcelona, digging through old chemistry books and enlisting the help of expert teams . . . and people. What is he ultimately chasing, though? And why?"

"Dude willingly abetted the destruction of his own organization to get where he is," Smyth said, then tapped his forehead. "Crazy. This situation could exist entirely in his head."

"The cultists don't think so," Lauren said.

"He's collecting items. Or following a map. Or stealing artefacts." Drake shrugged. "Whatever. We'll ask him when we find him."

"If we don't get taken off this thing first," Hayden fretted. "I mean, the entire team chasing one man?"

Drake scratched his forehead as Dahl wound through the quiet streets. "Don't be daft. The world's most wanted man, and a path of destruction and danger across Europe? Of course we'll see it through. Not to mention the personal angles."

A call came through, which routed through Bluetooth to the vehicle's phone system. Dahl touched a button.

"Yes?"

"Argento here. We have progress, *mi amico*. The woman is a ghost, a fringe-walker that nobody has ever heard of or seen before. How about that?"

"I'm not sure how that helps us, Armand," Hayden ventured as the Italian actually paused.

"She wasn't always that way. Take her story back many years and she was—and is—Sabrina Balboni, an Italian actress, singer and dancer. Very different back then, she fell into bad ways after gaining her fame and ended up convicted of manslaughter when a car she was traveling in killed a passerby. She and three other people, including the driver, were heavily under the influence of cocaine at the time. She did a stretch—a long one—completed her time and then fell off the map. Utterly. We haven't delved into the last twelve years yet, but she is a loner and totally devoted to herself. That's why she rolled over on Webb."

"I'll tell you this," Dahl said. "Those last twelve years? They taught her some furious skills. The way she moved . . ."

"Calm down." Kenzie patted his arm. "We'll get you an autograph."

"So what did she know?" Hayden asked.

"Webb contacted her because she has these 'furious skills', as you say. She has no equal, a reputation passed on only by word of mouth, and a contact protocol worthy of a president. Webb has always run in powerful circles and was made aware of her long ago. He paid a healthy monthly retainer just so, one day, he might be able to enlist her services. Now the time has come, it seems."

"But what are—" Dahl slowed for a red light "—these skills?"

"Basically, Sabrina is a thief. At a more complex level—she's Catwoman . . ."

"My favorite," Yorgi intoned with a deep Russian accent.

"Just so we're clear," Kenzie whispered under Argento's narrative. "She's not joining the team."

"Webb needs her services simply because his quest—whatever it is—gets harder with every stop along the way. The man needs Balboni's help to gain easy, fast entry to at least three more places, quite possibly because he can't take it slow and easy anymore. Not with the cult after him. He knows they're watching all these places. His solution is Sabrina Balboni."

Drake nodded. "Logical. Webb's not striking like a sledgehammer anymore. So where are these three places?"

"Ah, *mi amico,* the trillion-euro question. First, I have to ask, did any Alfa Romeos get hurt as your chase progressed?"

"Nope. Not one," Drake guessed, knowing the subject was close to the Italian's heart.

"Ah, good to know. That is good. Well, he explained to her where he was going next and hinted that nobody knew the final destination short of the country. He required her skills to gain access to one of Spain's oldest colleges, the University of Barcelona, which is why he agreed to meet amidst a hundred thousand people intent on watching the match. Her idea. She is governed by anonymity, this woman, just a face in a crowd that nobody ever remembers. They were headed to the university right away."

Dahl slowed the vehicle to a crawl. Hayden leaned forward. "And the final destination?"

"America," Argento said.

Of course, Drake thought. *Something else that just didn't make any sense.*

Dahl punched Seville into the satnav. "We can be there soon," he said. "Call the locals again, Armand, and have them watch the place."

"Already done. But it has been over an hour and a half."

"I know that," Hayden hissed, her frustration showing. "I friggin' know that."

CHAPTER TWENTY ONE

In typical and by now, expected fashion, the University of Barcelona had quite the multi-layered history. It had moved premises, been closed down, and changed buildings since its construction in the fifteenth century. In a stroke of good luck, though, they found that the Bourbon dynasty had closed the place down during the time Saint Germain had lived, perhaps even at the man's request. Who knew? The secrets, loaded decisions and inner conspiracies of the ruling classes were as deep and convoluted then as they are right now, from a town crier to a president.

Dahl pushed the minibus through sparse traffic, around sharp bends and down darkened streets as they followed the quickest route. Webb had a good head start. It occurred to Drake that Sabrina Balboni had always known this and intentionally dragged the questioning out, but he couldn't tell for sure until he met her face to face. The team readied themselves and checked all weapons, seeing the local cops up ahead, their cars waiting in the dark and giving off little reflection.

The building spanned the corner before them, stretching in both directions, its frontage higher than the walls and consisting of three arched entryways and ten arched windows, all dark. Trees swayed softly in front and higher structures to each side brooded in solitude, giving the appearance of watchtowers. The area was quiet, passing cars lending a peaceful and ordinary quality to the scene.

"One thing bugs me," Kinimaka said. "If Webb now needs Sabrina's talents to break into these places how did he get into this one?"

"She had time to explain it," Dahl said, "when they met. And, if they had comms set up, even as we chased them."

"One snake slithering alongside another," Alicia said. "You

and she might bond well, Bridget."

Not waiting for clearance, the SPEAR team moved out, seeing no reason not to head straight for the main entrance. The small security unit inside had been alerted, but reported nothing suspicious.

"Remember," Dahl said. "This man may now have less reach, less influence and less power, but he still has some very clever, influential and extremely resourceful people working for him. Eyes open, guns up."

The doors were unlocked, the interior darkened. The security unit met them halfway inside, again with shrugs. Spanish comment was passed, and even with no grasp of the language Drake knew they were all drawing blanks.

"Go," Hayden said and pointed. "Wait outside."

Argento had passed on Sabrina's information that Webb was only interested in the library, and the man's excited knowledge that Germain had studied there at will and convenience throughout his entire life *all the languages of the known world and more.*

Webb's words. Probably taken from some ancient script.

Meaning unknown. Drake thought it probably had to do with reading a map or following directions, maybe concocting something from the chemistry directives Webb took from Paris. They ventured carefully down one corridor and then an adjacent one, all the while closing in on the library. Darkness swarmed all around but fled from the soft, muted hallway lamps left on for security. As they closed in on the library door Hayden's pants pocket began to vibrate.

Holding up a hand, muttering that this was their only contact with the entire enterprise and reasoning that something urgent may have arisen, she quickly answered. "Yeah?"

"Oh, hello. Tyler Webb here. Is that Agent Jaye? Hayden Jaye?"

"Webb!" she hissed involuntarily.

"Oh it is. Excellent. Did the cellphone buzz in your pocket, Hayden? Did you feel me, vibrating through your groin?"

"Oh for fu—"

"Yeah, that was me. Think about it. In any case I have no time for that. Later, no doubt, when I have all the time in the world. If you survive."

Hayden held back all the words she wanted to say, all the threats she wanted to vent, all the lethal promises she wanted to make. "What do you mean by that?"

"Well, my friends have left a little . . . care package. A little revenge for stealing my thief."

"Sabrina set us up!" Kenzie hissed.

"No, no." Drake hoped she was wrong. "He always knew we'd come."

"One day," Hayden breathed into the cell. "Face to face."

"If not this then that day will be your last, Hayden. Oh and don't forget—I'm watching you. Always."

The line died. Silence fell like a ton of lead. Hayden stared at the offending phone and then at her friends and colleagues. "What now?"

Dahl gestured at the library door about ten meters ahead. "We go forward. It's what we always do."

He advanced and stepped on something hidden beneath the carpet. An ominous click sounded in the half-darkness, but from the roof above their heads.

Drake knew that sound. "Bomb!" he cried and turned to run.

As one, the team spun and fled, heading away from the library. In retrospect Drake realized they should have bolted in the other direction—Webb would never destroy the treasures of Saint Germain. As the clicks sounded and death neared, he made the fastest and hardest decision of his life.

"Wait!" he screamed above the noise. "We're going the wrong fucking way!"

"Oh, shit." Even Dahl vacillated.

Drake took their lives in his hands, grabbed Alicia, and hustled back past the detonation device. As he passed, a deep booming began; a resounding shockwave that stunned his senses and battered his ears. Above, he saw the entire length of the corridor's ceiling heave up and then collapse back down, swelled and shattered by the blast. He ran faster and lower, pulling Alicia and hearing the rest of the team racing behind.

Straight into the blast.

The corridor's walls bulged, bowed by the initial convulsion. Wooden panels smashed and shattered, some zipping across the corridor like deadly poisoned darts, passing between the runners and striking their body armor. Drake hid his face as they ran the gauntlet, grunting as objects abused his body.

Then the ceiling started to fall.

Plaster rained down, and concrete blocks. Drake hurdled one. A cloud of dust screened the way ahead.

"Drake!" Alicia cried out, and a heavy lump of masonry crashed down inches from his head. Behind, Smyth shielded Lauren, his arm constantly bombarded by falling shrapnel. Kinimaka plowed through the debris, kicking up almost as much rubble as fell around him. Dahl spun in mid-flight, seeing a descending jagged chunk and knowing instinctively that it would strike Hayden. He caught it momentarily in two hands, still running, then redirected its flight with a quick flick of the wrist. Beau twisted between collapsing curtains of wreckage, struck more times than he'd ever tell. Mai and Kenzie hugged opposite sides of the ruined walls, trusting that there would be no third explosion.

Drake staggered as a thick timber spar glanced off his shoulders, sprawling headlong, then rolling, still keeping up the speed. His body screamed, his nerves alight with pain. Dust filled his nose and eyes. They couldn't be sure what was happening up ahead and all the walls were destroyed, bristling with serrated wood and rough plasterboard edges. Beau kicked a ragged pole of wood aside. Mai used rubble the size of a boulder to leap off to avoid a hole in the floor. Kinimaka barged aside a cascading heap so the others could move quicker.

Drake gained his feet once more, using Alicia and Dahl as they reached arms down to him. The dust was clearing, the noise all but abated. Ahead, the library door appeared intact.

Dahl kicked it off its hinges, anxious to get out of the plaster dust and smoke and into what should be a safe haven. Quickly the team filed through, coughing and hanging their heads, staring at one another and seeing a ragged crew: white haired, white clothed and holding arms and legs where projectiles had struck.

"We all okay?" Drake panted. "Anyone badly hurt?"

All were fine, and then Hayden's cell rang again. She held it up so all could see the big screen.

Webb again.

"Don't answer," Dahl said. "Keep the bastard guessing."

"You know," Smyth said, holding his right arm extremely gingerly. "He could have killed us all back there. Wiped us off the map. What gives?"

"Impossible to say," Hayden said. "Lack of resources. Not enough time. Mistake. Design. Drake's quick thinking. My call is that the asshole thinks of this as a game, loves it more than family or power. Gets off on it."

"You think it gives him a boner?" Alicia wondered.

Drake and Dahl choked simultaneously, and not only on dust. "Jeez, Myles, tone it down to PG 13 wouldya? We don't need to hear that."

"It's what you were thinking."

Dahl blinked. "No actually, it wasn't at all."

"What about you, Yorgi? I bet you were wondering."

The Russian ignored her, which did the trick and stopped her conjectures.

Hayden pocketed her phone and took a three-sixty gander around the library. Stacks of hardbacks rose from floor to ceiling, all sizes, all colors, with no clear labelling system.

"Whatever he found here," she said. "Will probably stay secret."

Drake hated to, but tended to agree. "So that leaves us . . . fucked. We don't know what he's searching for. What he finds. Or why. Or where he's going to next. Fucked."

"Not yet." The words came surprisingly from Lauren. "I do have one idea."

CHAPTER TWENTY TWO

Drake sipped strong coffee whilst they all crowded around the two-way mirror, staring at Sabrina Balboni as the master thief stared back at them. Trying to read her was an impossibility. Drake wondered what it took to become one of the world's greatest burglars whilst also adorning yourself in anonymity. How deep the demands, how desperate the craving.

How overwhelming the guilt.

Balboni had chosen a profession that, by necessity, forced her to become a shadow, a true wraith of society. He wondered how her position now, facing prison, would sway her decisions in the next few hours.

Toward the good guys, he hoped. She was their last hope. After this, they were down to good fortune and a trip to Dubai.

Could be worse. He found his lips were curling up into a private smile, then realized he was staring straight at Mai. The Japanese woman noticed and returned it with warmth. He was caught, wedged between two stormy seas, the future an impenetrable cloud of impossibility. Thankfully, Hayden began to speak and he turned toward her.

"I will go in again. Reiterate the hard line. Then we'll let Lauren come in and propose the deal."

Drake listened as Hayden repeated the bleak future Sabrina had to look forward to and, try as she might, the thief just couldn't keep the horror from her eyes. Alicia took the time to rib Yorgi just a little.

"So what's it like, Yogi? To stand so close to a *real* thief?"

"What you mean?" The Russian looked suitably annoyed. "I am also real."

"Not on the same level, dude." Alicia pointed through the window. "That's a master. A genius. A light-fingered virtuoso with real-world expertise."

"I am master thief too!"

Dahl glanced down the passageway. "Hey, keep it down. We're in a police station."

"Well, you're good at impersonating a female, I'll give you that." Alicia turned the screw.

"I have proven my skills." Yorgi sulked.

"Yeah. Your eyebrows are amazing."

"I think you should leave him alone." Mai shifted slightly. "There is no time for this."

"Oh, and the Sprite leaps across the screen to the rescue! No time? Why not? Lauren hasn't even taught the thief how to do a proper Full Monty yet."

Mai blinked. "I don't know what you—"

"I do," Lauren said. "It is a stripping reference. And that's not what I'm doing here."

"Great film, great ending." Alicia was elsewhere. "And Robert Carlyle." She sighed. "Just leave me alone for a while."

Mai glared, then gave Drake a quick shake of the head. The Yorkshire man clapped Yorgi on the shoulders. Hayden waved toward the two-way window.

Lauren entered the room without comment, then took the room's third and last chair. She smiled at Sabrina, and Drake concentrated on what she had to say.

"There is a way out of this, Sabrina. A way you could help and make a difference."

Balboni's face remained neutral, which must have taken a huge effort. "A deal? I should have known."

"There's always a deal," Hayden said. "For those who know how to listen."

"We want Tyler Webb," Lauren said. "And right now, you're our best way of getting close to him. Real close. You're gonna be our inside man."

"Man?" Sabrina arched an eyebrow. "And Webb will know that I have been caught. He will meet me again only to kill me."

"Well, that's a possibility," Lauren told her. "But we believe we can coach you to pass his tests," she paused. "I've done it before."

Now Sabrina narrowed her eyes. "Really? In what way?"

"Doesn't matter. But I know I can do it."

"If I wanted to I could do it myself."

Lauren made a face. "Girl, I don't think so. We know all about you. Isolation from society is not a platform from which to engage Webb. He's a businessman, used to dealing face to face, and you don't have the interpersonal weaponry to fool him." Lauren spread her hands in response to Sabrina's stare. "You just don't."

"And you say you can show me?"

"Yup. Exactly that."

"And if I do this? What's the deal?"

Hayden sat forward. "At the moment, you're in a good position. All you did was meet up with Webb, swop stories, and slap my team around a little. That's okay."

Drake frowned over at Dahl. "Do you think she means it?"

The Swede nodded somewhat glumly. "Of course she does."

"We will give you immunity from prosecution," Hayden said. "And a free pass. For twenty four hours."

Sabrina pouted. "Is that all?"

"You're a mega thief, finally identified. What did you think was gonna happen?"

"Hey," Lauren added by way of compensation. "It's not like you don't have the skills to disappear again. Continue as a loner. Unhealthy though that could be."

"More unhealthy than staying on the radar?" Sabrina questioned with a defeated stare.

"We're getting off track," Hayden stepped in. "Our offer's good. And it's the only way you'll sniff free air again before you're past fifty. Listen, Sabrina, you're halfway credible already because Webb will totally believe you're capable of escaping." She spread her hands. "Because you are."

"Of course. So why don't I just do that?"

"Because you don't want to go to prison. I don't know what they call a supermax over here but that's where you'll be taken. And grand master or not, you don't escape one of those. Ever."

Sabrina flicked her chin over at Lauren. "So, what skills do you have?"

The New Yorker took that as a victory. "First," she said. "Take off all your clothes."

Drake couldn't help but lean forward, but then so did everyone else watching behind the two-way. Nine bodies were suddenly highly attentive, surprised by Lauren's words.

Then laughter. "Just joking. Like we said, Webb knows you have the expertise to escape. I can coach you into a believable scenario, the right words to use, and how to gain his trust. How to make him think you like him, respect him, and care about his quest. His beliefs. I can even coach you to make him believe you worship him."

"Are you serious? What kind of a cop are you?"

Lauren shrugged. "The best kind."

Drake relaxed his muscles. "Well, she sure knows what she's doing."

"Yeah," Smyth growled. "She has a way with prisoners."

"Oh, mate," Drake said. "Give her a chance. She's working for the good guys."

"Something is not right with Nicholas Bell," Smyth said. "And nobody except me seems to see it."

"What can he do? The guy's in a bloody supermax. Says he became tangled up with the Pythians and couldn't get out. He shows remorse. Good psyche results. He's never once mentioned release. And every lead he's given us has panned out."

Smyth stared fixedly at Lauren through the window. "And considering where he is, a Louisianan prison, the guy has everything he needs."

"You're not doing so badly yourself," Kinimaka put in.

"One day," Smyth grunted. "One day. You will see."

Drake watched Lauren talk to Sabrina. Time passed. More coffees came, this time with hard Biscotti. He trusted Smyth's instincts down to the bone and worried that they might all be missing something. But Louisiana was a long way from Barcelona and he saw Hayden fetching a phone in so that Sabrina could make a call.

Another hour went by as Lauren coached the Italian thief. Finally though, she allowed her to make the quick call.

Through the speakers Sabrina and Webb had a brief exchange and, immediately, they all knew the risk using Sabrina Balboni had already paid off.

"I am in Zurich," Webb told her after a few minutes. "Meet me there." The man actually sounded relieved.

"Well done, Lauren," Mai said. "Well done."

Beau also looked impressed. "She is good, yes?"

"Face to face will be harder," Smyth said.

"But she has given herself lots more hours," Kinimaka said. "To work on that. This is the best outcome, guys."

"Zurich then?" Drake studied the group.

The team inside the small room split up and left a relieved looking Sabrina Balboni alone for a few minutes. Hayden gave a sigh of relief when she returned to the group.

"What do you guys think?"

"I think we should go nail Tyler Webb," Alicia snarled. "Once and for all. To a fucking tree. Who's with me?"

Grim nods were made all around.

"Hold your horses, guys," Drake said. "There's another issue first. A big one."

CHAPTER TWENTY THREE

Drake finished his coffee before elaborating. "Forget Sabrina. Forget Webb. We have a crew of fanatics shooting up the Barcelona Motor Show. They're gonna need to be neutralized."

Hayden paused and then sighed. "Crap, I guess you're right. The cultists will be following Webb wherever he goes, but the head of the snake? I don't think so."

"Nah, that'll be sunning itself in Dubai," Drake lamented. "Of all places."

"So we split the team. One half to Zurich; one to Dubai."

"Sounds like a plan." Drake stared around, not voicing the disquieting thought that the team was pretty much split already. Professionalism stood foremost in their minds though.

"Drake, Mai, Alicia, Beau," Hayden said, "should head off to Dubai. The others to Zurich. And Drake, we need to keep Dubai under the radar. All of it."

Drake nodded. "Understood."

Mai watched Hayden. "You said 'we'. Are you joining us?"

Hayden quickly checked her emails. "It will be a good change, I think."

"And me?" Kenzie asked. "I mean, Dahl and I usually stick together but . . ."

The Swede winced. "Not by bloody choice, believe me."

Kenzie looked hurt. "I'm not sure I wanna be stuck with the B team. Even if Beach Runner is a part of it."

An already beleaguered group took stock of her words. A month ago they'd have been laughed off, but now Kinimaka gave Hayden woeful eyes and Smyth glared at Beau. "Maybe we should change places, bro."

Hayden rubbed her temples. "I need Lauren with Sabrina and *you* watching them both, Smyth. Mano, man up. And Kenzie, if you want to be part of this team you have to stop causing contention."

"It's just natural, boss. I'm not sure I know how."

Hayden motioned to Drake. "Seriously though, I can't stress how important it is to keep a low profile. The last thing we need is a brush with the UAE."

"We'll be careful, Hayden," he said. "All of us. Hey guys, take it easy. We'll meet you in Zurich." He started to walk away.

Dahl looked worried. "Drake?" he said.

"Yeah?" The Yorkshireman turned, pleased that the Swede cared.

"Don't fuck it up."

CHAPTER TWENTY FOUR

Karin Blake knew what hell looked like. She knew what utter defeat tasted like. And she knew the sensation of soul-destroying desolation. Since Matt Drake entered her life she had lost her brother, her parents, and recently the love of her life. She had tried to do good; fought on the side of the noble and the virtuous. She had checked all the right boxes—but somehow still lost out on life.

So she made Drake enroll her in a program, ostensibly to prepare a way for her into the team with confidence, into the field with some experience, and with more than just a dojo-earned black belt to call upon. The Yorkshireman pulled many delicate strings and cancelled out several favors to get the Englishwoman into the American Army program, but somehow managed to pull it off.

Fitting, actually.

It had a fateful sense of irony that Matt Drake had fought tooth and nail to sign her up for the months'-long, extremely intense, grueling super-program that would eventually—

Barked orders interrupted her train of thought.

"Enemy sighted. Stay alert, stay frosty. We're being told to engage."

Karin knew this was no drill, no extended training exercise. She looked forward to real-world action after training for so long. The months had been punishing, backbreaking, consuming her every waking minute and short hours of slumber. Soon after she started the proliferating exhaustion, she stopped remembering her dreams, which was a godsend.

Soon after that, the overwhelming pain and demanded effort robbed her brain of alternative thought processes, which also was a blessing in disguise. Being able to move, sleep where she could, wake on demand, know which injuries were serious and which would be laughed at, engage her genius intellect at select times, get along with the boys and earn their respect, stand up for herself when the need arose—all this and more crammed her day with details.

Guilt flourished, though, when she realized she hadn't thought about Komodo in twenty four hours. More guilt when she remembered a week had passed since she contacted the SPEAR team. Then the guilt compounded when she realized she couldn't remember the exact date when Ben and her parents died.

Emotions compressed inside her.

They became a raging sea, wild and untamed, kept in check only by the regime she followed. And in some rare moments of alacrity she knew—it was a damn good job the struggles expended her. A good job indeed.

Karin turned her rage toward the program. She became the best and the baddest version of herself, when either version was called for. Initial team sessions were hard, but first she outthought her fellow trainees and then she began to outfight them. What she lacked for in strength she gained in ferocity, in unfettered cruelty. She would strike at the most vulnerable place at the precise moment and without mercy. The men soon learned to take her seriously.

Another barked order. "We're now on point, people. Strap on and strap in. This just got very real."

Karin allowed the here and now to intrude. In truth, this was about as much thinking time as she'd had in the last few months. She decided now that she didn't like it. Bring on the goddam war, and bring on the friggin' pain.

The guys in her class sat all round her, filling the back of the high, black, unmarked truck. Palladino, Perry, Garrett and Winters, and many others, waiting with grim faces, little banter and unknown expectations. They had never been thrust into actual battle before—and now only through sheer misfortune. It was one thing to know you would be fighting a real enemy that day, quite another to stumble upon it during an exercise.

Karin stood up, braced herself, and peered through the

narrow rectangular window into the front cab. She wore black fatigues and a Kevlar jacket, boots and helmet. She carried a rifle and handgun, knife and other weapons. She had provisions, medical supplies, emergency necessities and Bluetooth arrayed around her body. She felt none of it; saw only what was directly ahead.

Two dirty white trucks filled with dirty white boys, running for the hills.

Palladino joined her at the window. "So that's Mullholland Drive, eh Kaz?" he muttered. "First time I seen it."

She accepted Kaz or Blake. She knew neither moniker showed disrespect.

"Just a road filled with soon-to-be-dead men," she said. "Any minute now."

Both trucks narrowly missed an oncoming car, the impact avoided through luck rather than intention.

"Civilians are in the way," Palladino said. "Bear it in mind."

"Civilians are always in the way," Karin said. "And often get killed."

"You never told us much about yourself," Palladino said with a perceptive touch.

"We're not here to get cozy, Palladino. We're here to learn how to kill these mothers before they kill us. Don't pretend you don't want to."

Karin ignored his confused expression, watching as the chase unfolded. Both white trucks swerved and bounced wildly around the bends and switchbacks, drivers becoming increasingly panicked and pushing overloaded vehicles beyond their limits.

"They're transporting guns," Palladino pointed out. "Sooner or later they're going to realize that."

Karin checked the truck's big side mirrors, and saw a phalanx of flashing black-and-whites following. "Yeah, and it'll be bloody messy."

"Now is that bloody? Or messy? Can't tell with that accent of yours."

"Palladino." Karin gave him the eye. "I don't want to be friends with you or anyone else. We work together. Concentrate on the job."

"Sure, sure."

Karin ignored everything around her to assess the unfolding events. Their driver—Callahan—steered carefully and with unwavering attention, staying close to the trucks but trying not to appear too threatening. The protests of the engine and squeal of the tires belied his efforts but his skills were obvious. As they roared along the asphalt a sharp, blind hill gave the trucks ahead some airspace, and Callahan didn't back off. Karin held on as the truck left the road, then crashed down, sending two men sprawling. She didn't move to help, preferring to keep her distance.

Outside, one of the trucks jolted along the grass verge, roof and sides shaking and jouncing against their padlocks, juddering as if from a localized earthquake. More guys crowded around.

"Move aside, Blake. Let someone else see."

Karin retreated, and that was when the shooting began. The back door of the rearmost truck rolled up noisily and bullets began to smash and punch through their vehicle. Karin ducked low and two of the guys went three shades whiter than pale.

"What do we do?" Winters asked.

"Don't get shot." Karin bent even further, figuring her position behind the front engine would also help. Four others figured it out too; some looked too scared to move.

"So this is what we've been training for," Hildreth, their current team leader bellowed. "You guys are exactly where you should be, just a tad earlier than expected. And on American soil." He added the last sentence a touch awkwardly. "Consider this a bonus."

Karin smiled grimly, noting the mixed emotions that crossed her colleagues' faces. All was not well there it seemed, and some might now willingly take the lonely walk down Washout Lane.

For the better, she thought. *I don't want losers watching my back.*

For now, though, they were a team. Callahan flung the truck around a sweeping corner; a bullet crunched through sheet metal and traveled through them, striking a small, young guy called Wu in the chest. The impact knocked him to his knees, where he waited for several moments, panting.

"I'm okay," he said eventually.

"Duh," Karin said. "We figured that when you weren't part of the stain on the back door."

"And a good job that wasn't me," said Perry, the tallest of their group at almost seven foot. " 'Cause it would'a taken my friggin' balls off."

There were a few guffaws, mostly nervous laughter. Karin knew how close they had come. Another bullet whizzed through, this time over head height, and when she chanced a look into the cab she saw Callahan fighting the wheel, windshield smashed to hell, and his co-driver nursing an arm wound. They were getting shot to shit up there.

"We have to do something," she said. "Or they're gonna die."

Hildreth might be team leader but he was still a new recruit. "What do you suggest?"

Karin didn't answer, instead smashing out the viewing panel and resting her rifle on the frame. When the trucks aligned she squeezed off half a dozen shots, scattering the men inside and winging one quite badly. It was a chaotic scene in there, with crates haphazardly stacked, some piled to the roof and listing badly, some with lids broken, jagged wood sliding around and men falling over everything, firing blindly as they rose up. Shots barely missed companions, some punching through their own truck. Others got lucky, flying over Callahan. Karin let loose her rifle again, adding to the general mayhem. Screams and shouts rang out and the truck incredibly tried to pick up speed.

"Take 'em out," Palladino whispered at Karin's side. "You got 'em panicking now, Blake."

"Amen to that, motherfucker."

Karin emptied her clip.

CHAPTER TWENTY FIVE

The rearmost white truck veered violently across the road, bouncing back off a carved cliff face, barely staying upright. Men and crates spilled inside the back, coming together with a crash and a crack and agonized screams. Two whole crates slid clear of the truck, smashing apart against the asphalt and spilling dozens of rifles and magazines. Callahan rode right over them, unable to safely avoid the obstacle. Karin changed her clip and sighted again, ignoring the questions that arose at her back.

"What happened?"

"Did we get it?"

We?

"Take 'em out, Blake."

She squeezed off more shots, hitting crates and one man's leg. The sitting ducks in back of the truck were now screaming at their driver to turn on the speed, realizing they were facing at least one trained shooter. Still they scrambled to and fro though, returning fire and rummaging through open crates to see what weapon they could take up next.

Screaming sirens filled her ears and, closer, the comments of her team. Karin caught Callahan's eye as the driver turned momentarily, nodded at the mouthed 'thanks', and told their co-driver to hunker down. *The tires,* she thought. Time to end the chase.

It had begun in east LA, a white gang taking delivery of weapons under the watchful eye of the DEA. Challenges had been issued and an assault made but the gang had proven too well-armed, and had made off toward the city. Several miles later they'd passed Karin's team involved in their own exercise up in the hills, and Callahan had tuned the army radio to take in the police band. A quick decision and they had joined the chase, radioing in along the way and receiving criticism from every angle. Nevertheless, once engaged they hadn't deemed it right to back off. Cop's lives were at risk and the Army couldn't lose face. The bandits were incredibly well-armed.

Karin squeezed off a shot at one of the rear tires, and saw her bullet take a chunk out of the road surface. Palladino breathed into her ear.

"I'd have made that shot."

Karin sighed. "Even with luck? Not a chance."

"Always better than you, Blake. Always. You know it, girl."

The friendly rivalry was out of place. Karin ignored it and re-sighted. The jolting of the truck, the bouncing of the wheels, the flitting back and forth of the men in back and their attempts at shooting, were mere disruptions to the deep inner and outer focus required to pull the shot off. If she . . .

Then everything changed.

One of the gunrunners smashed open a random crate and started shouting in his excitement. Karin took her eye off the tire to watch it play out. Other heads whipped toward the man. When his arms came up, scooping out dozens of small black objects, Karin turned quickly to Callahan

"Get ready to ram him."

The Irish driver was already goosing the gas pedal, on the same wavelength. The truck lurched, sending everyone staggering except for Karin. As she watched, the man with the grenades threw them haphazardly to friends and colleagues, an insane grin on his face. Then, before Callahan could close the gap, he hurled one at the approaching truck.

It bounced off, clattering down the road and into the grass verge.

"Forgot to remove the pin." Callahan shook his head in disbelief.

The next arced high into the air, triggering a violent reaction from the driver. He wrenched the wheel to the left, sending even Karin staggering.

"What the fu—"

"Take it easy, man!"

The loud protests went up. Karin regained her balance. The

grenade exploded as they passed, shrapnel peppering the side. After that it grew quieter inside as the men realized what had almost happened.

"Nice moves, Callahan," Palladino muttered.

Karin regained the viewing panel, knowing it was far from over. Callahan had the gas pedal mashed almost all the way to the floor; the faces of the men in the truck ahead all too visible. It was do or die as they moved within easy throwing range.

"Ahead," Karin said.

Callahan nodded in grim relief. A sharp bend lay just a few seconds away.

"Hang the fuck on," he grated.

The white truck flung itself at the bend, barely slowing, but Callahan sped up. In a second, their truck smashed the rear side of the other as it turned, flinging it into a broadside. Men sprawled and collapsed in the back, grenades flying up into the air and among the crates. At least two of the men's faces creased in terror.

"Nooooo!"

The cry echoed across the small distance as Callahan continued to push the truck into a spinning broadside. Crates and arms and legs rolled, spun and twisted in every direction, smashing against each other. The truck reared up on to two wheels. Karin screamed a warning at Callahan.

"Back off!"

It exploded three seconds later, the fireball washing over Callahan's cab and starting mini-fires inside the cabin. Both driver and co-driver covered up, bellowing as the flames came close to them, hairs singed, but came out the other side with barely a scratch. Karin swung away, grabbing Palladino and hurling him aside. A tongue of flame shot through the small gap for a heartbeat's span and then vanished. Karin elbowed Palladino.

"Saved your pretty face."

"I knew you had the hots for me, Blake."

But Karin was already back at the viewing panel, trying to take in the nightmare ahead. The shockwave generated by the truck's explosion had shunted their own truck sideways, off the road and across a sharply angled grass verge. Now Callahan was desperately trying to keep them running around the tight bend, their left wheels scrabbling along a narrow dirt track, their right several feet above that on the grass verge itself, their cab canted at a crazy angle.

To their left: a hundred feet of vertical drop-off.

Karin felt her stomach lurch; mouth suddenly dry as old bones. Above, still on the main road, the blackened, flaming hulk of the white truck lurched to and fro, the screams of its surviving occupants tearing at the hills. Black-and-whites flashed by, sirens whooping it up. Karin watched Callahan struggle with the wheel and the curve of the path ahead, all their fates in his hands.

"Shit."

She ran to the right-hand side, pushing at the metal side, screaming at her colleagues to do the same. Palladino was on it in an instant, the rest just a moment behind. They could all feel the sway and roll of the body. Their efforts threw the truck to the right just as a left-hand camber would have sent it tipping to the left and into the yawning valley below.

"Keep at it," Karin said, then leapt back to the viewing panel.

"Good job."

Callahan, sweating, bloodied and bruised, now flung the wheel to the right as a narrow gap appeared, bouncing and jarring off either side, but sending the truck through. Back onto the road. Cop cars littered the highway, swerving out of the way as the army truck bounced among them.

"Thought we were dog food back there," Callahan said.

"Not this lot," Karin said. "They ain't tasty enough."

"Thank God you didn't say 'too young to die'. They all say that."

"We're too old for that," Karin said emotionlessly. "And we don't cry. So let's take this last mofo out."

Callahan sighted between two cop cars at the last white truck ahead.

"Like your style, Blake. I really do."

Karin checked her gun.

CHAPTER TWENTY SIX

Mullholland twisted and wound through the hills; green, gray, brown and mottled like the hide of a huge snake, its sharp bends, sudden drop-offs and incredible views across LA as internationally famous as the city through which it slithered. Day trippers, joggers, dog walkers and a thousand others constantly walked its length and the environs all around, relaxed, peaceful and inspirational, but today the twists, turns and loops shook and thundered with something far less motivating.

An old, beaten truck hammered down the narrow roads, clattering and banging from side to side and forcing oncoming traffic into the dirt. Its rear door was raised and swarming with white men sporting facial tattoos and skinhead-cuts, their dirty white vests revealing lean, muscled bodies and baggy jeans, boxer shorts emblazoned with names like Calvin Klein, Hugo Boss and Tommy Hilfiger. They hefted automatic weapons taken from crates which they had at one time been trying to transport to the docks. Not anymore. Now, it was fight or die. Take 'em all with you. To the end, my brother!

Cops cars sped after them, sirens and lights switched on, an onslaught against the countryside. Then came a black-painted truck filled with army trainees.

Karin kept her gun aimed, and a full rhetoric going for the benefit of her fellow recruits. The guys hung on tightly, already bruised from stumbling around the rear of the truck.

"Hard right," she said. "Hang on."

Callahan barely slowed, flinging the vehicle around the shoulder and keeping inches off the police cars ahead. As they all straightened, the gunrunners raised weapons and continued taking potshots; some grinning, laughing and giving high fives, others sitting with sick looks on their faces among the crates. The mental state of these men followed a curve all the way from the "barely there" to "screwball insane".

Karin didn't care about that. Her thoughts and fears were for civilians and then the cops and her team. This was so much more than training now; this was the very thing they had been training *for*. The test of their mettle and their might; their critical skills.

Her mind flicked through the intense havoc that had been the last several weeks. Settling in had lasted mere minutes, whilst for the rest of the time she'd worked twice as hard as everyone else just to keep up. Before she started with these guys she thought she'd been fit. Now she knew civilian fitness and military fitness were measured on very different scales. An impossible feat for a gym rat might be an everyday exploit for a fully trained soldier.

Each day she grew stronger, fitter, more agile. Each day her knowledge grew. Though her brilliant mind suited her to geeky, indoor work, she pursued the outdoor vocations, following the narrative she'd told Drake to the absolute letter. She didn't believe her progress would be reported, but every angle should be covered. Her future plans were incredibly complex, and called for many months of intense toil to put into action.

The deaths of her parents and brother had affected her badly, hammering her already fragile mind into submission. Events in her youth where responsible and authority figures had failed to help save the life of her friend had damaged her forever, turning her into a pensive, soul-searching deliberate drop-out. The SPEAR team gave her a lifeline, a real purpose and became her rock when her family was killed at the hands of the Blood King. They had all lost somebody, and forged deeper bonds. Then, as life grew bearable again and an acceptable future with Komodo bloomed, her love had been snatched away once again.

Karin never stood a chance.

Never again.

She worked now not only to chase the past away, to destroy those creeping nightmares that hung and lurked all around, but also to build a barrier based on core strength and high principles. She wanted to be told what to do, to follow a regime, to train until it all went away.

At least for now.

This was more than she had bargained for, but more than welcome too. She sighted her gun on one of the men in the back of the truck and squeezed the trigger. Blood splashed a nearby crate and the man tumbled backward then fell onto the road, pinwheeling like a discarded rag-doll along the asphalt. One of the cop cars—already shot up through repeated attempts to kill the officers—swerved to miss him, leaving smoking rubber in its wake.

"Gonna be in a shitstorm when this is all done," Hildreth said.

"Dude," Karin said. "We're in one right now, along with unsuspecting mothers and fathers and hard-working cops. Do *you* want to give the order to back off?"

She looked around, and sensed Palladino do the same beside her. Hildreth stayed silent though, studying the far wall. Palladino leaned in.

"Want me to shoot a few? Give the girl a few tips?"

"I got a tip for you, Dino. Leave me the hell alone."

Callahan made the choice and swept past the swerving cop car, until he was nudging the back of the lead black-and-white. The trucks were by now dropping out of the hills and heading toward the highway and civilian centers. As Mullholland dipped it also performed a sharp switchback close to an on-ramp and it was here Callahan suggested a large force of cops would be waiting.

"No way will they let it on the freeway," he said.

Karin held on as Callahan gunned it once more. "What are you thinking?" she asked.

"That cops're gonna die."

He punched inside the leading police car as it slowed around a bend, skirting the dirt and shrubbery at the side of the road and jerking the truck from side to side. His right side mirror brushed the roof of the other car and then Callahan was in front, swerving again toward the rear of the first truck. To both sides, incredible vistas opened up, from some well-known backlot studios, to superstar residences and production buildings belonging to some of the best known names in Hollywoodland.

Karin sweated under her helmet and vest. Her mouth was dry,

her teeth gritted together like two bags of rocks. The stench of body odor permeated the truck. Muffled swearing came from every side and Perry sat at the back, looking as if he might throw up. None of the guys looked like they wanted to take her place. Except Palladino. He was game. Game for anything. She ignored him, knowing the future and a necessary all-destructive path. Now Callahan pushed the vehicle up to the rear of their quarry, this time staying as much as possible to the left and slightly blind-side, much to the grumbled annoyance of their co-driver.

When it happened, it happened fast. Mullholland dropped hard, and relatively open, unobstructed views spanned their horizons; the van driver must have seen the waiting road block. He jammed on, anchoring the truck so hard its back wheels slewed.

Bodies flew backwards, striking walls and wooden crates. A man appeared creeping over the top, hanging on for dear life, but as the truck slowed, producing a machine gun so powerful it required rolls of bullets to maintain its high-velocity rate, and fired bullets that could chew up a truck in under a minute.

Callahan bellowed in surprise and swerved right. The gun rang out, deep, heavy, like Satan's jackhammer. Karin rolled with the truck, bent her aim and angle, and zeroed in on the shooter. One shot and he was airborne, the gun toppling, the man winging it down toward the valley bottom.

"Blake," Callahan muttered. "I don't ever wanna let you go."

Palladino tapped her shoulder. "You get one?"

"Yeah, just one."

"Lame."

Karin barely heard the comment, concentrating now on what was happening up front. Somehow the rearguard had gotten wind of what was waiting for them—Karin could tell because all of a sudden they became intensely agitated. Weapons were fed through to the front cab and others distributed amongst those in the back. Without thinking, without aiming, they opened fire, panic setting their minds alight.

"This is gonna be so bad," Callahan moaned, twisting the

wheel so violently the truck again tipped up onto two wheels. Karin winced and waited, but in the next second rubber touched asphalt again and they were back to bouncing along. A bullet clanged off the framework of an already shattered windshield.

"Any ideas?" Callahan said.

"An RPG would be nice," the co-driver said.

"Ram 'em." Karin could see no other options. "Ram 'em before they hit the barrier."

Palladino gave her a pat on the back. "It's like you read my mind, Blake. I'll give you that much."

Karin held on. Callahan forced his right foot down hard, surging forward, straight into the back of the gunrunners' vehicle. The driver lost control.

The back end swayed and listed. Men fell from the open space like lemmings over a cliff. A stray, crazy bullet entered their cab and smashed through the roof above Karin's head, the jagged metal it left briefly smoking. This time their quarry's vehicle heaved up and then toppled onto its side, crashing down with a force of a mountain and then scraping diagonally across the road.

Karin saw Callahan stamping on the brakes and immediately turned, grabbed some guy ropes and started to make her way toward the back doors.

"Ready!"

The truck ground to a halt, momentum causing it to roll a little, then Karin pulled the silver handles that unlocked the rear. Sunlight flooded the space, glaring. She jumped down onto the hot surface, bent her knees and then twisted, staying low.

Men littered the road behind her, cop cars pulling up alongside. Weapons lay scattered from verge to verge. Around the side she crept in fluid motion, sighting along her rifle. Palladino watched her back.

They approached the broken and shattered vehicle with caution. A tattooed man lay in the back amid crates, unmoving; another crawled on his knees, probably unaware of which way was up.

When Karin saw a gun vaguely waving their way she potted its owner, putting the man out of his obvious misery. Cops ran down from the cars and up from the blockade, lending help.

The trainees picked among the wreckage, dragging the living into the open and binding their hands and legs. Karin watched Callahan on the radio and saw the grim curl of his lips. The outcome was immaterial if someone wanted to make an issue of this.

Someone *responsible*. Someone in charge.

Any incident could be finessed to further a white collar career. Karin knew she was close to where she needed to be with her training and didn't particularly need the rest. But it would still be good to get it under her belt, and good to have the extra weeks to prepare. After that, she'd have all the intellectual and physical skills she required to hatch—

Palladino nudged her. "We did good, Blake. Well done back there."

She couldn't help but stare. "We, Dino? We?"

"Hey, we're a team. Thought you knew that."

We'll see what you say when the recriminations start.

CHAPTER TWENTY SEVEN

Unlike many places he had visited, Drake found Dubai to be exactly as he'd imagined. Colossal airport with heightened security, rank upon rank of limo drivers brandishing cards emblazoned with people's surnames or flight operators. Broad walkways where passengers could feel relaxed rather than shoved along in a tide of humanity, and a duty free shop to end all.

"Y'know," he said. "I could just as well spend the night *here*."

Alicia flicked him a glance. "Eh, saucy. They have rules about that kind of thing in the Middle East."

"That's not what I meant, love. A guy could actually get lost in here."

Beau pointed out just a few of the hidden cameras. "I am sure they would find you."

Hayden hefted her carry-on. "Which should tell you all to keep your heads down and get a move on. We don't want some eagle-eyed airport employee tagging us all together."

The Frenchman looked a little aggrieved. "Well, it is not me they will recognize, I assure you."

"Nah," Alicia coughed. "It's the 'extra package' you got in your trunks. Ha ha."

Hayden couldn't help but smile. Drake leaned in close to Alicia. "Love, it's a little off-putting when you talk about your old boyfriend's knob right in front of your new boyfriend. Just so you know."

Alicia battered her eyelids. "It is? Oh, well."

Drake sighed. "Yeah. Good talk."

Outside, the heat struck them immediately and everyone removed their jackets. Drake took a look at the group and broke out into a smile. After so much military work he'd gotten used to seeing everyone in combat gear and now it felt wrong to see Alicia in jeans and a T-shirt, sporting a thick rainbow bobble,

Hayden wearing three-quarter baggy pants and the incongruity of a gold watch, Mai dressed in a flowing black dress with slits up the sides, and Beau in formal wear. For himself he'd gone for the Yorkshireman's uniform of choice: T-shirt and jeans, a black military watch—Chase Durer for the rugged quality—and brand new white trainers. The team had already made a play of shielding their eyes every time he walked ahead of them.

A taxi whisked them away from the airport, its size and shape still capturing Drake's attention. Soon they joined traffic and saw familiar shaped hotels on the horizon, and famous shapes, rows of restaurants, car showrooms and local stores along the side of the highway. Drake wasn't surprised to see much of the local fare was interspersed with well-known American names—Wendy's, McDonalds and more.

The Burj Al Arab appeared and flitted off to their right, a little misty in the distance, its sail-like appearance unmistakable even in a city stippled with splendorous vistas. The road meandered lazily before them.

Their driver half-turned and spoke in good English, "Is the temperature okay for you? Not too hot?"

"Leave it where it is, pal," Drake said. "It's nice to be warm. Where I come from the winters can leave you in a dozen pieces."

"We are approaching the Jumeirah Palm," the driver told them. "From here, all is man-made."

Drake knew much of the story around the famous Dubai palm islands. Designed in the shape of palm trees topped by a crescent, they were entirely artificial, built on sand dredged from the Persian Gulf and protected by breakwaters containing several million tons of rock. Each rock was placed individually and given a GPRS tag.

The Palm Jumeirah itself—the one they were interested in— consisted of a tree trunk, the main highway through, a crown with sixteen fronds, and a surrounding crescent island forming the breakwater. Adding to the Dubai coastline itself, each frond housed hundreds of multi-million dollar homes and status symbol addresses.

A much more interesting fact for Drake was that the entire

island was built only from sand and rocks—no metal whatsoever was used—and was the brainchild of the Prince of Dubai, who came up with the idea for the Palm Islands and also their design.

A hands-on boy, Drake thought. *And not a man we want noticing us today.*

And a forward thinker. The islands were primarily constructed as a tourist attraction to counteract the drop-off in revenue as oil reserves diminished in the region. Drake could see their appeal to the casual vacationer.

The taxi driver took them to their destination, Frond F; basically a long curving road with exclusive houses built on both sides. Gardens were greener than emerald jewels and every palm tree was lopped just right, perfection personified. Drake lifted his sunglasses up for a minute to get a better view but the glare bouncing off the white walls and the brilliance of the horizon sent him back under the shades.

"It's quiet," Hayden remarked as the driver pulled up.

"Not many live here all year," he said. "Mostly vacation homes. Some American, some European." He shrugged.

Drake didn't have to voice what they were all thinking. The group, even dressed as tourists, were going to stand out like flies on a wedding cake. Still, tourists *did* visit the fronds, if only for curiosity.

"We shoulda hired a car," he said.

"I can organize that for you," the taxi driver said.

Drake blinked. "You can?"

The man laughed. "This is Dubai. We make everything happen."

Hayden touched him on the arm. "Have it sent here, keys under the front wheel. Soon as you can."

"I will need you to authorize a credit card."

"Of course," Hayden said. "And here's something extra for you."

With the transaction complete the taxi driver held her gaze one more second. "And why leave the keys under the front wheel? This is the Jumeirah Palm, not New York."

Alicia whistled. "I do believe Lauren might call you on that."

Hayden cracked open the door, allowing the intense midday heat to rush in. Drake followed the others until they were all standing around on the sidewalk, fake cameras in evidence, baseball caps slung low. In truth Drake actually felt more like a tourist than a soldier at that moment, a little awkward and a little dubious in the bright, hot, mega-rich area of Dubai. Hayden suggested they saunter up the road until they came closer to their destination.

Sounds reached their ears at last. The hum of a lawn mower, the clatter of a sand raker. Even a smattering of whispered conversation from places unknown. All the windows were dark and the upper balconies on every house were empty. Drake paused to stare up and down the wide road and saw no vehicles in either direction.

"Weird," he said.

"Must be the time of day," Beau offered.

"Maybe."

Another ten minutes sauntering and they were nearing their destination.

Drake felt the absolute focus descend over him. He scrutinized every window, wall, hedge and door; every discreet garden and thick palm; the driveways and double garages; a parked 4x4 across the road. The house they sought looked very similar to all the others; except now there were several signs that it was being lived in. One of the two single garage doors was slightly raised and a yellow car sat in the driveway. Three adult pushbikes lay on one of the front lawns.

"Somebody's home," Mai said.

With no weapons, no comms systems save for their phones and no Kevlar, they were not best prepared. Still, they were exactly where they needed to be.

Hayden smiled and pointed at the horizon, leaning in as the others crowded around. "We walk up to the door. We look around. Got it?"

"Any sign of weapons?" Beau looked doubtful. "Or guards?"

Negatives were muttered all around.

"I feel naked," Alicia complained, "without my armor."

"God forbid," Mai muttered. "Talk about visiting horrors upon the world."

Alicia looked like she might stamp her foot. "Have you ever *seen* me naked, Little Sprite?"

"Are my eyes fried out of my head?"

"They could be." Alicia turned on Mai, but Hayden hushed them with a word. Drake could see the exponential advance of the new enmity expanding between the two, and worried. The paths of their lives were coming together fast, and hard. The end was unknowable, but there was no way it would end up pretty.

It would be best to end it all, he thought. *In our finest hours. In* all *of our finest hours.*

The driveways were short, just over a car's length. An arched front portico led to a solid oak door. One side of the house was inaccessible, blocked by what looked like an electrical box and then dense shrubbery. The other side looked more promising.

Three steps led up to a narrow pathway leading around the side of the house. The five of them ducked under the window ledge and made their way to the path, watching every angle and houses across the street. No sudden shifts were apparent, no movement of any kind. Hayden stopped at the bottom of the three steps.

"Ready?"

Beau slipped around her, nothing but smoke and shadow even clothed in his civvies. Low to the ground he pressed ahead, disappearing around the corner.

"I guess we're clear then," Drake grumped and followed Hayden around.

Alicia and Mai brought up the rear—bad planning perhaps but then this operation couldn't be rationally organized. Even the SPEAR team were well out of their comfort zone.

The path was dark, secluded and narrow, its chest-high wall bordering right on next door's property. Drake was surprised at the near proximity of the next fifty-million dollar home; he'd imagined money would bring legroom. But it did help their cause.

Drifting along, Beau paused at a side door, tried the handle, and gave them all a nod. So far the Dubai gods of fortune were

The Treasures of Saint Germain

liberally showering them with luck. Or, more likely, this was the norm for the Palm Islands.

Drake followed Hayden inside the house, hyper-alert, finding himself inside a kitchen whiter than white with contrasting smooth, polished black units, tables and even picture frames hanging on the walls. The floors were clean enough to eat off, mirror-polished enough to brush your teeth in.

"Spread out," he said, feeling crowded. "We—"

A tall, thin man walked into the kitchen, clapped eyes on them and gave a slow wave.

"Hey."

Drake paused in mid lunge, eyes widening in surprise. The man wore a white thawb with mirror sunglasses, and limped along at a languid pace, at peace with the world and his surroundings. Drake backed off, allowing Hayden to push forward.

"How you doin'?"

"Pretty good, sister. Pretty good."

Drake watched the man head for the fridge, expecting him to pull out a beer, but was surprised to see a bottle of juice. He leaned toward Alicia. "Are we in the right place?"

"Headquarters of a vicious cult, hell-bent on protecting some ancient dude's secrets without caring who gets killed in the crossfire?" The blonde studied the kitchen. "Who knows?"

"Are you . . . surprised to see us?" Hayden asked carefully.

The Arab took a swig before answering. "It's all good," he said. "Grape juice is right there. Fruit on the patio outside. They're preparing boats for later."

He headed for the door. At that moment two more men wandered through, stared at the newcomers, and offered greetings. Drake saw no signs of drug or alcohol abuse, heard no party noises, and tried to accept their graceful, languid attitude.

"How many are there of you?" Hayden asked, forcing a laugh.

"A couple of dozen. Every day is different," the same man said. "C'mon. You'll enjoy."

Drake trod very carefully, wary beyond expression as he followed three languorous Arabs into the strangest, dreamiest nest of vipers he'd ever seen.

CHAPTER TWENTY EIGHT

Beyond the kitchen a pearlescent-walled hallway gave onto four more rooms. Their euphoric guide led them into another room where a huge picture window looked out onto a deck, a pool and a private beach that led to the glistening sea. The room was highly populated, both Arabs and Europeans lounging on plush sofas and drinking water or juice whilst chatting to their neighbors. Drake managed to keep his mouth from falling open, but only just. He turned purposely toward Hayden.

"This has to be the wrong place."

"This address was verified by three different mercs in three separate rooms and at different times. Same address." She watched everything. "This is the place."

"Or what they wanted the mercs to believe." Beau leaned in.

Alicia picked from a golden platter heaped with fruit. "Can't say it's been a wasted effort though. These strawberries are amazing."

Drake studied faces for the one that they might know. The merc closest to the cult's leadership had provided them with a sketch of a distinctive looking man with a well-trimmed beard and piecing blue eyes. Their last piece of information was his name: Amari.

Drake tapped a young woman on the arm and spoke the name. Her face lit up and she pointed at the picture window. "By the pool. Say hi for me."

The team made ready, still distracted by the spaced-out ambiance. It was rare to see villains living it up so carefree and unprotected; even rarer to see those around them so content and trusting. Drake felt confident with Mai and Alicia at his back, but couldn't help turning to check they were okay. This environment wasn't right, and made him disbelieve most of what he was seeing.

They approached the picture window. A double set of open patio doors gave onto an elevated, concrete deck. Tiered pools lay to the right and an eating area to the left, and straight ahead steps led straight onto the beach. Tanned bodies swam and lounged and walked this way and that, taking in the beautiful day. Drake made his way poolside.

"Make ready," Hayden breathed.

Scrutinizing the faces, he saw a man surface, water spilling down his face. After the man wiped it away, blinked and then locked eyes, Drake knew they were in the right place.

"Amari? That you?"

"Join us." The Arab slipped into a comfortable backstroke. "We have spare bathing suits, even for the women."

Alicia frowned. "What does he mean by that?"

Drake skirted the pool, watchful as Amari glided toward the pool steps. No threatening moves were made, but he was also mindful that half a dozen other Arabs were stroking for different exit points. And the laughter had stopped.

Amari climbed out, curtains of water sluicing down his tanned body. "Would you like to join the party?" he asked as politely as a man could.

"Not my style," Drake said. "I'm a bangers and burgers on the barbie kinda guy to be fair."

A blank expression said it all.

"Answer's *no*," Alicia translated. "But we do need to talk."

For a few more seconds Amari studied them, considering, perhaps dissecting their intentions. Drake was aware of the six other men climbing out of the pool, all empty handed but none less threatening.

Nobody moved, nor spoke. Drake found himself in the middle of yet one more perplexing situation. No threats had been made, no peril was obvious. This could still be a mistake. What was the answer?

Alicia found it in just two words.

"Saint Germain."

It electrified the entire area so much Drake thought a lightning bolt might have struck. Amari went rigid, blue eyes blazing and the six onlookers gasped as if in chorus.

"You are not my guests!" Amari cried, looking inexperienced, raw and strangely shocked to the core.

"What the hell are you people?" Hayden drawled. "You don't come across like . . . terrorists."

Amari's mouth fell open. "We protect. We preserve. We defend."

"And, mate, I'd love to hear the one about the rich Arab who fell in love with the long-dead Transylvanian count." Drake grinned.

Amari surprised him with a bit of venom. "The Ascended Master is *not* dead. And one day, he will reward us."

The Arab spun and ran, bare feet slapping the mosaic tiles. Drake went one way around the pool as Beau went the other. They reached the point where the top pool stepped down to the next amid a little waterfall. Amari bent down to rustle among shrubbery.

Warning bells grew to claxon quality in Drake's mind. This may be the oddest leader of the oddest terror cult he'd ever come across, but one bad guy was just the same as another. As Amari turned with the handgun in his hand, Drake was already leaping aside and shouting out a warning.

Beau flipped out of sight, clearing the top of the pool and landing amid sun-loungers. Hayden, Alicia and Mai fell away, scrambling for cover. Drake found the bushes as Amari's trembling arm swayed from left to right.

"Stay away," he cried. "We are not fighters, but we can fight. We *will* fight. To protect the Master."

Drake now guessed these people handed down attack orders through a phone connection, insulated and oblivious to the terror they caused; uncaring, happy in their bright fantasy world. Fanatical in one way, utterly green in the other.

"Put the gun down," he called. "We can talk about all this."

"No, no! You will hurt the Master. You are questing the world for his treasures just like that other American! You have no idea, not even the faintest inkling, of the supreme power you are up against." The next phrase came out as four separate words. "He. Is. A. God."

A living man become a god? Drake thought. Where did these freaks come from?

Without further idiosyncrasies, Amari pounced down the steps. His six acolytes flowed with him, saying nothing, but seemingly attracted to the magnet that was their leader. Alicia's head popped up from behind a low wall, and then Mai's.

All seemed surprised there had been no gunshots.

"We're dealing with a different kind of animal," Drake said. "But no less dangerous."

The team sprang in pursuit. Around the top pool and down to the lower one, then circumventing its kidney shape. A straight dash toward the steps that led to the beach and a glance in the direction that Amari was running.

Brushed sand led all the way to the sea, a sparkle and a shimmer dancing atop the playful waves that ran between the mind-warping fronds. A small dock had been built into the water, where half a dozen small speedboats were moored. Amari raced toward the furthest.

"Crap," Alicia moaned. "I can see where this is going. If I get seasick—" she yelled at the escaping men "—one of you is gonna be shark bait!"

Drake leapt down the steps and hit the sand running. Amari and his acolytes were already in the first speedboat, two of them unwrapping the thick rope that held it in place. Amari sat behind the wheel, looking straight ahead.

Refusing to believe he was being forced to run? *Unable* to believe it? Pampered. Veiled with untold luxuries. Pretending that he was just nipping to the shops for a pint of milk, millionaire-style?

The engine roared to life. Drake and the team arrived on the dock a few seconds later but the craft was already moving. Of the seven men sitting or standing aboard the speedboat, not a single one glanced back.

Drake shook his head. "Fucking loony toons town, that's what this is." He climbed carefully aboard a light blue speedboat, expecting and finding the keys to be in the ignition. "Press start," he said and the engine roared to life.

Trainers hit the deck at his back and then Mai shouted, "Go," and Drake pushed hard on the throttle. Water churned from the rear and the prow lifted a little. Bright skies glared down in warning but Drake was safe beneath his shades. Safe, but leaking sweat from every pore. He spun the boat and curved an arc in the water, blasting toward the center of the sea passage and the end of the frond. Was Amari heading out to sea? He hoped not.

"No signs of pursuit." Hayden had been scanning the whole area. "Or cops, for that matter. Does anyone know what the hell is going on?"

"I could hazard a few guesses," Mai said, holding on tight as Drake accelerated. "Wealthy parents, bored kid. Somehow develops a fixation. Has the resources to carry it all the way through to its unwise end."

"Well, he's clearly not under duress," Drake shouted as spray flicked at his face. "Or any kind of stress. Hold on!"

The speedboat skipped a small wave, left the water and came crashing down with a bump. Drake hung onto the wheel as he flexed his knees to absorb the impact, and followed the getaway boat as it sped into the distance. At this speed they could clearly see the shape of the fronds to either side as they arced gracefully through the sea, artificial wonders and tributes to the ingenuity of man. Every rear garden led down to a private beach and a small jetty; every jetty held several types of craft.

Amari aimed straight for the center of the passage at first, then began to drift to the north as the frond's outer edges appeared. Drake whistled as an enormous plot came into view, a mansion half built at the very end of the frond and surrounded by high walls and pre-grown palm trees.

"Now there's a pad," he said. "Whaddya say, Alicia? Wanna go halves?"

"Too bloody big. We'd never find each other."

Mai coughed. "Not to mention . . . elegant."

Drake rammed the throttle wide open, ignoring the knife-edge banter and concentrating on closing the gap to Amari. The lead boat hit a bit of chop, slowing it down whilst Drake luckily skimmed across a mirror-flat surface. Still, nobody turned around, all preferring to ignore the fact that they were being pursued. Amari started to pull his craft closer to the coast.

"Is he beaching it?" Beau asked.

Drake kept arrow straight, using every ounce of the speedboat's power to get closer. The boats were evenly matched. It was Amari's errant driving that allowed Drake to come to within twenty meters. After that though, the Arab gave the boat all of his attention, staying just out of the shallows and flicking the boat at a fast clip around the end of the frond.

Waves slapped Drake's hull as he completed the same maneuver, not far enough out to sea for a proper swell, but the deep brine choppy enough to send Alicia both green and white.

On the boats raced, passing across the channel of the next frond and seeing another enormous space being cleared at its end. A three-story structure was already going up here, with the aspect of a hotel.

Amari threw his boat down the next channel. Drake breathed a sigh of relief because he'd already noticed it was the last. Beyond it sat the crescent breakwater and then empty, open sea all the way to Iran.

Now a hard left turn, the boat heeling, the passengers holding on with white knuckles, spray coating them from head to toe. Amari cleared the turn perfectly, much to Drake's annoyance, but then the man had probably done it a thousand times. He followed the boat as it drifted toward the beach around the final frond and noticed a bridge up ahead; a concrete structure carrying a monorail that spanned the entire waterway.

"Maybe he'll hit it," the Yorkshireman said despondently.

"Don't worry." Alicia patted him on the shoulder. "He has to stop sometime."

"Oh, that really helps."

Gradually, a new structure began to take shape on the right.

"Oh bollocks," Drake said. "I think I see his intentions."

They all did, and anxiety set in. Until now, this chase had seemed destined to have only one ending. Amari couldn't outrun them. But now . . .

The sprawling Atlantis Hotel rose high and multi-colored,

encompassing most of the last frond by itself: thousands of rooms, restaurants, shops and a waterpark. Thousands of people. A million places to hide. If Amari got a head start on them in there, he and his people would be gone.

Drake gave it his all, choosing the slackest water and the widest arch through the bridge. He inched closer. Their quarry was only twenty meters away, still ignoring them. Drake blasted through the bridge just as a monorail passed above; he saw the faces of people staring down through the glass. To all intents and purposes this was a boys' race—nothing more.

He twisted the wheel hard as he cleared the bridge, skimming the bottom of the craft across a flat surface and closing the gap to under twenty meters. Beau rose to his feet and approached the edge of the boat as if preparing to jump.

Alicia laughed. "Are you serious?"

"No. But I am ready."

Drake saw they were angling hard toward shore now. Another jetty stuck out just ahead, but Amari ignored it and rammed the speeding boat up the sandy beach. The men inside must have been talking at some point, because they all hung on for dear life and then rose as momentum decreased. Drake went all out, hitting the beach at full speed, taking the jolts and trying to stand even as they plowed practically sideways.

"She's gonna roll!" Hayden cried.

Luckily, she didn't. Even so, Beau leapt gracefully from the tipping, sliding craft, landed like a cat, and took off after Amari's men.

"Hate to say it." Drake struggled down to the beach. "But that French bastard has skills."

The way ahead was at best dubious, masked by hundreds of planted trees, meandering walkways and doors leading to different wings of the hotel. A huge pool dominated the center, sun-loungers and tourists arrayed ten deep all around it. Bars, rental huts and coffee shops added to the SPEAR team's misery, all adding to the potpourri of distractions.

Drake spied Beau disappearing around a bend up ahead. He reached the place just in time to see the Frenchman run into a totally unexpected tree branch to the face. One of the acolytes must have stayed behind to take Beau out. Brave, ballsy, and incredibly naïve.

The Frenchman did stagger, even covered his eyes, but it was the slippery paving—wet from a recent watering—that sent him to the ground. The acolyte ran off. Beau nursed a bruised nose and a twisted ankle.

The team kept up the pace. Knots of tourists slowed them down. Sunlight bounced off the high hotel walls. The team were shocked when they turned a blind corner and ended up facing Amari and his six pals who were waiting just outside a small side entrance to the hotel, every man holding a small handgun.

"You will back off. Leave us alone," Amari said.

"Amari is right," another piped up, voice almost failing. "We haven't hurt you."

Drake pulled up, knowing he shouldn't be surprised but taken aback all the same. "Haven't hurt . . . how insulated are you people? Do your parents know you're not in your rooms?"

"We answer only to the Master. Other than that, we do the same as everyone else. We party, drink lots of water, socialize and sunbathe."

Drake wanted to plug his ears. The sheer ignorance of it staggered him. But he plucked on a likely thread. "The Master talks to you often?"

Utter disbelief and scorn poured out at him. "The Master talks to *no one*. His legacy will remain intact. At. All. Costs." More one-word sentences.

Drake couldn't fathom the depth of idiocy—or rather the extent of fanaticism—he was seeing. But the guns—they were certainly real and required addressing.

He backed off. "No problems here."

Amari already had his hand on the door. "Do not follow us into this hotel. We do not want to hurt you."

Drake allowed them to leave, still astonished at the turn of events and the lack of attendant mercenaries. The cult clearly preferred to work from afar, directing operations with a wave of a sheaf of thousand-dollar bills and reluctant to shake hands with their unwashed employees. When the last man disappeared into the darkened interior, he followed.

Hayden held him back. "They're desperate men, deep down."

"All the more reason to corner them," he said. "And I don't see a man among them."

The team filed through the same door, into the hotel. A welcome blast of air conditioning struck their exposed skin, almost as good as the relief from the constant blue glare of the skies.

Amari and his acolytes stood dead ahead of them, staring down an inner hallway with guns drawn. Hotel guests milled between them.

"I warned you!" Amari screeched.

"No—" Drake managed to cry.

The sound of gunshots drowned him out.

CHAPTER TWENTY NINE

Torsten Dahl found himself, unexpectedly, in a coffee shop in Zurich. Sabrina Balboni had been allowed her freedom to help catch Webb, and had been directed to head for the Swiss city. Now, the rest of the team had traveled after, knowing that where Balboni was so too would be Tyler Webb.

And the mercenaries. Let's not forget about those.

Dahl believed he'd had his fill of these so-called soldiers of fortune lately. From Arizona to New York they'd plagued his every waking hour, and then even during a much-needed vacation in sunny Barbados they had attempted the unthinkable—to hurt his family. Dahl didn't think any hired killers survived that day,

Balboni, to her credit and desperate need to stay out of prison, had played her part well. She'd taken the time to convince Webb even though he already respected and revered her skills. And she knew her job, which at the moment was all about Webb. She knew her Saint Germain history.

Zurich was the place where, according to old accounts by various public figures including Sir Francis Bacon, Saint Germain had founded Freemasonry. The Count had spent some years here, perfecting that particular formula, before transplanting it to Venice and also Paris. Dahl cared about none of that now. He only cared about stopping Webb.

"Any contact?" he asked Kinimaka.

The Hawaiian held the cell that was Sabrina's point of contact. "Not yet," he said. "Shoulda implanted that tracker, brah."

"Too obvious. And Webb wouldn't hesitate to kill her if he found it. I believe she'll come through."

Kinimaka scrunched his face up, the old CIA suspicion still evident. "She's a thief. Why the confidence in her?"

"She's not *just* a thief. She is different. Proven in most ways and lacking in just a few. I believe she's redeemable."

The Hawaiian laughed. "Like your new girlfriend? Careful, Dahl, you'll end up surrounded by your own sympathies."

"Kenzie is not my girlfriend," Dahl said crossly. "Stop believing everything Alicia tells you."

Hearing her name, Kenzie looked over from the table beside them. "Talk to me, boys, not about me. So, when are we setting off after this screwball thief?"

Dahl swallowed a harsh retort. "We allow her to settle in, gain Webb's total confidence, and then she will call. Have faith."

Kenzie grunted and returned to staring into the black depths of her coffee cup as if she could read their future in what grounds remained.

Dahl stared into space, ignoring the comings and goings all around. Since Barbados and the terrors his wife, children and he had been put through by his old enemy, his life had been through more twists and turns than a corkscrew. Johanna, at first willing to try again, was already starting to pull away. The children were holding up well, bouncing back with a vengeance, and not even suffering nightmares after their ordeal. *There was always a silver lining*, he thought, *even where the storm ran deepest*.

It seemed there was nothing more to do, or try, short of quitting his job. Even then, would an initial euphoria turn to dust once whatever kind of new life they made grew mundane and he began to miss his true calling?

So here he was in the heart of Zurich, in the middle of another job and trying to find a solution to his marital problems. Not easy when the other half of the solution sat thousands of miles away.

Zurich itself was an impressive city. Located at the northwestern tip of Lake Zurich it had been called the wealthiest city in Europe as well as the city with the best quality of life. Theatres, art galleries and museums were in abundance, bringing tourists from all parts of the world. Gathered around him now were an eclectic bunch: backpackers, business men and locals pecking away at computers.

A standard cellphone tone caught his attention. Kinimaka

stared at the screen before nodding and holding it to his ear.

"Yes?"

Dahl watched his face as the hustle and bustle around them went on uninterrupted. This could change things. Set them in motion. The Hawaiian's face remained impassive for a while and then a telling reply.

"Where is it?"

Dahl felt a surge of energy and smiled at Smyth. At last, movement. This would help occupy their minds, divert their attentions.

Kinimaka nodded as he spoke. "We're on our way. We'll try to—"

Clearly then the line went dead as he stopped talking and stared at the screen. "Hope she's okay," he said, and then let out a long breath.

"And so do I," Dahl said. "But stay tough with her, Mano. Don't forget we have the means to test her too."

The merc they'd questioned in Paris earlier had listed all the places both he and his fellow goons had been tasked to guard. They had that list now, and would be matching it closely with what Sabrina gave them in the future.

"I have coordinates. It's not too far but—" He looked downcast.

"What?"

"She said something like—'bring your skis'."

Dahl could understand why Kinimaka might look so glum. "Shit, and you find it hard to walk in a straight line."

"I know." No protests came from the Hawaiian side.

Smyth knocked on the table. "So, get the coordinates tapped in. Let's scope this bad boy out."

Dahl watched Lauren push her laptop into the center of the table. She had been researching Saint Germain and Zurich, and the history of Freemasons. The wealth of lore and hearsay surrounding the Count, however, was challenging and quite fascinating.

Considered a secret agent of King Louis XV of France he appeared to have gone with a British commander to India to actually fight the French, highlighting an incredible talent for being able to go back and forth with leaders of warring camps and nations. An agent, a spy, a "singer who plays the violin wonderfully, composes and is also completely mad", according to Horace Walpole.

In Freemasonry he was considered not so much a Mason, but a member of the Higher Brotherhood. Modern-day Masons tried to distance themselves from involvement with the Count, citing the ridiculous accounts surrounding his alchemical discoveries, great feats and long life as proof that the man was an utter charlatan.

But Lauren pointed out the stark facts: kings courted him; battle commanders traveled with him; composers sought his company, theaters his compositions. He facilitated the marriage of a Dutch princess to a German prince, to establish a "fund for France". All statements of fact.

Why?

The Brotherhood called him an Advanced Adept, and many branches still did not deny him. His intrigues, travels and successes certainly pointed to a man of power, moving within influential circles and swaying minds.

Dahl was more interested in the place he'd stayed whilst visiting Zurich. "Lauren?"

"Yeah, it's up here." She jabbed at the screen where a 2D map of Zurich was displayed. Mountains marched beyond the lake and the city, some snow-capped. Lauren's fingers tapped at one of the tallest.

"We have a GPRS locator?" she asked.

Dahl nodded. "My old job. Never go anywhere without one."

Kenzie tapped him on the shoulder. "Um, except Barbados, eh?"

"That was different. Stop jabbering."

He ignored the bleat of protest, listening as Lauren suggested a simple route to a location close to the foot of the mountain in question.

"Webb's there now?" he asked.

Kinimaka nodded. "Like a virus that can't be shaken."

"Kenzie." He stood up without looking at her. "Get the check."

*

Sometime later around lunchtime, the team crowded out of their rented minibus, opened the rear hatch, and took a look at the assorted clothes and implements they'd thrown there. Only Dahl and Yorgi sported smiles.

"Don't worry," Dahl said. "It looks more cross-country than hill climb. A totally different kettle of fish."

The team reached inside the van for jackets, trousers, headgear and then the dreaded skis. Dahl didn't say a word when Smyth gestured for help or when Lauren fell over, just made sure the guys were okay. Their weapons were secured last, and then Kinimaka sent a final communication over to Argento at Interpol.

They set out, leaving the minibus parked in a large area alongside other vehicles and following tracks already laid out in the snow. The glare was high, the skies bright. Dahl tried to show the others, particularly Kinimaka, how best to employ his poles to help him glide across the snow-covered terrain. The Hawaiian was a fast learner, but in his own words had "no real experience with the white stuff".

"Use the alternating technique," the Swede said. "And look on the bright side, it's not too far."

The snowy landscape stretched far and wide, rolling hills ahead leading to higher and higher slopes. Dahl felt a chill in the air but knew it would soon dissipate once the team started their cross-country walk. He took the lead, looking back often and shouting encouragement. This was just what he needed, something to interfere with his train of thought and a way to help. When Kenzie fell on her ass he even scooted over to pull her up.

"People actually do this for fun?" she asked.

"Of course. You get used to it, like any pastime. Give it a chance."

The first rolling hill secreted a sharp slope down which both Kinimaka and Lauren went sideways and tumbling. Dahl helped them up and they continued, checking ahead and seeing at least three more similar hills. To the far right a cable car passed them, trundling slowly up highly tensioned wires.

"See the tracks?" Dahl panted as they paused, his breath pluming. "The popular path veers off that way."

Kinimaka raised his goggles. "And we go . . . ?"

"Straight on." Lauren pointed. "Across virgin snow."

"Crap, that's just great."

As a team they persevered and struggled through. Dahl helped when he made them slow down, wary of any lookouts Webb may have posted. There were no more communications from Sabrina and already the day was growing old, the shadows long. They crested a final slope and paused in the shadow of a huge boulder.

Ahead, a gentle slope ran to the base of the mountain. As Dahl studied the terrain a gentle snow flurry skipped up all around them, stinging their exposed faces with bits of ice. Kinimaka complained surprisingly more than Smyth.

"He's just cranky," Kenzie pointed out. "Problems at home."

Kinimaka swore at her. "Keep it to yourself."

"Relax," Kenzie said. "She's fine. I'm sure someone's taking care of her right now."

Kinimaka turned his back with obvious melancholy and asked how close they were to the coordinates. Dahl checked his GPS. "A few miles," he admitted. "Might be best to get a move on."

Another hour of relentless shambling and they were close enough to their destination to remove skis and continue in thick boots, much to everyone's relief. The air had already grown noticeably colder and the sky was fast losing its shine. The slopes of the mountain had been rugged for a while, before flattening out into a wide plateau. As the group came up the final part of the hard climb, they peered over the apex and saw a wonderful thing.

Rocks dotted the plateau, which led all the way to the mountainside. Nestling at the foot of the next rock face was a medium-sized house, bland in appearance but ancient; its brick structure weathered and its surrounds being retaken by the mountain. From this distance they could discern no more until Dahl broke the field glasses out.

They crept over the edge and lay amid a clump of trees, snow spilling out beneath them. When Kinimaka bumped into a low branch heavy with snow and dislodged a white shower that covered them all, everyone complained but Dahl—who used the field glasses to see if the movement had been spotted.

Through the lenses he saw golden light beaming through undraped windows, its radiance spilling across the landscape. Each window gave up a secret—the presence of suited men, a table full of untouched food and unused glasses, rows of leather-bound, hardback books lovingly preserved, and more.

Nobody he recognized.

Upstairs he went, training the field glasses carefully. With a slow turn of the adjustment wheel he compensated for the slight change.

And focused in on the face of Tyler Webb, staring out the window and across the landscape back toward Zurich.

Dahl almost gasped. Surprise made him tighten his fists around the glasses, an act that didn't go unnoticed amongst the team.

"What is it?" Kinimaka and Smyth said at once.

"Webb," he breathed. "I don't believe it. Tyler bloody Webb, large as life and twice as ugly, standing before a window on the top floor. Dozens of guards below though. This place belongs to a high-level player."

Kinimaka grunted, a feral sound bearing all the hatred and pent-up fears reaped from months of stalking both Hayden and he had endured, from afar and from intimately near.

"We go," he said, forgetting the cell and their line to Sabrina. "We go now. Hit it. Hit it hard."

Kenzie moved in the snow, her body making it crunch. "Hey, Mano, if you'd used your own advice on Hayden you might still be together."

The entire team ignored her. Dahl rolled onto his side, snow spilling, and regarded them. "Prepare for a fight. Are you ready?" It was a rhetorical question. "Try Sabrina quickly, Mano. Then we move."

CHAPTER THIRTY

Drake exploded into action as the shots rang out, darting left and wrestling a whole cluster of tourists to the ground. Hayden sprang right and Mai down the middle, flinging people aside if need be. Windows shattered behind them as the bullets flew high, darkened glass jettisoning outside in a prickly shower. Drake thanked the gods that these men were not true terrorists and fired only to aid their getaway. He slid off a pile of tourists.

"You're welcome," he said as they complained.

Hayden rushed over to him. "It probably won't help, but heads down. We could be in deep when they review the footage later."

"It won't matter then," Drake murmured. "If we do this . . ."

He sprinted off after the cult leaders. Hayden groaned in his wake. Alicia flew at his side, body language set in grim distaste. The way ahead was highly polished, reflective and lined by high windows containing super-expensive items. The whole place was darkened, the ceiling lit with gold. The floor shimmered and shone with inlaid tiles in swirling patterns. Amari and his friends were already at the far end, running hard and still refusing to glance back.

Drake stayed low, his head bent as much as was safe. They quickly approached the corner and slowed, inching around, but no shots came. Bands of tourists huddled in shop doorways or headed toward staircases and a bank of elevators. Drake led the other four the length of another opulent walkway and saw a large space opening up ahead. A sign mounted above read: *Lobby*.

"They're heading outside," he guessed. "Guys like these. Locals. Wouldn't surprise me if they had vehicles all over the bloody place."

Again they slowed as the vast lobby approached, and their vigilance paid off. A marble statue beside Mai exploded into

The Treasures of Saint Germain

pieces as a bullet zinged into it, the pieces momentarily masking her surprised, scarred face. Another bullet hammered into the filigree-work overhead, showering them with plaster. Drake jumped aside, casting eyes behind to make sure no inquisitive guests were following.

"By now, you'd have thought these guys would realize we ain't got no guns," Hayden said.

"They're not thinking that way," Drake said. "Because they're not trained to do so. We're dealing with wealthy sheltered citizens who have no real grasp of the consequences of their actions."

"Doesn't make them any less deadly," Mai said, flicking marble off her clothes. "Or answerable."

Drake crept backward to get a better angle into the lobby. Screaming filled the area and the shrieks of police sirens could be heard in the distance. He spied a security guard heading over toward Amari and knew they had to act quickly.

To his right and left were an array of small potted plants. He hurled them inside one after the other, distracting Amari and catching the guard's eye. He waved the man back. More shots filled the area, then the sound of running.

Alicia sprinted into the open.

"Whoa." He took off after her, and slipped in the residue spilled from the plant pots.

Alicia entered the lobby as Amari fled. Check-in desks stood to her left, concierge and information straight ahead. An enormous ceiling-height object filled the center of the lobby, something that looked like blown glass. As Alicia approached, two of Amari's acolytes stepped around it and pointed weapons at her.

"Look out!" Drake's call.

She sighed in exasperation, then stepped in and batted one of the guns aside. The other wavered as the man squeezed the trigger, but Alicia was nowhere near it, ducking to the right and driving a palm up against the man's elbow. A scream and an airborne gun attested to the fact that he certainly felt the blow. The first man adjusted, but Alicia slipped behind him, wrenched at the wrist and disarmed him. As she sought to twist them against each other, tying them together, she sensed rather than saw another attacker at her back.

She spun. Too late. The butt of a gun came down on her nose, making her see stars and blood. But none of that mattered. Alicia pushed through it, focusing on the deadly weapon rather than the man. It wasn't in play at the moment; held and used more like a rock than a lump of deadly metal. Nonetheless, as blood dripped down her chin, she spun into the third man, gripped the arm and twisted, making the gun fall to the floor.

Three disarmed.

Facing Drake she saw him pound toward her, the team at his side. Then all three cultists turned on her and the blood got in her eyes, stinging. A few punches that barely registered struck her forehead and stomach. Then one of the men thought to trip her and she collapsed onto one knee.

All three men turned tail and ran hard, following Amari toward the big exit doors.

Drake slid in next to Alicia. "You okay?"

"Of course I'm fucking okay. Go get 'em, you idiot!"

Mai stopped and held out a hand. "Guess with your broken nose and my scar we're a pair now, hey Taz?"

Alicia ignored the offer. "Nose isn't broken." She rose to her feet.

"Sure you don't need a little help keeping your feet?"

"Touch me and I'll bite your arm off." Alicia saw Drake, Hayden and Beau converging on the exit door and struggled along to join them. The exit narrowed and then gave way to a sprawling, sloping parking area, extensive gardens and a taxi rank. Numerous vehicles were parked to the left, some bright and expensive, others dull rentals. Alicia tore her gaze away from the myriad hiding places and watched the others.

Drake barged through the doors, sensing his quarry was close and panicking. Amari was dead ahead, flying down the slope and across the hotel's winding drive at breakneck pace. Beyond that, the hotel gave way to a road and then the final breakwater that formed Atlantis's island, then the endless, glittering waves stretching as far as he could see.

Amari's route couldn't be aimless. Drake believed that even a wealthy, tranquil owner of a coveted Jumeirah Palm address had to have come up with some kind of escape plan. These guys were fit though, able to stay ahead of the SPEAR team. Money could certainly buy fitness, if not perfect happiness.

"I will cut them off." Beau angled left, predicting they might cut across the gardens toward a larger side-parking area.

Drake pounded in pursuit. The sunglasses came loose, fell down his nose and needed scooping back up again. A busload of tourists gaped down through their windows, chattering away. Busboys and limo drivers scurried out of the way, one caught by Alicia and sent sprawling as she barged through with little ceremony. The SPEAR team were plagued with the added burden of ensuring they always had somewhere to hide in case Amari turned to fire, and constantly shouted at people to take cover. In the next moment all of the acolytes who still had guns turned and fired. Drake backed off.

Hayden caught his shoulder. "Too many civilians around."

"Agreed. The bastards are desperate."

"No," Mai said as she caught up. "They're just the same, and making a little extra room for their next move. Look."

Amari pounded out of the hotel grounds without slowing, hurdled a decorative wall, and then sped straight across a busy road. Cars swerved and collided. Fenders caught rear ends and one SUV slammed straight into the hotel wall. Amari's acolytes used the chaos to skip between or slide right over the massed vehicles. Drake, Hayden, Mai and Alicia hurried straight for the heart of it all.

As they neared the confusion—now made worse by more arriving vehicles and approaching flashing lights—they were stopped dead in their tracks by Amari's antics. The cult leader jumped atop the wall that separated land from sea, a breakwater from rolling waves. Glancing back, he nodded toward his acolytes and flashed a brilliant, white-toothed smile.

Drake read his lips.

"The Ascended Master will need us more than ever now."

He jumped. His six followers rushed up and followed suit, bodies filling the air and the horizon, leaping over the wall and down toward the dazzling blue brine. Hayden held up a hand so the team slowed.

"Split up," she hissed. "Check it out, then melt away. Get back to the city any way you can. We can't be arrested here."

Her instructions were part fuelled by the arrival of police vehicles, the gathering of people along the wall to check out what had happened, and the influx of hotel guests. The team scattered and then pressed against the high wall, peering down to the seas below.

Drake swore. Amari clearly had more than six close friends. The drop was little more than ten feet, straight into deep water, and floating close to shore was a large, fast looking speedboat. Amari was already inside, with his friends fast approaching.

Drake put his hands on the wall, thankful the cultists hadn't simply leapt to their glorious deaths. He was ready to jump into the fray. Then he paused and glanced across at Hayden. Beau was ready too, staring his way.

Hayden struggled with it. Drake cursed silently. There was only one way this was going to go. The cops were scrambling out of their cars. Mai was already drifting away at the edge of a pack of tourists. Alicia was crouching down with a local, examining the damage to his car and making comforting noises. If they continued the pursuit they would end up packed into a Dubai prison, and as much as Drake would like to get a look inside a cell where the cop cars were Ferraris and Lamborghinis he didn't want to end up taking an extended vacation there. Not whilst Webb was still on the loose.

Maybe next time.

A tourist standing and watching the speedboat, turned away and Drake latched onto him, asking what was happening. They engaged in conversation and wandered back into the hotel. Several glances back confirmed the cops were still catching up, trying to make sense of what had happened and probably assuming all the perpetrators were on the boat.

He saw the signs for the monorail that led from the hotel to the edge of Dubai city and paid for a ticket. Amari's escape was bad, a major setback to their cause. The previously oblivious man would be in full crazy mode now. Drake wondered how that might affect Tyler Webb and his efforts to find the treasures of Saint Germain.

Badly, he hoped. But now they had two primary enemies to track down.

He wondered how Dahl was doing.

CHAPTER THIRTY ONE

Dahl led the painstakingly slow, watchful and meticulous raid on the house in the snow-covered mountains around Zurich. Following his sighting of Webb, they had mapped the house, guessed at the layout and number of guards and tried to get in touch with Sabrina Balboni. Not surprisingly, the super-thief didn't answer their calls, so Dahl had decided to take the initiative. Webb was in their grasp. They had weapons, the element of surprise, and three well-trained soldiers. Four, since sometimes Dahl counted the Mad Swede part of himself as an extra person.

The six of them crept out of hiding, careful not to shake the trees, and scuttled through soft snow. Yorgi led the way, his watchful prowess coming into play now. Kinimaka came in the center, hoping his bulk wouldn't get them seen. The truth was, despite very careful observation they could find no sign of an outer guard. Dahl couldn't wait. Webb might be in there for hours, or days. This was an isolated spot with little chance of escaping unnoticed. Chance was in their favor.

They pulled up against another set of three lonely trees, halfway to the house and with a white-covered garden spread out before them. The garden was a hodgepodge of replica vehicles, statues and collectible items, all seemingly errant as if an eccentric might be hoarding them. Dahl leaned in to Yorgi. "As soon as we reach the door you fall back."

The Russian nodded. "Dah."

Kinimaka's phone rang. He'd forgotten to mute the sound and the tone rang out clear in the wintery stillness. The Hawaiian's eyes went huge as he rummaged through thick, zippered clothing for the black rectangle.

"Crap, crap, crap . . ."

Dahl studied the house, the windows, the doors. Nothing moved. Nothing changed.

Kinimaka jabbed at the phone without checking the caller ID. "Hi. Can I help?"

Smyth rolled his eyes.

Dahl listened in, recognizing the dulcet tones that belonged to Sabrina Balboni filtering through the tiny speaker.

"You must stop calling me. You put me in danger."

"You're our asset," Kinimaka breathed. "We needed you."

"I said that I would call you when I was safe. That time is now. I have news."

Kinimaka waved them all to stand down. He held the phone out but didn't turn on the speakerphone. "Go ahead."

"Webb has come here, an old haunt of Saint Germain's, to learn the secret of the next treasure. The idea, the conception, of Freemasonry was born here, in this place. A High Master lives here now, safeguarding it as a sanctuary, offering assistance only to those who can prove their worthiness. Webb was beside himself with pride, telling me this. The disgusting worm. He sweats when he's excited, you know."

Lauren made a face. "I know the type."

Dahl listened carefully.

"This High Master will tell Webb all he needs to know so that every Freemason in the world will be answerable to him. Doors previously locked even to him will be thrown open. The world will be his playing field. This is in addition to all he has already learned about alchemy and the mastery of languages. And this Webb—he was already crazy."

Kinimaka endorsed her with a grunt. "The lust for power drives him like nothing else. But it is all a perversion. He perverts all he sees and touches."

"Well, Freemasonry was envisioned in this house and lives here still. I am not allowed into their discussions, but will quiz Webb when he comes out. He is stupid. Can't wait to tell me all and show what a big man he is becoming. We must make him regret it. We must."

"We're close," Dahl said. "Any advice?"

"How close?"

"Come to the window. I'll wave."

"Oh, that is good. The guards are all wearing robes. They have swords. They have knives and ninja stars. They number almost one hundred. The High Master is a true adept of everything you can imagine, a being seeking ascendance. The house is devoid of technically advanced controls. It does not need them. There are a few old-school defenses in the grounds. I hope you brought the Swiss Army."

"No," Dahl muttered. "Just the knife, I'm afraid."

"Oh. Did you think assaulting a potential ascendant's house a formality? Did you assume an attack on the very bricks and mortar of Freemasonry would be easy? I thought you people were at the top of your game?"

"We didn't know," Dahl said. "And we're short staffed."

Sabrina didn't deign to reply.

"You did say ground defenses," Yorgi put in, his accent toned down. "I see only ornamental objects. A statue. A pair of Aztec pillars. A rusted tank from one of the wars. A birdcage. And a bright red UK phone box. Good touch, that."

Sabrina came across as confused. "It was one of Webb's remarks. Listen. I am locked in my room but they will come soon. I have to go. So I have one more item to give you."

Dahl glanced around the hungry pack. "All right. Let's have it."

"Upon our arrival, as we drove into here, I quizzed Webb as to our next destination. I figured it would be good to know, to prepare. For you."

"Clever," Dahl said. "What did he say?"

"He waited until we were inside, behind the locked door for security I think, and then blabbed it all out like an old woman. We go to London, he said. The Haymarket."

"The what?" Kinimaka looked blank. "What's a haymarket?"

"Somewhere Saint Germain spent time," Sabrina said. "Research it."

"We will," Dahl said. "Now, be ready. We're on our way." He was pleased that nobody, especially Kinimaka, revealed that the name was on the merc's list, and even more so that Sabrina appeared to be a kosher asset.

"If you all die our deal is void and I will find a way to disappear."

"We can't stop you. But it would save many lives if you would at least help take Webb down."

"Once I am safe, I will see."

Dahl nodded at Kinimaka. "Let's end this."

The Hawaiian wound it up, and then they were staring at the house again, this time with new eyes.

"Tighten your armor," Kenzie said. "That bitch said 'swords'. Friggin' *swords*." Her eyes shone. "I can't wait!"

"Nothing's moving out there," Smyth said in some exasperation. "Nothing. If they have defenses, they're lower profile than a painted-on tire."

The team re-checked their weapons then drew them for use. Another moment passed before they considered the area one last time, scrutinized the doors and windows, and made their move.

Bending low, running silent, the six-strong team padded through deep snow toward a totally incongruous row of canons. A statue stood silent to their left, the old tank to their right. A second statue showed no signs of life, no slanted eyes suddenly coming alight and shining like full-beam headlights. Dahl reached the canons first and hunkered down, still watching the doors and seeing no movement.

Satisfied, he turned back to check on the team.

Kinimaka came next, slipping and sliding on the soft surface but holding up well. Smyth and Lauren ran close, not speaking but clearly not wanting to be too far apart either. Yorgi came next and then Kenzie, the ex-Mossad agent, suddenly sporting a skip in her step.

Dahl's jaw hit the floor.

The big gun on top of the huge tank was tracking them, swiveling silently, its enormous barrel following their every step.

"Oh, shiiiiiiiiii—"

Death exploded from every direction.

CHAPTER THIRTY TWO

Dahl's warning sent the entire team leaping like acrobats, away from the assumed impact point. It came a split-second later, a totally insane, unexpected blast from the turret gun of a rusted tank, the shell slamming into the piled snow and exploding, flames shooting for yards all around and shrapnel detonating. Most of the shards shredded the snow, peppered the canons or stuck into trees but a few sharp particles passed among the team. Dahl added a cut wrist to his scar collection; Kenzie a gouge to the abdomen. Lauren got a nicked ear, whilst Smyth was lucky enough to see deadly slivers deflect from the stock of his gun.

The door to the house flew open and a steady stream of screaming, black-robed sentries rushed out, all brandishing swords. Kenzie's reaction was on the verge of orgasmic.

"Oh, come to Momma. Get your sweet, sweet-tempered ass over here!"

She met the first to arrive with gleeful abandon.

Dahl kept his head, raised his handgun, and conserved his bullets. One shot, one man. Around him, his team followed suit.

Smyth ran at the tank, man versus machine, growling and gnashing as if he might chew his way through the bulletproof exterior. The gun barrel stayed still, its occupants probably reloading. Smyth jumped at the vehicle, hit the side and jumped again from a tiny ledge, landing on top. The entry hatch lay before him, as old as the tank and as rusty and vulnerable. He stamped on it, then struck it with the butt of his gun, gratified to see chunks flying off. When the latch broke he hefted the lid and dived away, rolling to the front of the tank. Sure enough, bullets zinged up through the hole, shooting straight up at the sky. He wondered briefly how far they might get and where they might land, and then wished for a grenade.

No such luck.

Dahl shouted at his team to vacate their positions as Smyth hit stalemate with the tank. The robed swordsmen were still coming, half a dozen down and dead, but others leapt over their comrades and poured forward like rats deserting a plague ship. Dahl shot one point blank, the descending sword whistling over his shoulder. The next he barged aside. He deflected a blade with his handgun, clenching his teeth to keep the pain inside, and fired off a quick shot. This man fell to his knees, but then another leapt onto his back and flung himself at Dahl, snarling, robe flying in an impression of Batman or Dracula, sword slicing apart the very air that surrounded them, first left, then right and then left again all in the blink of an eye.

Kenzie whooped it up, disarming the first man who reached her. Free of him she spun and brought the sword arcing down, slicing clean through the arm of her first opponent, whose hand and sword spun away at an alarming rate. On the backswing she sliced a stomach, and then caught the next sword on her own, the clang of metal loud as the churned up ice and floating snow spun all around them, creating a magnificent vision. Kenzie pirouetted, confusing her foe, then left him bleeding. She stabbed and thrust and chopped, taking on battle after battle, and never once looked troubled.

Lauren and Yorgi stayed behind the others, planning their shots well and covering when magazines needed replacing. None reached them, but the enemy kept on coming.

Kinimaka planted himself behind Dahl, a solid rock against which all enemy waves broke. Firing to both sides he also ducked under two sword swings and then brought his bulk up hard, sending his opponents into the air in messy, graceless cartwheels. Fast shooting ensured they were dead before they hit the ground, clay pigeons destined to die.

Dahl backed off a little. The front door of the house continued to belch forth hooded killers. He took a bead on the door and emptied a full mag, filling it and blocking it with twitching bodies. He picked up one man and then another, throwing both into the pile. Kinimaka covered him, and Lauren and Yorgi covered the Hawaiian. Behind them, Smyth wrestled with the tank.

Kenzie twirled at the heart of a melee, bright blade flashing, snow and ice swirling and churning all around her, stirred up by the ferocity of her passing. Gouts of blood flared through the snow, screams erupted, and wherever the fray moved to, it left a pile of broken bodies behind.

A hand reached over the top of the tank's hatch, but Smyth was ready, firing and blasting away the fingers. He leapt at it, firing straight down, pummeling a body with bullets. The tank didn't stop humming, but no further sounds were heard. Smyth swore at it and thought his skills might be useful elsewhere.

Kinimaka's text tone rang out in the heart of battle.

"Crap, hang on."

Dahl doubled his efforts, guessing what the Hawaiian might be thinking. Sabrina might be suggesting a plan or directing them to Webb. At that moment Kenzie swept toward him, a majestic Queen of Swords, dripping the blood of her enemies and grinning from ear to ear.

That woman is so unbelievably dangerous.

Hard. Relentless. Confrontational. He was sure she cared deep down, but if that were true then the emotion was locked away behind impregnable doors.

Smyth jumped in too, taking the pressure away from Dahl. Feline-fast, he whirled toward Kinimaka. "What is it?"

"Not good. Our thief is out of the house. With Webb. Covered by guards." He looked around. "Side door!"

Dahl saw it. Another black-robed torrent flooding from another angle, toward the far side of the house where the edge of the roof met the rock of the mountain. Even as he watched, the stream reached the far side.

"Webb!" he cried. "Right there." He saw Sabrina's black hair and Webb's frame and the stick-thin figure of another man near the front of the pack, probably the High Master. The unmistakable sound of a garage door being rolled up prompted his next reaction.

"With me!"

To a man and woman they all broke with the Mad Swede, firing sideways, stopping sword-wielding maniacs in their tracks.

Dahl hurdled a canon, sidestepped a bright red telephone box and used a frozen ice sculpture as a screen to race closer to the escapees. As he came around into the open an engine roared to life. Robed sentries spotted him and broke with swords upraised. Dahl slammed home a fresh mag and fell to one knee.

"Come get some, assholes."

CHAPTER THIRTY THREE

Dahl squeezed the trigger, loosing shot after shot, aiming for central body mass. The wave of attackers didn't slow, a dozen men and then more flooding toward him with swords brandished high. From the left came even more, the remainder of those who had exited the front door.

Dahl's team were spread out, but still coming and fighting hard. Kenzie slashed at those seeking to join the new wave. Kinimaka and Smyth ran low, firing constantly, trying to reach the Swede's side. Yorgi and Lauren stayed several feet back, surveying the battle from a different, cooler perspective and picking off threats the others didn't have time to see.

At the side of the mountain, engines roared. The big treble garage was open and swarming with active bodies. The first sign of a vehicle emerging was when a short white nose eased out straight onto the ice. Dahl knew immediately that they had problems.

"Oh, shit. That's a—"

He didn't have to finish. Three more vehicles shot out, all different colors. Blue, green, midnight black. Snowmobiles, loaded with people and revving, ready to go. Dahl took off like a streak of lightning, firing constantly. Two sword-wielders came close. He barged one in the chest, hurling him backwards and hit the next practically head on. A withering sack of meat bounced off the Swede and shriveled away to the floor. Another came close, swinging his sword. Dahl ducked under then caught the arm and threw the man overhead, not able to spare the time to see where he landed. Kinimaka was behind now, ducking the airborne attacker and locking onto the snowmobiles.

"No time!" he cried.

The white tracked vehicle shot forward, one of the less popular two-man versions. Not content with that, two robed assassins also clung to the vehicle, somehow perched on the back and holding onto a leather loop. The driver still held his sword but squeezed the throttle with his spare hand and held on.

The second snowmobile, light blue, held Webb and three guards; the third—green—Sabrina and three guards. The last held the thin man and a gaggle of sentries. All at once all four snowmobiles were speeding across the ice and churning up plumes of snow, engines bellowing like angry charging rhinos.

Dahl saw them coming but was still fifteen meters away. He couldn't shoot with any accuracy on the run and the snowmobiles were already up to twenty miles per hour. They would race past him and be gone before he got anywhere near. A quick glance back showed Kinimaka and Smyth right behind and Yorgi and Lauren tracking them to the side. The robed killers had amalgamated now and were still chasing. Kenzie flitted around their edges like the shadow of death, administering lethal judgment wherever her steel chose to kiss.

He kept running. *Never give up.* Most of the guards around the garage were gone now, clinging to the protesting snowmobiles, so the interior was open and clear. The view inside was galvanizing to say the least.

Dahl grinned. He turned. "Cover the perimeter," he said.

Dahl ran as Smyth and Kinimaka laid down a screen of lead, quickly whipping a mag out and slamming in a fresh one. Yorgi and Lauren came around the back, whilst Kenzie broke away and jumped over a kneeling Smyth, holding her new sword high.

Dahl roared up atop a new snowmobile. "Ya got one of those things spare?"

Kenzie hopped on board. "Why? Are you about to go wild?"

"It's never far from the surface."

Kenzie found a discarded blade quickly, plundered from the guards they had shot whilst the tracked vehicles made their escape. Then, a sword in each hand, she leaned over Dahl's right shoulder, her lips close to his ear.

"Ride it hard, Torsten."

The snowmobile pounced faster than a striking panther. Kenzie's head whipped back and Dahl hunched over the controls.

He jerked a hand at Smyth. "Four more back there. Get a move on, mate."

The vehicle felt heavy, tracking over the packed ice and then the soft snow, but the handlebars turned easily and the windshield offered good protection. He ignored all the little buttons, trusting that all he needed was speed and power. He already knew where the brake lever was, but had no intentions of using it. In the mirror he saw Yorgi and Lauren emerging from the enormous garage, both astride snowmobiles and angling them toward Kinimaka and Smyth, who continued to hold off the robed sentries. Their job was made easier by dozens more men heading into the garage to view what was left.

Should have disabled the rest.

No time!

Gliding and springing over the snow and unseen bumps, he swerved in the tracks of the rearmost vehicle. They were gaining as their enemies were heavier, hampered by unbalanced men, and having to closely follow three other vehicles; clearly with no distinct plan in mind.

Dahl tried sighting over the windshield whilst guiding the handlebars with one hand, found it didn't work and almost sent them somersaulting into a tree. Kenzie rapped him on the top of the head.

"Get closer, idiot."

"Thanks. I figured that one already."

They raced closer. Behind, Kinimaka clung to Yorgi whilst Smyth looked, not surprisingly, rather unhappy seated behind Lauren. The New Yorker chewed her lips like gum as she concentrated hard to steer and keep them safe. A horde of sentries screamed after them, but now with no chance of keeping up. In the far distance Dahl heard the sudden roaring start-up of more engines.

"We have to end this."

"Just get me close."

The tracks slipped and leaped, never still. Dahl shifted the handlebars, taking the bumps in his stride. Lauren roared a bit closer, prompting Kenzie to slap him hard on the back. He pushed it to the absolute limit, sensing he'd held off a little for safety's sake. He could see the thin man now, the voluminous robe wrapped around him and yet still billowing out. Swords bristled all around him. Dahl was conscious that they had to get past almost every snowmobile to reach Webb's.

"Don't worry," Kenzie said as if reading his mind. "It's a long way back to Zurich Town."

"The light will start failing soon."

The day was dwindling away, he knew. And although a vast illumination of light guided their way now, revealing every pitfall, he'd hate to be forced to take this route by night. Something told him the guards knew the way.

"Get ready, Kenzie."

She rose, black-haired and lithe, a sword in each hand. She balanced on the footrests as Dahl squeezed a drop more power from the screaming engine. They came alongside the black snowmobile; the closest sentry swung his sword down in one hand whilst holding on tight with the other. Unbalanced, he appeared ungainly, but the blade came down no less sharply. Kenzie deflected it and sent her second sword thrusting into his midriff, then withdrew quickly. The man grunted and fell away, bouncing in their wake and spraying blood across the snow.

Another took his place.

Dahl inched the vehicle closer, tracks almost touching and spray pluming up all along the sides. The thin man merely stared at him. Kenzie fenced with the rear guard, deflecting and searching for an opening. A sharp hill made her stagger, their snowmobile catching air for three seconds alongside the other, but on landing she caught herself and sliced down at her opponent's wrist.

The sword fell away, still attached to the hand.

The man jumped over at her, hitting their vehicle with a crash. She caught him and dropped a shoulder, sending him spinning over the seat. His remaining hand managed to catch hold of her foot, but the rest of his body dangled over the side, his feet scraping chunks from the earth.

Kenzie kicked him point blank in the face and turned her back as he tumbled away.

The next guard didn't bother holding on, just came at her with both hands clasped around the hilt of his sword. Kenzie blocked as the two snowmobiles blasted over a stretch of level ground. Dahl saw an opening, steered again with one arm, and raised his handgun in the other.

Sighted on the driver.

The thin man—the High Master—suddenly came to life. His frail-seeming hands, until now clasped together, twitched and sent a black object spinning at Dahl. It struck the gun arrow-straight, made him drop it to the floorboards and let out a grunt of shock. *What the hell?* He'd seen the flash and gyration of a ninja star and was grateful it hadn't lodged in his neck. Another twitch of the fingers and Dahl ducked, inadvertently swinging the snowmobile away. Kenzie staggered and the Swede felt a nick across the side of the face.

Don't fuck with the Mad Swede, bro.

Kenzie was screaming in anger and surprise, but Dahl had no time for that. Teeth grating, he swerved the vehicle sharply with a quick turn of the handlebars.

They came together hard, ice and snow exploding all around the impact, sparks kicking off the engines and chunks of metal ripping free. Dahl clung on grimly, shouting at their enemies, still turning the handlebars so the vehicles stayed together. Kenzie grabbed hold of her opponent and tugged him free, jumping up as he tumbled clear off the back.

The last guard engaged her. That left the High Master and the driver.

Dahl took that responsibility.

At that moment, Lauren came speeding past, gliding along at high speed and then Yorgi, struggling with Kinimaka's bulk but tweaking the throttle gamely to hang on to Lauren's slipstream.

Dahl leapt across to the black snowmobile, planted his feet on the floorboards and faced the High Master. With one hand, and without looking, he made a motion. Kenzie's spare sword flickered through the turbulent air, spinning, catching light, and then his fingers were clasping around the hilt and bringing it slicing down in a single motion.

The thin man held up a hand as if to ward off the blade.

Dahl shuddered as his sword came down on a heavy metal wristband, making it ricochet away. A thin stiletto appeared from under the black robes and darted at Dahl's midriff. He fell back on the long seat, and brought his legs up under the man's chin.

The head whipped back hard, neck muscles creaking. The driver glanced back, eyes terrified as they met the Swede's. Dahl rose, sword high and brought it down hard. Behind him Kenzie parried and thrust, every second a blow, until her enemy was run through and falling, falling like an old marionette whose strings had all frayed away.

Dahl skewered the High Master, then bounded up beside the driver.

"One chance," he said. "Jump the fuck off right now."

The man complied. Dahl saw their own snowmobile, miraculously still attached to the black one, was now starting to drag, presenting a danger. He glanced back at Kenzie.

"Hop over there, love, and set that thing free. And throw me that handgun."

Ahead, the battle raged.

CHAPTER THIRTY FOUR

Dahl saw Lauren come alongside the green snowmobile, her objective Sabrina Balboni, but trying to hide it. Yorgi ran his own vehicle hard in her wake. Two more motored on ahead: Webb's and the lead one. Dahl looked over at Kenzie who now sped along at his side.

"Wanna help?"

"Not my forte. But hey, now that I have a sword I'm pretty much open for anything."

Dahl pressed his mic. "Careful with the asset, Lauren and Smyth. Could still be useful."

Yorgi went full throttle and swept up alongside and then past Lauren. He was in pursuit of Webb, someone they *could* take down with acute prejudice, and he had Kinimaka in tow. The Hawaiian weighed the back of the snowmobile down but clung on gamely, no doubt seeking any kind of vengeance being so close to Webb.

Dahl let Kenzie jump back aboard and then brought her close to the rear of the green vehicle. A sentry, brain no doubt frazzled with relentless rhetoric, actually leapt straight for them, arms and legs akimbo in mid-air like a flying lizard. The long blade he held vibrated as winds struck its fine steel.

Kenzie rushed forward, covering Dahl who didn't bat an eye, just kept driving. She caught the oncoming blade six inches from his skull, kicked the descending man hard as he landed, breaking ribs and sending him tumbling overboard, crashing through the snow. Dahl swerved to avoid the body.

They sped up again. It would look suspicious if they didn't attack the thief's vehicle. Sabrina sat with her head down, eyes peering from under a hood right back at Dahl. Around her, sentries raged.

Kenzie grabbed the handlebars and shrugged. "Just shoot 'em."

"Really? Have you had enough swordplay?"

"I want to get to Webb."

"Yeah," Dahl admitted. "Me too." He fired three bullets and three men cartwheeled away. Sabrina stayed low, unthreatening and the driver didn't even look around. Dahl gauged their submissiveness would be enough to pass them by.

"Now." Kenzie balanced on the footrests again. "Be my rock."

He smiled.

On to the blue snowmobile, and Dahl came up on the left as Lauren and Yorgi fought for position on the right. A swirl of sleet, a blinding blizzard, blew up all around the speeding contestants. Webb was trying to order men around. Dahl saw the confusion and despondence in their eyes. Today, they had lost a leader.

Where would they go next? At least three-quarters of them seemed to think sacrifice was a good idea. Kenzie stepped up and caught the onslaught of two men at the same time, their swords clanging together as they all hung off the sides of the vehicles. Dahl held it perfectly steady, Kenzie's 'rock'.

Kinimaka's huge paw held a handgun which he used safely to pick off a robed man on their side; Smyth did the same. After that there was no more safety; the glide, bounce and swerve of the runners were always imperfect.

Ahead, Dahl saw the long slope coming up against a sparse forest and beyond it, he knew, lay the run into Zurich. It stood to reason that the Freemasons would have had a plan.

Then his thoughts were fully occupied as the treeline passed and they were suddenly among thick, branchless trunks. Kenzie knelt down to aid balance as Dahl swerved barely in time to miss one deadly obstacle and then skimmed straight past another, scraping paint from the vehicle and shavings from the tree. The white snowmobile, well ahead, came even closer, losing a mirror and a guard to an extra-wide trunk and twisting roots. The worst thing was that the hapless man just stuck there, in the roots, splayed as if caught in a spider's web, instantly dead.

Dahl motored past, passing the command along to ensure everyone stayed low. Another huge trunk came up and then he flitted left and right past two more, a lethal chicane and one

Drake would be pissed to know he'd missed out on. He grinned smugly.

The ground was terrifyingly uneven, one bump sending them high into the air, unable to steer, and aiming for low branches and the stem behind. At the last moment the runners hit the sparse snow at an angle due to Dahl and Kenzie's desperate lean, then shot off past the tree. Their slant brought them sideways into Webb's blue snowmobile, shunting it off course. It struck Lauren's, then shambled back into forward position, its jarred riders stunned. Dahl was forced to veer widely away again as a giant pair of knobbled trunks blocked their path.

"You see that?" Kenzie called out.

Dahl could see nothing but snow and wood and hanging branches. "What?"

"A road ahead. If it's the same one we came up on then it's a direct run into Zurich. This can't be blind luck."

"So that's it." Dahl nodded. "Knew there had to be a reason."

The snowmobiles plowed on, the fighting paused for now as the drivers struggled to keep everyone alive. The white leader took off over a ramp-shaped pile of snow, its driver standing, and came down with a double bump, now past the forest and careening toward the ribbon of black tarmac—prominent amongst the fields of snow.

Thunder shook the skies.

Dahl looked up, and although darkness stole among the white-gray clouds he easily spied the running lights of a pair of helicopters. "The cavalry," he said.

"Or the cultists." Kinimaka jumped on the comms.

"Too coincidental." Dahl eased off the throttle as the edge of the forest approached. "How we doing for ammo?"

"Pretty damn good." Kenzie wielded her sword and grinned.

The others sounded off; not bad after such outright warfare, but then they had come prepared. *Not in all ways,* he thought, glancing at the beast he straddled and then at Kenzie standing tall with her bloody blade. But the Swede had a soldier's mind, a soldier's brain, and made the next decision without pause.

"Lauren, Yorgi, you're closest. You get Webb. We'll go after the choppers."

Easy to say, but the framework was clear in his mind. If they harassed the choppers before they landed the pilots would be forced to evade. He then got a look at the men sat inside the helicopters.

Not robed, not locals. Somehow Webb must have had them stationed in Zurich, and on stand-by. They wouldn't back down.

Men leaned out of the descending choppers, feet planted on the skids, weapons pointed.

Dahl knew they were sitting ducks. But something didn't quite sit right. Webb had called these men, sure, but where were the Freemasons going?

He pulled on the handlebars, spun the snowmobile behind a wide trunk as hellfire erupted from above. Bullets stitched the wood, driving huge splinters from the tree. Dahl and Kenzie ducked low. Through the comms he heard Kinimaka and Smyth grunting as they were shunted to safety and the remaining snowmobiles carried on.

Dahl didn't take defeat easy. He leaned around the trunk, held the Glock in two hands and drew a bead on one of the chopper pilots. Return fire mangled his aim and the bullets shot up toward the clouds. All three remaining snowmobiles had stopped beside the road and one of the choppers was coming down hard, aiming right for the middle. As it neared asphalt mercenaries dropped out to take up perimeter positions.

"Too many." Smyth cursed. "Too desperate. But they still have our asset."

Dahl didn't want to do this all again. He couldn't fire blindly because he didn't want to hit the master thief. "Next time," he said, for no real reason. "We're bringing grenades."

Kenzie looked a little hurt, and Dahl had to admit she'd done more than her fair share for the team. Another volley of gunfire swept the treeline, keeping them pinned down. A new sound now roared out of the encroaching darkness, and bright lights flashed and bounced from earth to skies. Dahl knew that sound.

"4x4s," he said. "Coming up the road. So that was the Freemasons' getaway."

The helicopters boomed, their rotors spinning mightily as one took off and the other pulled up. Dahl saw only the robed warriors remaining and the face of Tyler Webb pressed against one of the chopper windows. The man was grinning.

Got what he came for.

But Sabrina was in there too. The day wasn't totally lost.

"Now," he said. "Let's go grab ourselves a couple of vehicles."

CHAPTER THIRTY FIVE

The team exploded from hiding, engines revving and runners skidding. The robed men heard them coming and formed a cordon around the 4x4s, but Dahl had no intentions of slowing down. As the line came up he blipped the throttle, and saw the looks of fear flash into his enemies' eyes as they saw his intentions.

"Don't fuck with me," he growled.

Smashing men aside, he threw the handlebars sideways and the vehicle into a slide. Kenzie slashed down with one hand whilst holding on with the other. Her sword clanged once, twice, then cleaved through bone. Men went sprawling. Dahl lifted his gun as the snowmobile slowed, squeezing off three shots. From the right came Yorgi and Lauren; Kinimaka and Smyth laying down the fire. The robed warriors ran at the slewing snowmobiles, fanatics to the last, some striking at the metal with their swords, others falling as they slashed at those aboard. The car engines roared as their drivers saw what was happening.

Dahl leapt from the footrests, came down on two feet and blew the side window from a high black vehicle. Blood splashed and a figure slumped, the engine note withering away. The second 4x4 shot forward in a gravel-churning skid.

A sword swung at Dahl. He skipped back, letting the blade pass an arm's width away. He kicked the owner, seeing the sword fall, and then rendered him unconscious. Another attacker screamed in from the right but Kenzie caught his plunging sword with her own, jerking the man's weapon free and almost breaking his wrist in the process.

Dahl saw a gap to the bloodied 4x4 and clicked the comms. "With me," he shouted out. "Fast."

They ignored their few remaining opponents and ran hard for the 4x4. Dahl jumped through the open front door and kicked the dead driver aside. The engine was still running. A robed figure came at him and he closed the door against the man's face, wincing as metal struck bone with an ungiving crunch.

Kenzie remained by the passenger door, fencing with two men and keeping them at bay. Smyth shot one as he jumped into the back. Yorgi and Lauren jumped off their perches and dived in lengthways, tangled and sprawling in the footwell. Dahl pressed the accelerator hard.

Kinimaka bounded into the back.

The Swede set off in a black cloud of rubber, racing hard into the heart of Zurich.

CHAPTER THIRTY SIX

Drake sauntered along, a tourist alone returning to his hotel in the heart of Dubai. They had chosen a place near the Dubai mall, both because of its distance from the Palm Jumeirah and proximity to the main airport highway. He entered the lobby now, holding the door open, casting around to see who might lie in wait.

All looks well.

The interior was bright and shining, the staff all smiling. Guests came and went, despite the late hour. Drake made his way through carefully, went for the stairs and paused on the first landing. All was quiet. In truth, nothing set his alarm bells ringing.

Looks like I'm safe, but what about the rest?

Their strategy hadn't worked well—a fail for the SPEAR team. They had endangered civilians and themselves. Questions would be asked . . . somewhere. He was unused to failure, especially during the last few years. Sometimes a man might be forgiven for thinking he was a little superhuman, but elite Special Forces soldiers were trained to deal differently, to think differently, accomplish feats those without the preparation of decades of experience might think unachievable.

It had to be said they were working on the back foot though. Webb was clearly following an agenda he'd had in place for many years. The cultists were reacting . . . until now. *Now,* he thought. *They will be putting new schemes in place.*

He entered their room, close to the fire escape. Heads swiveled and a shadow moved to the side, but Drake knew immediately that the figure was Mai.

"Took your sweet old time," Alicia commented.

"Hey, less of the old."

Hayden rose from her seat by the window, the lighted-up

skyscrapers shining beyond. "So, we're all here. Thoughts?"

The group fell into a discussion relating to what had happened. Hayden fielded a call from Argento and the team considered what to do next. The mood was despondent; nobody liked losing. And whilst they hadn't strictly lost, the outcome was not good. Drake consoled himself a little when he found three boxes of pizza, all half-eaten. With care, he fished out two slices of pepperoni and drank a full bottle of water.

Hayden called Dahl.

The Swede answered immediately, sounding out of breath. "I hope you have better news than us, Hayden, because we just damaged half of Zurich and lost Webb." He paused.

Drake munched disconsolately.

"We screwed up big time," Hayden said. "Lost Amari and his boys. They could be halfway to Europe by now."

Dahl asked them to wait a moment whilst he gathered his thoughts, then said, "So, Webb was meeting with a High Master, some Adept and a big knob Mason, I guess. The lad was guarded to the max by some sword-wielding loonies who chased us down a bloody mountain."

Alicia pursed her lips. "Sounds like you had a better time than us."

"It had its moments," Dahl admitted. "Anyway, Webb took off in a chopper which we tracked all the way to the city. Caught him close to a helipad, chased, rode through some red lights. Crashed." He sighed. "I'd like to say it was Kenzie's fault, flailing that bloody sword out of the window, but it was my hands at the wheel."

Drake stopped mid-munch. "Kenzie has a sword now?"

"Yeah, I keep trying to get it away from her but . . ."

"You don't have the balls?" Drake asked.

"Yeah, that's the real risk."

Drake winced a little as Dahl went on. "So, a crash, but we plowed on. Webb slammed through a shopping district and across a bridge and that's when the police got involved. Argento asked them to let us take the lead but some local hothead ignored him and went head on with Webb. The outcome was not pretty."

Hayden gauged the room. "Yeah, same here."

"Webb's mercenaries did not hold back and even though he only seemed to have three or four of them it was enough to help block the roads with police cars and make his escape. Luckily for us he has Sabrina with him."

"She stayed?" Alicia looked impressed.

"She did. I have faith in her. And her information matches the merc's list. Despite having the chance to escape, she remained with Webb. We have Interpol searching, but given Webb's proclivity for disappearing, I believe she is still our best chance."

"What did we learn about Webb's trip?"

"Very little," Dahl admitted. "Saint Germain helped found Freemasonry here, so maybe their secret chants or handshakes are what he needs to progress, but Sabrina intimated that it may well be something to help pave his future. An introduction to a million open doors, or something. Who knows? The point is—he's on to the next place now and Sabrina already told us where that is."

Drake cracked open another bottle of water. "My guess is Europe. The Count seems to have traveled further than bloody Boeing."

"And you would be right. The next stop for Webb is London, and the Haymarket Theatre. Lauren is no Karin when it comes to computers but she did find that Germain composed songs, and performed there."

Hayden scratched her head. "So now he's a composer and actor too? Jeez, who the hell *was* this guy?"

"Interesting," Beau spoke up. "You're on the side of the 'dead' camp."

"Whaa . . . say again?"

"You believe he is dead."

"Of course he's friggin' dead. The man was born in 1712!"

Beau said nothing. Alicia looked like she wanted to get a huge and sarcastic comment off her chest, but reined it in as she met Drake's eyes.

"Is it because you're French?" Smyth rumbled bluntly. "You know, the romance of it all, the nostalgic passion and whatever?"

"Aye," Drake nodded. "The French sure love a weepie."

"What happened over there in Dubai?" They heard Kinimaka's voice.

"We lost 'em," Hayden said very simply. "But the guy has at least six primary followers and can't handle weapons. I don't know yet how he ended up obsessed with Germain but he *is* a fanatic, a crusader dedicated to his cause. Amari is different again though—pampered, affluent, out of touch. Believes everything happens at the click of a finger, probably because all his life, it has. I truly believe the man has no grasp of the consequences of his actions and no sense of human life. Of course, that doesn't help us much."

"Anything at his home?"

Hayden clucked. "Another mistake. We cleared out of there in fast pursuit and now the cops have the house cordoned off. Must have traced the trouble back to him already. Bottom line is—we can't access the house."

"So what next?" Dahl asked, more of a rhetorical question because everyone knew the answer.

"So we're heading for London," Hayden said. "We'll meet you there, guys. But just remember, everything has changed now. It's sped up. Grown more dangerous. Amari and his cult know they're being hunted, but my guess is they'll still stop at nothing to protect their precious Count and all his treasures. He's totally invested now. This is where it really begins. This is where the shit really starts to happen."

Drake nodded and rose to his feet. "Webb will follow his set of clues all the way to the end. If need be he'll raze everything in his way. Same for Amari. At the very least we need to catch up with them."

"See you in London," Dahl said.

"See you, Torsty." Alicia said with a smile. "And don't forget—Kenzie's a bitch. Don't get on her sharper side."

"Yeah, thanks. I think I'm already there."

"Believe me," Alicia muttered. "You're nowhere near."

CHAPTER THIRTY SEVEN

London was dismal the following morning, drizzle falling constantly from a gray slate sky. A cold wind whipped the lackadaisical Scotch mist to and fro, all over London Town, making the residents and the tourists miserable, cold and wet. Drake remembered thinking this kind of weather was "just for the sake of it", something his mother used to say during the long, usually cold autumns north of Woolley Edge. The mood all around was dour, and wasn't helped by the fact that Dahl's team had been waiting for hours.

Piccadilly Circus buzzed with activity; its flashing signs grabbing what attention they could; its statues standing tall, hard and cold, as leaden as the skies; its bright stores and restaurants standing closed, a non-tourist hour this, allowing its residents brief respite so that they might take a breather from a relentless life.

Alicia looked up from underneath her hood. "You'll have to wait for me," she said. "I never, ever, pass a Cinnabon without opening my purse."

Drake tried but couldn't restrain a healthy guffaw. "Purse? As if."

Alicia sniggered. "Yeah, that didn't come out right. Chuck us a fiver, love."

In the end, Hayden managed to fish some crumpled English money out of a zippered pocket, leaving Drake wondering about the last time he'd made a personal purchase. In truth, he couldn't remember. Their lives did not revolve around comfort and belongings. As Alicia came back, lips covered in cinnamon-dusted icing, he wondered what it would be like to lick it off.

"C'mon guys," Hayden interrupted his fantasy before it grew too intense. "Incredibly, we go down this road here called Haymarket."

"Just shows how important the theater is," Dahl said.

"Ah, but what was here first? The road name or the showhouse?"

The Swede laughed and paused at the wide curving junction where cars and buses appeared to have full leave to aim at the scuttling road-crossers and slow-moving older people. The team waited for the lights to turn green, feeling a little out of place in traveler's London, standing among the drifting crowds.

As they waited, Hayden's cell rang and she directed them all into a shop doorway. "Sabrina," she said, then answered.

"Are you okay?"

"I am now," came the hushed but still fiery Italian tones. "So long as you keep that sword-wielder you have away from my face. Many times she almost cut me. I am traumatized."

Kenzie grinned and leaned forward to say something but Hayden cut her off with a stare. "Sorry, she'll never do that again."

Dahl held his hands out, palms up. "You weren't there. We couldn't have done it without her."

Drake nudged him. "Sorry to break it to you, pal, but you *did* fuck all except cleave a bunch of monks."

"Ah. And how did Dubai go?"

"Better than your vacation, for sure."

Dahl looked ready to take it further, looking beyond disgruntled now, but Drake's attention was grabbed by Sabrina.

"We came by jet some time ago and ever since have been prowling the Haymarket Theater. Webb talks to me of his quest, how important it is and *he* is. How I might be invited to worship his glory in the future." The thief sounded sick. "He is a vile man. But he knows no better. Wait . . ." Moments passed as she moved to a better position, the phone rustling in her pocket.

"I am back. First, Webb already knows where the next and penultimate clue will be found. He has not explained further but I think I remember his words as being 'at the place of his death.' So now, this Saint Germain has a connection to the London theater scene. The greatest philosopher who ever lived, who always looked forty five, no matter at which country house, treaty, or party he was spotted, also had an extraordinary proficiency for the arts. The violin. Harpsichord. He was an improviser, an inventor in all walks of life."

"You memorized all this?" Smyth barked.

"No. I have had it drilled into me for many, many hours," Sabrina sighed back. "Torturous hours. I'm sure that I will dream of this long-dead Count tonight."

Hayden chewed her lower lip. "Better than dreaming of Webb, believe me."

"So, he was a composer, this Count. His works were given to Tchaikovsky and Lobkowitz whilst at least two others were played at and gifted to the Haymarket. In 1745 and 1760, it seems. Webb says the next clue is in the composition, the words or notes of the song."

Hayden looked up through the drizzle, to the top of the highest buildings. "Of course. He would hide vital information in something that would live long after he was gone. I guess, if a follower has gotten to this point, the Count may already believe he is worthy."

"I can't talk much longer and will then be unavailable for some time, as we'll be moving on to . . . wherever. I do not know. Webb says our next stop is our penultimate prize. I suggest you move quicker."

"Does he have backup?" Hayden asked quickly as Drake gauged the road ahead and their path to the Haymarket. "Men? A trap? Anything?"

But Sabrina was gone, called away by Webb himself it seemed. The team took a long look around.

"Busy as all hell," Smyth said. "And getting worse by the minute. But if Webb's there right now . . ."

"Worth a shot," Drake said. "Or two."

Hayden headed out, followed by Kinimaka and Dahl. Drake came next with Alicia, Mai and Beau and then a final group traipsed along—Kenzie, Smyth, Lauren and Yorgi, watching the rear. A tour bus rumbled by as they passed shops almost covered in scaffolding. A steak house and signs for Dover Street Market. Lauren pointed out a Planet Hollywood across the street for

Kinimaka, but the Hawaiian turned his nose up at it.

"Not the same. I like rock with my burgers."

"How is the shot glass collection going?" Drake asked as they walked and reconnoitered.

"Growing," Kinimaka admitted. "My buddy Nigel posts them from all over the world. Either he's better traveled than us guys, or has lots'a friends."

A theater, another burger place, and then Drake could see six white pillars and multi-colored banner advertisements hanging down across the sidewalk and guessed they were nearing the Haymarket. Again the group slackened off, taking the time to scrutinize the area. Drake saw no threats and picked up nothing on his trusted inner radar. Within a minute the team were attempting to gain access to the theater, calling up the locals for clearance and then waiting for some to arrive. All the time the clock ticked and Webb grew closer to his goal. By mid-morning the team and half a dozen skeptical looking coppers were entering the sacred innards of the Haymarket Theater.

They spread out, searched the place. They asked the manager to open locked doors and old, unused rooms, archives. They searched for an hour and found no clue that anyone else had been there.

Drake paused at the balcony of the first tier, looking below at the seemingly small stage surrounded by gilded fittings, drapes and mirrors. To see it empty like this, embellished and adorned with finery but desolate, lacking the one thing that filled its rafters with life, was a little unsettling. He just hoped to God that Alicia didn't take to the stage and break out in song. That would really bring the place down.

He leaned with hands clasping the tiny rail, staring into the distance. Had Sabrina ever been here? Was she playing them? Where in the world was Tyler Webb? More importantly—when would Mai actually come out and say she was unhappy with how things had gone?

And what then?

The last thing Drake wanted was two of the deadliest women in the world fighting over him. Hayden took that moment to use their comms system to admit there was no sign of Webb or Sabrina—or anyone else for that matter—and called the manager to the stage.

Drake headed that way himself, seeing Dahl and Beau and Kinimaka also striding toward the rendezvous. Hayden waited. The theater's manager was an indeterminate man, tall, gangly and wearing a jacket that was too tight and a watch that was too big. Oddly, he also sported a ponytail too, which maybe he thought was rakish.

Alicia's eyes were on it the moment she arrived. Drake warned her off with a raised brow. Hayden gained nothing from quizzing the man, not so much as a shifty sideways glance. Drake knew she believed he'd probably allowed Webb unfettered entry in exchange for a hefty paper wad—it was her CIA training—but saw no deceit in the man. After several minutes she altered her line of questioning.

"What do you know of the history of this place?"

"The last twenty years? Most of it. I have been manager a long time." He looked happy with himself.

"Further back," Hayden said. "I was thinking more mid-eighteenth century and a dude called Saint Germain."

"Nah, I definitely wasn't manager then." He tried a smile that fell flat, then rubbed the back of his neck. Again Alicia's eyes lit up as the ponytail started to bounce.

"But you know this place wasn't the Haymarket then, surely?"

Hayden frowned. "It wasn't?"

"Nah, the original building is a little further north. Same street, but redesigned in the early 1800s."

"And its . . ." Hayden struggled for the right words. "Works of art. Paintings. Compositions. Songs."

The manager creased his entire brow. "Well, those are always sent to the British Museum. In particular, if they were donated to the theater."

"Saint Germain donated the songs," Lauren affirmed.

Drake took it in. "And, my friend," he moved closer. "You've told nobody else this in let's say . . . oh, the last hour?"

"Umm . . . no. But if I did does it mean I'm in trouble?"

"Was he alone?" Hayden rubbed the bridge of her nose in frustration.

"No. He came with a young woman, his daughter I thought at first. But not so. They were entirely different."

"No . . . bodyguards?"

"Nah."

At that moment Hayden's phone chirped. She held up the message for all to see.

Breaking into British Museum right now. Come quick!

"She is useful," Alicia admitted.

Hayden spun to one of the local cops. "How far to the British Museum?"

"You can run it in less than fifteen minutes. Unmarked cars might take almost as long."

"Then let's go. And call for backup."

"What kind?" The cop was running and digging his radio out at the same time.

"Everything. All of it. There's no telling what this bastard has up his sleeve this time. Not to mention his enemies."

"Look on the bright side," Drake said. "This time we have guns."

Kenzie huffed softly. "Mere curios. I'd do better with my katana."

"Your world—" Dahl winced at her "—is not ours."

Drake caught Alicia reaching out for the ponytail even as she started to run. "No," he growled. "Do you have to tug on everything that dangles before your eyes?" The he cringed and started to sprint. "Don't answer that, for God's sake."

Out into the drizzle they ran and then ran even harder; the man who would rule the world only minutes from their grasp, his wild and devastating plans on the brink of fruition; the men who would destroy him at any cost no doubt concealed and planning an attack.

Lives and livelihoods; war and peace; death and destruction:

It all hung in the balance.

CHAPTER THIRTY EIGHT

Hayden followed the lead cops out into the eternal drizzle and cast a glance at the gunmetal skies. The low-hanging clouds matched her mood, and she could see no change coming in the near future.

Alicia jogged along beside her. "Having fun?"

"What? No. For some time now life has been about as much fun as a bullet in the back."

"Well, you would know."

"I feel that I don't know my own mind, can't trust decisions that I make."

"Why's that?"

"Because every big decision I make is wrong."

"So this is you. Running beneath a gray sky. Physically and emotionally."

Hayden sent an inquisitive glance across. "Is that really Alicia Myles?"

"New and improved. I've changed, or rather I'm trying to change but it's a lot harder than you think."

"I get that you've stopped running. But you've found what you're looking for. I haven't."

"Ah, bollocks. So I have." She stared at Matt Drake for a moment.

"Maybe I'll never find it because of the job we do."

Alicia nodded. "Fighting. Running. Chasing. Never stopping. I guess I got lucky."

Hayden managed a smile. "So I get the next pick of the bunch, huh? Who's that? Smyth? Beau? Yorgi?"

Alicia whistled. "All damaged goods."

"Yes," Hayden whispered. "We don't know the half of it. We're all damaged goods. Once that childhood innocence lifts away—we're all damaged goods."

She put her head down as they passed the National Opera and then cut past the tube station at Leicester Square. Here, droves emerged onto the sidewalk with little care for those already walking past and the area turned into a free-for-all. Dahl found a way via the road and zipped between slow-moving cars. Hayden's cell reverberated at that moment and she fished it out automatically whilst on the run.

"Jaye."

"Hi, Miss Jaye, this is Bob Todd calling from the President's office. Is this a good time?"

Hayden pulled the phone away to stare at the screen, doubting her ears. The number was not identified.

It could be better, she thought and said, "Sure, we're good for now."

"I'll be brief then. The President feels this business with Robert Price has opened a few doors."

Hayden's thoughts flicked back over the recent *ex*-Secretary of Defense and his betrayal of the United States. "It has?"

"Well, first there's a new Secretary of Defense. And Price's . . . bad decisions . . . give us opportunity to change."

"They do?" Hayden was concentrating as they passed the Cambridge Theater, Foyles and then hung a sharp right down Denmark Street. She heard Kinimaka grunting something unintelligible about the old Forbidden Planet store, but tuned the Hawaiian out.

"In basic terms the President feels your team should be relocated. Somewhere new. Fresh. And secret."

"A secret base?" Hayden blurted.

Bob Todd chuckled. "Exactly that, yes."

Hayden bit her tongue, managing to cut off the *ooooohhh* sound only a second after it began. She thought she'd gotten away with it.

"Sounds good, yeah? We'll be getting on that right away but be prepared to travel and let your team know in the next few days. In related news, our new Secretary has been chosen and she will be in office very shortly."

"She?"

"Yes. Miss Kimberly Crowe is a woman."

Hayden filed it all away as the Shaftesbury Theater passed by and then they were on Bloomsbury Street. The cops waved and pointed out an imposing building up ahead. Hayden opened her mouth to end the call but closed it quickly as Todd offered up a little more information.

"Miss Crowe has expressed an interest to meet you all very soon. We're trying to arrange it even now."

"That may be, um, tricky."

"Understood. But that is part of what Secretary Crowe is all about. If she thinks somebody or something is worth taking the risk—nothing's gonna stop her."

Hayden shook her head. *Shit. How the hell do I explain the attributes of this crew?*

"Maybe wait until we get back home," she said tactfully. "It's gotta be easier."

"That sounds very amicable. It will be arranged." Todd signed off before she could reply.

Hayden looked up. The British Museum was larger than she'd imagined. The truth that then settled was that it could take all day to find a determined man in there. She looked over at the cops.

"Can you get the curator down here? The manager?"

"Which one, ma'am?" One of the cops tried sarcastic.

Alicia still stood at her shoulder. "You can get Santa and all his fucking elves if they'll help, boy. Just do it now."

Hayden took a moment to relax and look over the imposing structure. Inside was a man who'd dogged her dreams and waking nightmares for far longer than she cared to remember. In addition, she remained certain that Amari or his cronies would make some kind of appearance. If they'd been watching the previous locations then they would be here too. She looked up as a man came running down the steps.

"The curator," one of the cops said.

"What on earth is the meaning of this?" the tall, self-important man asked them, his voice a piercing wail. "I am a busy man, you know."

Drake stepped into his face. "We ain't exactly lounging around, pal."

Alicia said it best. "Look, man, shut the hell up and answer her questions. The faster you do it the less chance there is of you getting shot." She viewed the area. "Best be quick."

"Shot?" The curator faltered.

Hayden pushed him toward the museum. "Move it, move it. Faster." The team followed the now sprinting curator all the way up the steps.

And to whatever hell waited beyond.

CHAPTER THIRTY NINE

Splendorous hallways that merged the old with the new, the ancient with the cutting edge, led a multitude of ways inside the British Museum. Drake watched Hayden as she followed the curator, her attention focused on some volatile middle-distance, her body language as tense as ever he'd seen it. Like Alicia, Hayden could be a fiery package. He wouldn't like to be the man on the wrong side of her.

Kinimaka plodded along beside him, concentrating as ever on walking straight and not knocking down ancient statues and filigreed pedestals on his way past.

"I can't reach her anymore," he told Drake.

"She still loves you, mate. Give her time."

"She may still love me, but she's already gone. She doesn't waste her time once her mind's made up."

Drake tended to agree, but kept his own counsel. "Remember the good times, mate. If you're sure that you could have done no more then . . ." He paused. Who the hell was he to be giving out relationship advice?

Kinimaka planted a huge arm across his shoulders and then leaned in. "Thank you, brah. But I'll tell you this. You got a big reckoning coming. You. Alicia. Mai." He pursed his lips and blew out a heavy breath. "Judgment Day."

Drake felt the weight increase across his shoulders. "Thanks for that."

The vaults were vast, dusty and incredibly disorganized. Hayden quizzed him about Saint Germain but it took time to boot up a computer and search the digital archives. Only after that was done could the man point them to the right area. "Two compositions," he said. "Donated around the mid-1750s. Are they of significance? I do hope I haven't missed anything."

The team calmed him, then sent him back to relative safety.

Drake was already prowling the dusty passageways, keeping to the darkest of byways and listening hard. Ancient tomes and curled scrolls lay on unending wooden shelving, the only movement they ever knew just the motes that sifted all around them. Bare bulbs flickered overhead, though most were dead. Drake found it in contrast to the sparkling halls above; down here it seemed the forgotten relics resided in age-old dreams. But then, like people, not all of them could be put on display all of the time.

"Creepy," Alicia muttered at his side. "You don't really know what they have down here."

"Prehistoric hounds," Drake said. "Chained zombies. Voodoo priestesses. Or so I heard."

Alicia gave him the elbow. "Don't be a co—"

Mai clicked her tongue. "Shut up, Taz. I can't hear anything over your pathetic whining."

"How about my knuckles? You think you'll hear those?"

It was escalating.

Drake ignored it.

A row of chest-high crates continued the row to the right, their lids in disarray, some nailed fully shut whilst others were broken into jagged pieces. Drake saw pottery, small statues and a broken mirror. Red lights blinked everywhere, catching his eyes, sensors to catch would-be thieves, and the security up top had been first class. This was one of the main reasons Tyler Webb had recruited Sabrina Balboni.

He turned the next corner and Tyler Webb was crouched on the floor, his back to them, rooting around inside a low cardboard box. Drake blinked in disbelief, came to an abrupt halt, and just stared.

Alicia froze as if she'd just been turned to ice. The rest of the team crowded around the corner and paused; shocked, but all hardening very quickly.

Webb scrabbled about inside the box, jeans and coat thick with dust, surrounded by a dozen ripped apart cartons and a shelf that had clearly broken. Sabrina, crouched before Webb and watching, met eyes with Drake but said nothing.

Webb cackled away to himself. "It's in the song. The song is all. Where to next, my equal? Where to next? You traveled far and wide. You traveled near. Europe was your playground. Kings and queens your friends. But where are you now? Where will we end?"

Each sentence was punctuated with a ripping of paper or a scroll being flung to the side. Drake wanted to listen longer, conscious of the clues that may be dropped, but Hayden only saw the man who'd once stalked her every move from dusk till dawn, and made sure she was the first to speak.

"Stand up carefully, Webb. This is as far as you go."

He stiffened, then clapped his hands together to free them of dust, sending plumes into the air. He rose slowly, and Drake saw he held two fragile looking sheets of paper. "Found you," he said softly.

Then he turned.

"Hayden Jaye." He smiled in a lewd way. "Been a while. You look slimmer in person than you do on CCTV. And Mano Kinimaka. Is that beef or is it fat? Wait, I'm sure I have some pics. Oh, and the inimitable Matt Drake. Your memory involves Mai Kitano. Let me know if, sometime, you want to relive it. Oh, and the rest of you . . ." He waved and flapped and backed away. "Email me. I'm sure I have all you want."

Drake restrained Hayden as she stepped forward in anger. Webb was entirely too confident and nothing they did was ever so easy. He saw Webb pass over Beau with disdain. It couldn't be easy seeing your old bodyguard who'd always been a double agent. With purpose, he gave Webb one more chance to spout his malice.

"Come to think of it, *Hay*," he spat out Kinimaka's nickname for his lover. "I don't think I've ever seen you stood upright before." He cackled. "And Alicia? Does Drake satisfy you the way Beau used to? Hmm, 'cause I have the audio and I know. Mai Kitano? I'd love to relate sometime. Oh wait, I'll call you. Have to watch from afar first. And dudes, bitches, guys—I *will* watch all of you. I *will* have the resources and endless, endless hours of time."

"You think you know everything because you're an utter creep, a sliver of scum with resources. But you don't know us. You know nothing," Hayden spat at him.

"You think?" Webb's face opened and a light in his eyes spoke of pure honesty and viciousness mixed. "I know one of you is a lesbian. One of you is embarrassed all the time. And one of you is dying. I know that. I know one of you killed their parents in cold blood. One of you who is missing is far from what you believe. One of you will die by my hand in three days' time *just* to wring those tragic emotions from those who remain. One of you cries themselves to sleep . . ."

"You do seem utterly confident you're about to escape," Dahl said blandly.

"It's the only reason you're all still alive."

Drake felt a cloud of suspicion and disbelief start to settle in.

"I don't understand," Dahl admitted.

"My big plan. My *master* plan. Did you actually think it began when I started this last final search for Saint Germain or do you think it began *before* I formed the Pythians? Truly?"

Drake searched the shadows, watched Sabrina, racked his brain for clues.

"You're gonna be shocked." Webb laughed.

Alicia aimed her gun between the man's eyes. "I'm ready. Shock me."

"You're all still alive so I can stalk you forever. Understand? My plan started twenty years ago. Yes, it's had adjustments, most recently to accommodate every last one of you, but the structure still stands. The bones of it—" he chuckled "—and the meat."

"He's a fuckin' loon," Smyth grunted. "Somebody just shut him the hell up."

"Happy to." Alicia squeezed her trigger.

But Webb held up a hand. Sabrina backed away, still playing her part for as long as she was able.

"Really," Webb said. "I have enjoyed letting you follow me."

"Nobody followed anyone," Dahl said. "We found you out and you got lucky. If not luck then it was absolute recklessness and your disrespect for human life. In chaos, you thrive."

"Ooh, good one. I'll write that down, commission a T-shirt. But really—everything you have done has been at my whim."

"But how?"

"Because that is as it should be. I am better, of godly stock. I am a master of the human race. And you shall all bow down before me."

"Really?" Alicia grunted sarcastically. "And how will you make us do that?"

Drake couldn't believe the audacity, the utter belief of this man. Truly, completely, he knew that he was born to be superior. Webb glanced back at Sabrina and said, "Get ready."

And then whipped his head around.

"Don't kill them, Beau," he said. "But hurt them just enough."

He started to run.

CHAPTER FORTY

The whirlwind started inside his head—a horrifying mix of incredulity and doubt—quickly becoming a physical presence as Beauregard Alain finally showed his true colors and betrayed them. The man of smoke and shadow flitted among them like a wraith, taking every advantage of their shock and reluctance to believe.

First he felled Lauren, the New Yorker at his side and totally unprepared, going down clutching her throat. Then he took out Smyth, the soldier totally focused on Webb and collapsing in agony from a blow to a nerve cluster behind the neck. Next, he went for Mai, probably realizing her reactions were the quickest, and won on the trust factor. Even as she whirled to see him coming at her she just didn't believe what she was seeing. Then, Yorgi and Hayden and Kinimaka with single blows, whirling like a genie released after a thousand years of captivity, darting and striking among them, every punch a blow of devastation.

Hayden was incapacitated, lying on her back and able only to claw feebly at the air, trying to catch her breath. Kinimaka fell hard on his face, blood splashing into his eyes. Then Beau was spinning at Drake, Dahl and Alicia, and still only seconds had passed since he acted. The latter two still hadn't turned around, still processing, but the Mad Swede was swiveling, reddening, and inclined to trust his own gut.

The punch came around, a fraction of a moment too late to impact against Beau's skull. The Frenchman was inside, feeling relieved, and dealt out a painful flurry. Even then Dahl manned it beyond Beau's expectation, catching him with a sharp jab as he went down and then kicking out. Beau's feet tangled for a moment, but he was fleet and fit enough to skip free.

Right into Alicia. Her eyes were wildfire, pits of magma, her features firm with disbelief. Beau wiped it away from her with two fists, unfeeling, uncaring it seemed. The perfect, emotionless weapon of death.

"You live or die by my will alone," Webb shrieked back. "Remember that."

Drake faced Beau.

"Why?" the Yorkshireman managed. "We trusted you. And what about Michael Crouch? Is he—?"

Beau assailed him like a bullet and a battering ram, making him feel little like a Special Forces soldier and very much the backstreet kid. Pain erupted from several nerve masses and his legs went to jelly. Still, he barely believed.

"*Why?*"

The Frenchman was already leaving, following his master, but glanced back with a snarl of disdain.

"The thing Webb seeks. The thing he will find. It will make me live forever. When you people lie old surrounded by your deathbed memories, *I* will still look like this." He preened.

Alicia, on her knees, somehow managed to look up and croak: "A big cock?"

Then Beau turned and was quickly gone. Footsteps could be heard behind as the cops came along to investigate and the SPEAR team tried to recover. A long, heavy minute passed.

Drake contemplated all that Webb had told them.

Then came the explosion, deep and terribly dark, so powerful it shook the entire British Museum to its foundations.

CHAPTER FORTY ONE

Dahl dragged himself to his knees, ignoring several rivulets of fire streaming through his system. Even with their protection Beau had struck unerringly at their weak spots. Part of the problem this time was shock; it wouldn't happen again. He crawled among the others, encouraging and helping where he could even as the walls and ceiling rocked and rained plaster all around him.

Images of Johanna and his children darted before his eyes. Dahl staggered upright, pulling Hayden with him. The cops swayed and shouted into their radios. A high stack of shelves began to crumble, showering timber and paper confetti upon their shoulders. He watched Drake help Alicia to her feet and then moved over to aid Kinimaka.

"Up you get, pal. Was this you? I mean, what on earth did you knock over now?"

The Hawaiian managed a weak smile. Hayden came to his side and asked if all was well and Dahl thought that a kind act. Smyth was cradling Lauren, whose eyes were open but swimming with agony. The woman could barely croak.

"Fucking Frenchie's gonna pay for this," Alicia gasped first. "How'd he do it?"

"Well, you certainly didn't help," Mai said, rubbing her shoulders and neck.

"Bitch, explain yourself."

"Everyone here lowered their guard as soon as you started . . . shagging him. Shame on us all."

"Who I pole bounce is my own concern. Not yours."

"Wrong." Mai narrowed her gaze. "It *used* to be."

"Look," Drake said. "Can we stop blaming and get running? This room ain't gonna repair itself in a bloody hurry."

The cops bolted, one of them shouting that the explosion was localized and bore no threat to the actual building. Probably extra insurance to aid the escape. Drake dragged Alicia away from Mai and bolted in the midst of his team, racing the collapsing ceiling, the crumbling shelves and the disintegrating crates stacked thirteen-high as the cave-in came down all around them.

Staggering, falling headlong, he grasped Alicia's arm in one hand and reached out to pull at the shadow on his other side, who had slipped in deadly wreckage and stumbled to her knees.

It was Mai.

Grimly, he heaved them both along.

CHAPTER FORTY TWO

Tyler Webb was ecstatic, proud, practically orgasmic. The fruits of long years, the labors of his lifetime had finally come to fruition.

So to speak. He cackled aloud.

London was a crackling hub of movement and motion. Webb melted among the crowds, slipped through the comings and goings, wondering when the locals might employ their much-vaunted CCTV facial recognition software on him.

On *them.*

The two mortals he currently allowed to share his air: Beauregard Alain, his magnificent triple agent; and Sabrina Balboni, the master thief come major betrayer. French and Italian. Cunning and fire. The hardest part was treating them like the human beings they clearly were. Webb was above all that now—in his mind already ascending. The trail of Saint Germain had been tough so far and fraught with danger, but someone worthy—like him—took one more step toward immortality with each passing day.

And now he had the great composition that Germain had gifted to the British. And what had they done to it? Thrust it into some deep, dark and grimy hole in the ground *beneath* a thousand lesser treasures. Later, he would visit a special kind of retribution down upon them.

The godlike powers of his master were absolute. Years before his supposed birth in 1712 it was believed that Saint Germain— under a different, famous title—faked his death, attended his own funeral, and made his way from England to Transylvania where the new legend was then born. The Count's 'magnum opus' was the search for the Philosopher's Stone that, far from being an inanimate object as many believed, was actually a living, breathing, scorching alchemical substance able to impart immortality into those who drank it. For centuries it was the most sought after prize among men.

Very few found it.

Webb didn't believe every legend, every myth, but his investigations into Saint Germain and the man's many attributes, accomplishments and dealings pointed to truth. Who else in history could mix a previously unknown substance for the good of man one day, compose a sonnet the next and then head out to deal with kings and commanders in the hopes of staving off a war? This romance, this brilliant and wondrous narrative, captured his imagination long ago but became more and more intriguing as months and years of deep investigation rolled by. Webb became convinced. He'd learned of Leopold and the scroll and used Ramses' last bazaar to obtain it.

Full circle. The crowds thickened as Webb headed down Piccadilly. Maybe he should have taken Regent Street for even more anonymity but the decision was made now. Then he saw an *Eat* on the corner of Swallow Street, headed up that quiet road and switched to Saville Row. The police would be out in force. Webb needed to hide, but he also needed to move forward.

Germany next, for the penultimate prize and then . . .

He faltered. *Nobody knew.* Where was the ultimate goal, the final objective?

Shaking it off, he gripped the composition tighter. It held clues for the Germany trip. Interestingly, it was full circle for Beau too. He tapped the Frenchman on the shoulder as they hurried past a shop named Huntsman and Son.

"I have to admit there were times I had my doubts, but you did well, Beau. You switched sides so easily. Made them believe."

"They believed Michael Crouch. They believed Alicia Myles. The hardest part was convincing Crouch. He is wily and intellectual. But the time I took won him over. It was good we began so early."

Webb agreed. "And despite all that business in New York, which we did not plan for, all seems to be right with the world." He then turned slowly to his other companion. "Except for you."

Sabrina had made no move to leave them. She knew of

Beauregard's reputation and Webb's hidden arsenal. Her face, acceptably, was turned to the floor, her shoulders slumped. She made no comment.

"For years I held you under retainer, paid your way. I always kept you in mind for this, the final chapter of my mortality. You. *You, Sabrina!* My chosen acolyte a decade in the planning and . . ." he tailed off, unable to accept her deceit and wiping at the tears in his eyes. "Truly, I am shocked."

"Shall we . . . drop her off?" Beau murmured.

Webb shrieked a gout of laughter. "Don't be an ass. Despite her stupidity she is the best thief in the world. We still require her skills, of course, for the next job and then, potentially, the final one. It would be cutting at our noses to spite our faces if we . . . dropped her off now."

Beau accepted this in silence.

Webb contemplated the middle-distance. "That doesn't mean she shouldn't be taught the error of her ways," he mouthed. "When opportunity knocks."

Sabrina made no movement save for walking. Beau allowed a brief nod. The threesome twisted along several side streets, crossed Oxford Street and headed toward Bayswater. Webb stopped in a street behind a hotel and nodded at the man standing outside, smoking a cigarette.

Beau shifted slightly. "Friend?"

"I have none. But the best hiding places usually go to those with the biggest wallets and there is a, shall we say *dastardly*, shadow network of bellhops, doormen, hotel receptionists and restaurant serving staff operating in London that can find you the quietest of places to hole up for a while."

"Interesting."

"Isn't it? These people are the true heart of this city. Little happens here that they don't see. Few people pass by that they don't note. Everything and everyone is currency to the network."

"And we are?"

"Rich and privileged." Webb laughed and approached the smoking man. In moments they were off the street and being led through dark rooms that appeared to have no purpose, along a corridor that hadn't been cleaned in years. Webb wasn't fussy where they ended up so long as it gave them some breathing space.

He needed to study the composition.

"Four hours," he told the man. "Then, an unmarked taxi. I'll tell him the destination en route."

"Just ring the bell," an eastern European accent rang out, and the man indicated a button set into the wall.

Webb settled in one overstuffed chair. "Get comfy, people. Sabrina—I do believe it's time for Beau to deal out your comeuppance whilst I read quietly, don't you?"

"If you want my help you will hold your fists," the Italian sputtered.

"Then you will assist me when I command it. Is that understood?"

"Only if your pet freak leaves me alone."

Webb felt the pull of the composition almost as if Saint Germain was calling his name, calling him toward the extraordinary. Without a nod for Beau to refrain he opened up the old papers and began to read.

"Here we move into legend," he said. "And the Devil take all who oppose us."

CHAPTER FORTY THREE

Drake stumbled as an entire shelf of books thumped and clattered down his back, hard edges hammering his spine. Ahead, a stack of crates toppled, hitting the floor with an ear-splitting crash and filling his vision with dust and debris. Dahl cleared a path through, kicking and wrenching the wreckage apart. Another shelf, this one over eight feet high, threatened to crash among them and the tottering heavy pots and urns, the statues and oversized artefacts, promised more than just bruises if they fell.

Mai pulled away. Drake herded Alicia past the last shelf as it collapsed. Dahl made the exit door, then turned to help Lauren and Smyth through. Hayden found herself propelled by Kinimaka so that her feet practically skimmed the ground. Yorgi sprang, nimble and fleet as a cat, picking his way through the destruction. Kenzie came last and then, only inches behind, Drake. As they raced, the rumbling eased and quieted, the shake of the building stopped. Only seconds had passed since the localized explosive went off.

Drake slowed, staring back the way they had come. No chance of them following Webb; the floor was nothing but rubble, the endless high stacks crumpled and ruined.

"Some treasures never see the light of day because scientists can't explain them," he said. "We learned that from the Odin thing. These treasures . . . stored, hidden perhaps, now spoilt, will end their days in devastation."

"Don't get over-weepy," Alicia huffed. "Most of them do."

A sense of the surreal and the incredulous hung over the team. Drake summed it up in true Yorkshire fashion. "So that French arse-end is gonna need a slap, no mistake."

Dahl, for once, just nodded. "I'll be happy to oblige."

Hayden made a phone call, explained the situation, and asked for all eyes to be turned toward Webb. She also mentioned they might still have an ally in Sabrina without tabling the question as to the thief's fate. All there hoped Webb had further uses for her. Truth be told, he had to have known she was compromised in the first place—yet still he'd desperately used her services. And the quest was not yet done.

Dahl cleared his throat noisily. "And may I address the brand new elephant in the room?" He paused. "All those things Webb was spouting? Are any of them true?"

Drake didn't like to think too hard about them, and assumed the rest of the team needed some time to ponder. "Let's chat later," he said. "I need some air."

Almost in silence, they trooped along the corridor and found a way to the museum's entrance. Fresh air helped revive Drake and he was soon casting around, wondering what the next move might be.

Then Alicia surprised them all by pushing her way into their midst. "Look, guys," she muttered. "I'm apologizing here. I don't know how," she shrugged. "But I'm sorry my relationship with Beau helped keep his cover." She drew a heavy breath. "That's it."

Drake smiled at her. The new and improved Alicia Myles, and even more startling with each passing day.

Mai ignored the apology and turned to Hayden. "We won't be able to rely on Sabrina anymore. If she's still alive."

"I know." Hayden bit her bottom lip and looked over at Lauren. "I seem to remember a snippet of conversation, do you?"

"Yeah. Webb's a talker, all right. He told Sabrina the next clue will be found 'where he died', or something like that. Obviously that doesn't mean Webb, but the crazy obsession he lives and breathes—Germain."

"I dunno," Smyth grumped. "Sounds like a long shot."

"Oh great," Lauren said. "Now you don't believe a thing I say."

"I didn't say I didn't believe. I said—"

"You're both right," Hayden interrupted quickly. "Webb was referring to Germain but he rambles and fantasizes and builds all his castles in the air. It's a leap. But . . ." She gave them a small smile.

"We see if it matches the merc's list," Yorgi said.

"And," Dahl said, "it is what he told Sabrina so I'm inclined to believe. She has become a true and believable asset."

"Calm down," Kenzie muttered. "Don't forget the ole lady."

Dahl frowned. "Eh?"

"Yer main squeeze." She effected an accent. "The old battle axe."

"You probably know her as 'boo-bear'," Alicia put in.

"Oh, you mean Johanna?"

The two laughed.

"Maybe he'll never get out of London," Kinimaka offered.

"He will find a way behind our backs," Mai said with a sly glance over at Alicia. "The slippery ones always do."

Drake almost gulped, but luckily the Englishwoman was still feeling a little humbled and brooding over all that she had said, and most likely her relationship with Beau. How many times would she replay their conversations through the next weeks and months? Drake ignored Mai and found himself thinking about all that Webb had said.

Some gigantic bombshells dropped.

And such personal information. But then the man who boasted of private footage of Hayden Jaye—ex-CIA and at the top of her game—no doubt had the resources to breach any wall, delve through any record. Our personal worlds were there for all to see if a despicable individual knew where to look.

"Shouldn't be hard to find out where Saint Germain died," Drake extended the option.

"Already done," Lauren said. "The merc said northern Germany and there's a place there called Eckernförde. On the coast of the Baltic Sea. The town's history contains an interesting anecdote. The Count de Saint Germain was buried in Eckernförde near the Saint Nicolai church. His grave was destroyed in 1872 by a storm surge."

Even Smyth had to affect a wry grin. "Convenient," he said. "No body."

"It all adds to the conspiracy and the legend," Lauren said. "No remains. No proof he died at all."

The Treasures of Saint Germain

Mai snorted. "Do not tell me you are buying into this immortal nonsense."

"Me?" Lauren drawled. "I'm from Manhattan and believe absolutely nothing that I'm told. I just paint the pictures, darlin'."

"I imagine this Eckernförde is a big place," Dahl said. "Maybe Webb thinks the old grave site is intact? He would go there."

"And what was Germain doing in Germany?" Kinimaka said. "From what we know of him he always seemed to travel with purpose, not by whim."

Hayden turned her nose up at the London drizzle. "So unless there are any objections we're out of this murk."

"And quickly," Drake urged them. "Maybe this time, with the manhunt slowing him down, we can actually get ahead of Webb. I don't believe we should wait. Fact is, even with measly resources he'll be able to fly anywhere in the world."

"So let's go." Alicia was the first to move. "Because I know one big, fat penis with whom I want to set a very special date."

CHAPTER FORTY FOUR

The German town of Eckernförde was a popular coastal town, well-liked by tourists. The team flew to Hamburg and then choppered toward the coast, lines of communication always open for word of Webb or Sabrina or even the new Secretary of Defense, Kimberly Crowe. But the wires remained silent, as did most of the team.

Dahl quietly evaluated Webb's words.

I know one of you is a lesbian. One of you is embarrassed all the time. And one of you is dying. I know that. I know one of you killed their parents in cold blood. One of you who is missing is far from what you believe. One of you will die by my hand in three days' time just to wring those tragic emotions from those who remain. One of you cries themselves to sleep.

It struck him that most if not all of these statements were true. Yes, Webb would profit from sowing unease among the team, but despite all his terrible flaws he wasn't known for lying. He had no reason to concoct such wild yarns. Some of it didn't even matter, but there were a few profound statements there that Dahl wanted to make sense of. In addition, he was worried about Sabrina. Despite her crimes, her past sins, she had been forced into helping the team.

"You look like you're moping." Kenzie nudged his knee with hers. "Thinking about the old ball and chain?"

Dahl shrugged. Johanna hadn't figured in his thoughts today. "Maybe," he said. "And Sabrina. I feel for them both."

"Well at least now we know who the lesbian is." She chortled at him and flicked eyes at Drake, who couldn't hide a smile.

"Don't encourage her," Dahl stretched his legs out as the chopper cut through the clouds. "What happens to Sabrina Balboni will be on us."

"Not on me," Kenzie blurted. "I am but a follower and she a nasty criminal."

"She actually never hurt anyone," Drake said. "Unlike you, Bridget."

"I only kill in retaliation," she said. "Or for revenge."

"Sweet." Drake turned away as Alicia tapped his arm.

Dahl tried again with Kenzie. "Then let somebody in. There's a real, caring person hidden deep within you. I know. Let her out, even for just a minute."

"You're wrong, Dahl. Inside me there's only ashes. Barren emotions. And longing. I long for a redo."

"A redo?"

"In life. I want to go back to before. Do it all again differently. I want my family to be alive."

"I'm sorry."

"You can't possibly know what it's like."

The Swede skimmed over recent near misses. "I agree. I can't physically stomach contemplating it."

"So where would I find my heart?"

Dahl swallowed drily, unable to answer. Drake came to his rescue in inimitable fashion.

"Dudes, just follow the unwritten Matt Drake rule. When you're talking and start sounding too much like Taylor Swift, it's time to end the conversation."

The helicopter descended toward Eckernförde, seeking out a helipad. The team were operating under Interpol's dominion, but locals would always be around. Sometimes they were helpful, most times not.

Dahl watched his friends and team-members jump down from the chopper. From old comrades to new they all had their secrets.

But who fitted which ones?

He exited, knowing that, even now, he was running from a decision. Recently he'd learned he couldn't juggle family life with a soldier's lot. The two would never gel. So where did he go from here?

Outside, the German town was bathed in sunshine. Hayden herded them all into a hangar where a large vehicle waited and Lauren chose that moment of relative peace and quiet, and dim coolness, to transmit all she had learned during the flight.

"I believe I've found what Saint Germain was doing here. Apparently, he decided he would die here after arrival. He was weary of life, careworn and melancholy. Feeble. He died leaving nothing, not even a gravestone. He was the guest of a man called Prince Charles of Hesse-Kassel, who would later give no details of Germain's death, or of what he had left behind, and turned the conversation every time he was asked. Further discrepancies exist. Reliable witnesses say he died here in 1784, yet the documents of Freemasonry, relatively reliable, say the French took him as their representative in 1785. The Comtesse d'Adhémar reports a long conversation with him in 1789, a matter of record."

Lauren took a long breath. "But I digress. This Prince of Hesse-Kassel also had a vested interest in mysticism and was a member of several secret societies. Gems and cloths were passed around, it seems, and Charles was convinced that Germain could invent a new way of coloring the cloth and preparing the gems. He then installed the Count in an abandoned factory in Eckernförde." Lauren grinned. "Which was later converted into a hospital."

"How the hell did you learn all that?" Alicia asked.

"As I mentioned, it's a matter of record. This is the greatest part of Saint Germain's mystery—that all the facts are out there, in the public domain, and attested to by princes, kings, queens and heads of state. We're not talking mysterious grails, legendary kingdoms or mythical weapons. We're talking fact after fact after fact. Alchemy. Freemasonry. The arts. Diplomacy of the highest order. Councilor. Linguist. Virtuoso. Every title earned and documented. This mystery—" she shook her head "—runs deep."

"To the Philosopher's Stone and the secret of immortality?" Mai said wonderingly. "Now you're back in fantasy land."

"I've been to Fantasy Land," Dahl laughed. "There's no Saint Germain ride there."

"Mock all you like," Lauren said. "The facts, as they say, will out."

"All right," Hayden took up the reins. "So Germain's final

workplace was a laboratory, you say? Converted to a hospital. Where is it now?"

Lauren reeled off an address not thirty minutes from where they stood.

"We moving out?" Drake asked.

Hayden hesitated. Dahl knew she'd be wrestling with the facts. Hospital or gravesite? Or even this prince's castle, where Germain had stayed? More importantly, were they even in the right country?

"Workplace," she said. "So far, it's all been workplaces. The bedroom in Versailles. The library. The first laboratory. The compositions were removed from where they were written, which was the initial clue." She looked relieved. "It's the workplace."

Dahl liked her reasoning and was anxious to get into gear. "So wrestle it into the satnav and let's go." He took the shotgun seat whilst rummaging through the supplied holdall that held the real things.

"Do we think Amari's cult will make it this time?" Alicia asked. "Missed those little weasels in London."

"Could be they were watching the old theater," Hayden returned as she fastened her belt. "Could be they don't have all the details. Could even be they left London alone as it's so well guarded and chose—" she nodded out at the hills that surrounded them, the big sky and the small town "—this."

The vehicle set off, Smyth at the wheel. Forewarned by Hayden's lateral thinking the team checked and readied weapons. The busy, narrow streets soon gave way to wider, less populated roads and a rolling hillside. Smyth turned the air conditioning up high and tapped at his communication device.

"This thing's so friggin' quiet I thought it was busted."

Dahl agreed. "No help. No info. Not even DC chasing our tails. And Armand? Where's he? On any normal day you have to make him shut up."

Hayden double-checked her cell. "You shouldn't say it out loud. Could be the calm before the storm."

Drake stared out the window. "Since this is the penultimate clue I'd say you were right."

"Fuck, yes," Alicia said. "This would be a good time to stop him."

"Perfect," Drake said with satisfaction. "So close but so far. No closure for Webb, ever."

"And here we are." Smyth slowed outside the hospital and searched for a parking space. Dahl viewed the structure, finding it entirely incongruous to be at the tail end of what had been a varied but classical journey so far. The walls were square, rough gray concrete, spanning two floors, with dirty, draped windows in uneven lines and a small entrance out front. Patients, workers and visitors used the sidewalks and threaded through parked vehicles. An ambulance filled the road directly outside the entrance, awaiting some calamity.

Dahl pointed out the obvious problem. "Easy access," he said. "For everyone. But only Webb knows where he's going. Yes, it's a small hospital, but where do we start?"

Lauren held up both hands and several sets of eyes swiveled toward her. "Beyond me, I'm afraid. Maybe Karin could have dragged up blueprints from the depths of the Internet. Maybe not. But I sure as hell can't."

Dahl blinked on hearing their missing companion's name. He missed Karin Blake and wondered when she might return.

"Assuming the lab or factory was knocked down to make way for the hospital," Hayden said. "Assuming Germain was savvy enough to know what might happen, the true lab would be underground. Hidden. And it would still be there."

"Mahalo." Kinimaka nodded. "My thoughts too."

True as it was, it didn't help them much. "We need the manager of the hospital," he said.

"No," Hayden said, now smiling. "We need the *janitor*."

"Ah, so do you mean the tunnels? Or the secret passageways?" Dahl stared and seconded Drake's outburst: "Come again?"

"When you have an old site and you build on top, on top, on top." The janitor used his arms and fingers to explain just as much as his words. "Soon get . . . many passages. Unused places. Forgotten storage and boiler rooms, sewers and access passageways. Soon—" he threw both arms aloft "—you have warren. Hidden warren. *Secret* warren."

Dahl studied the man, who looked as old as the hospital. Rat-faced and clean-shaven from the top of his head to at least his chin, standing wrapped in a protective sheet, he looked a little like a missile. Oddly, he also resembled the manager from the Haymarket Theater to a certain degree. His fingers were uncomfortably long and Dahl wondered if some of the patients had nightmares after catching a glimpse of the janitor flitting up and down the corridors.

"The hospital don't . . . police it?" Hayden asked, looking like she couldn't find the right words.

"They have more important things on their minds. So, tunnels or secret passageways?"

Drake's face took on an expression of intense excitement. "Let's make it both."

Dahl shook his head at the Yorkshireman. The child was never far from the surface.

"I am Lars," the janitor said. "Follow me."

Hayden fell in behind the odd apparition, Kinimaka not far behind. Dahl respected the two intensely for not letting personal problems get in the way of their work. It had to be tough. And if Hayden's mind really was made up then she'd already be in another place.

Just like Johanna.

Dahl tried to compartmentalize the conflict of emotions, but struggled. For a short time their crumbling world had started to steady, but again the decline had set in. His heart ached for what it might do to the children.

You're not the only couple ever to separate. Kids usually do just fine.

But . . . but . . .

Lars the janitor swooped down familiar passageways, passing open doors and locked storage rooms, at home in the clinical white sprawl. Predictably, he seemed to be working his way toward the back of the hospital. As they walked, Hayden quizzed him.

"Anyone else been sniffing around recently?"

The janitor spun with a flourish. "Sniffing?"

"Looking. For the tunnels?"

"Ah, no. It is just me and the ghosts back there, I'm afraid." He bowed. "But don't tell the management, eh?"

Dahl found the man more than creepy. Reminded him of some old horror movie, and definitely assimilated with the legend of Saint Germain. If this was the site where the Count worked in his final days then perhaps his specter still haunted these halls. Perhaps it judged them all even now.

He grunted, shrugging the weird feeling off. All about him was real, from the medical rooms to the receptionist's desk and chair. Unused to the eerie, he concentrated on what he could see and feel. The janitor led them deeper into the bowels of the place, and the lights began to dim. Strip tubing fizzed and popped, and some were empty. Dahl was aware of the incredible weight of concrete above his head, in particular when he saw the wide cracks in the walls. The janitor made no comment, despite the many viewpoints that had a negative bearing on his job.

Through a large archive they walked, threading their way among tattered, dusty cardboard boxes and old desks, then came up against a heavy steel door with a chain and padlock across its pull bar.

Lars shrugged. "Keeps the undesirables out."

Dahl wondered, but didn't question. His first thought was: *And what does it keep* in*?* But such absurdities vanished from his thoughts in an instant. Lars produced a long key and unchained the door.

"Wait," Hayden said. "Is there another way into the tunnels?"

Lars rolled his arms and shoulders. "Many ways. Once you get back here the old rooms all have access to the building's former areas. Long-forgotten they may be, but potentially serviceable. It costs too much to keep them all properly maintained."

"CCTV?" Kinimaka asked without hope.

"Only where it is crucial. Never back here."

As Lars pushed through, the team unobtrusively prepped weapons and made ready. A narrow corridor, still clearly part of the hospital, led past several locked rooms with grimy viewing panels and one open area complete with padded sofas, a wall-mounted TV, and water cooler. Abandonment hung over the area like a stain.

"Love these old deserted places." Lars smiled happily. "Gives you a sense of belonging. You know? To the past."

Nobody commented as the man's supersized fingers flickered toward the way ahead. "To the tunnels."

"You mentioned secret passageways," Hayden said.

"Oh yes. Around us now, inside the walls, are two parallel running passages, also leading to the tunnels and formed when the waiting area was built. Partitioned off—" he shrugged "—to make the space feel nicer."

This put Dahl on his guard. Webb could be around them even now. Listening. Watching. Doing the thing he loved most in the world. A place like this was a stalker's wet dream. They proceeded down the corridor and came to an intersection. Lars pointed to the right.

"An old staircase takes us to boiler rooms and other storage areas. Then wall access points give to the sewers, electrical inspection tunnels and forgotten corners bricked over and ignored by the new build. To the left are archives and disregarded offices. Which would you like?"

Hayden studied the janitor. "How well do you really know these areas?"

"The truth? I rarely go home." He grinned.

Dahl swallowed the distaste. "You mentioned places that were bricked over. We're interested in the history around here. Apparently there was once a factory?"

"You are correct and then you are not." Lars gently swept his arms forward in a sliding motion. "The factory is still there."

"Show us," Hayden said with urgency. "Show us now."

Dahl knew they could be as little as an hour behind Webb, or a day ahead. If the man had made it they'd be sure to find signs. He moved next to Drake.

"What of these Dubai-based fanatics?" he asked. "Do you believe they're irrelevant now? Lost?"

"I can't shake the feeling that they're still in the running," Drake said. "Yeah, they're protected from it, aloof and seemingly unaware of the nightmares they sponsor, but these guys have been watching for years. They're dedicated. Organized. Obsessive guardians. It doesn't seem right that they wouldn't know about Germaine's deathbed factory."

"On a brighter note," Alicia butted in. "Whaddya think of the brand new secret base idea? How cool is that?"

Drake raised an eyebrow. "Dunno, love. Cool is relative. What if it's in Antarctica?"

"And the new Secretary of Defense is a woman," Lauren added. "An interesting change."

At the end of the corridor a staircase rose out of the floor. Hayden stared at its base. "Ummm,"

"We have to go up," Lars said. "To go down. I thought it odd too, but maybe it serves as a façade."

Dahl blinked. An odd façade, considering it blended old secrets with new. Such concealments spoke of vast conspiracy and suppression. He shook his head at the follies of men. Always focused on the wrong things.

Up they went, winding around a spiral until Lars brought them onto a wide landing. Ahead a larger spiral twisted down and down, its handrails mostly thick with dust except where the janitor's fingers had previously touched. To the right an old, forgotten, stained-glass window stared out across the landscape.

Kenzie stepped up to it. "See the patterns in the glass? This kinda thing *starts* conspiracy theories."

Dahl approached her, supremely careful not to get too close. "We don't have time for—" He paused. "Now that's odd."

The team halted in their strides, Drake coming over. "What you on about, mate?"

"The seven men stood watching the hospital from the far parking lot . . . they're all Arabs."

Drake shouldered him aside. "What?"

Hayden came over too. "Amari? Looking for Webb?"

"I think so." Drake squinted. "Eyes aren't what they were."

Mai nodded toward Alicia. "Clearly."

The Treasures of Saint Germain

"If he's close—" Hayden said.

"Chaos ain't far behind," Drake finished. "And what's he doing there? What the hell is he doing with his hands?"

"Counting," Dahl said with a feeling of sudden, freezing horror. "He's using his fingers to count down."

"And there." Drake pointed. "Mercenaries rushing at them. Shit, there's gonna be a full-scale battle in the car park."

"No," Hayden said. "Amari ain't running. They're *his* mercs."

"But why?" Drake wondered.

Hayden's phone went off just a second before Drake's and Dahl's, and then everyone else's. Tones of impending doom filled the landing area, grim expressions lining every face.

Argento said it first.

"Amari," he said. "Has just called in a terrorist act on the hospital you are currently inside. His message: If I can't safeguard the Master I will destroy every single trace. And that includes your hospital." The man's tone was uncharacteristically lacking in enthusiasm, heavily laced with fate.

Alarms exploded throughout the building and the team turned to face one another.

"The mercs were running," Dahl said. "Because they left something behind."

"God help us all," Hayden said.

Argento's scream: *"Get the hell out of there!"*

CHAPTER FORTY FIVE

When a man or woman is faced with death, any death, they can make one of only two decisions—fight or die. To fight might encompass a world of choice—battle, flight, hide, a jump into the unknown. But to die—that was easy. *If there's a choice,* Drake thought. *Fight!*

Fight to live with all your being. The alternative is very bleak.

When the explosions began the whole team listened hard, feeling and testing and listening to their gravity, their depth and range. Drake knew they were deep. Leaning over he saw windows blowing out and mortar crumbling. Shocked, he saw a wide crack traveling from the foundation to the top floor, concrete parting and discharging clouds of dust.

"I'm pretty sure my legs ain't turned to jelly," Lauren said. "So that's the building shaking."

"Oh . . . what have they done?" Hayden gasped.

Drake couldn't imagine the mindset of a person who would destroy a hospital full of people to safeguard a forgotten room from another century, but he could visualize his next set of choices.

"Amari's right there," he said, swaying. "With a dozen or so mercs, and he's fast decelerating into insanity. Webb's probably below us or already moved on to his final undertaking and, knowing Webb, that can't be good for the world. I'm sorry, guys, but there's only one decision here."

"This building's coming down," Hayden said.

Kinimaka was already headed for the door, Dahl alongside.

"The people," Alicia said. "The patients. Oh my God."

In the midst of all hell, they ran. Chunks of plaster, lighting and plasterboard trim were already breaking free and hanging down, swaying like deadly pendulums. They pounded back to the populated wings of the hospital, saw doctors and nurses running this way and that, patients shuffling along the corridors, and heard the screams of the trapped or the hopeless.

"We get them all out," Dahl said. "All of them."

And he darted away.

Drake picked up a nurse who slipped beside them, looked around. "Where's the . . . hey, where did that bloody janitor go?"

"Slipped away," Kenzie growled, angry, then quickly changed her expression. "Wished I'd gone with him."

Alicia swept her aside. "Then go, bitch."

But the ex-Mossad agent was there with them throughout the terror. Drake set his mind and helped each person as they came along, shepherding those who wept to the exits, herding a six-strong crowd who couldn't find their way, carrying air-tanks for a slight nurse and making sure one of Lauren's tasks was guaranteeing the consistent arrival of elevators. Mai and Kenzie swept in and out like angels of mercy, aiding where they could and ferrying patients to the elevators or stairs.

A constant stream of people crowded the way down and tried to make way for those racing up from below. Another barrage of explosions shattered even the chaos of noise that filled the hospital, quieting every man, woman and child for just a moment.

Then, like another detonation, the panic erupted once more.

Alarm bells shrieked like desperate banshees. Glass shattered out of windows due to the pressure of failing walls above. Strip lights tumbled. Life-saving machines slid to the extent their wires would allow. A drinks machine tumbled over, its glass panel exploding. Hayden ranged along the corridors, ensuring no one was left behind. The staff fought hard too, toiling and risking it all for their patients.

A nurse screamed for help. The room she stood in suddenly skewed. Kinimaka rushed to help, and the view out of the window changed, becoming narrower as the entire building sagged. The nurse was stuck with her hands under the patient, unable to lift him, frustration creasing her face. The Hawaiian grabbed the man under the shoulder and heaved whilst the nurse grabbed whatever paraphernalia he was still attached to and then the two ran, side by side, toward the stairs.

Drake saw the bent walls, the crumbling ceiling. The halls were empty; a couple of lone doctors checking rooms.

"How are we doing?" he cried out.

A nod, a thumbs up. The elevator dinged, still serviceable but not for long. The risk had paid off, though Drake had originally had his doubts. But without their help almost half a dozen patients would still be up here, stranded, just waiting to die.

Sirens screamed from the parking lot. Drake drove the patients downstairs as they parted for paramedics rushing up. "All clear here," he told them as the doctors arrived, and relief lit their faces.

"Just the ground floor then."

Drake inclined his head. "What's it like?"

The paramedic turned a flinty eye to the roof as several trickles of plaster and mortar rained down. "A shitstorm. How long we got?"

"Judging by this—" Drake barely moved as a chunk of concrete shattered at his back "—not long."

The crowd thinned; the exit must have been flung open, maybe all the windows too. Drake hit ground level last of all his colleagues and saw them in action; making split decisions and taking impossible burdens. The weight of the hospital bore down upon them. What would it take to bring the place down? Why was depraved and detached horror the core principal of so many wealthy men?

Drake came to a room inhabited by four patients and two desperate nurses. The patients were children. He moved in, grabbed two and lifted. Couldn't quite manage the balance. There was only one thing for it. Against the instincts of a soldier but running with personal compulsions, he dropped his weapons to the floor. No need for them here. If he ended up weaponless, facing mercs outside then so be it. He could only carry the utterly essential.

Freed from extra burdens now, he managed to juggle three children, wrapped them tight in his arms and moved out into the hallways, approaching a wide window. Here, the more able patients were climbing to safety.

Drake deposited the kids into the arms of waiting people—

made up of doctors, nurses, civilians and even patients already ferried to safety, and ran back for the others. All else had already faded from his mind. There was no Webb, no Amari, no Beau or Sabrina or even any other mission. The innocents about to be crushed under the weight of another's madness were all that mattered.

The team rallied. Partitioned walls collapsed: bending, shattering and crumbling, sending plumes of dust billowing forward. Critical walls and pillars held for now, but everyone could sense something vital was shifting. The hallways widened, flowed together into the lobby, once a confluence of seating, desks, a pharmacy and a coffee shop and filled with lots of light, but now transformed by all the elements of a battle zone.

Drake spilled into it with many others, saw a man lying prone on the floor, arms flapping, and hoisted him to his feet. He saw now why the crush had eased so quickly. The whole glass frontage had burst out, either by the weight of the building or explosives, but a wide hole had been breached. A stroke of luck. He scanned the lobby.

Kenzie and Alicia worked together to free a man from the remains of a false wall, his skull and shoulders bleeding. The two antagonists did good work, their differences forgotten for now. Mai helped a paramedic trying to resuscitate a man on the spot, shoulders not flinching as mortar rained down upon them. Kinimaka pulled rubble away from a doorway behind which people were trapped. Some of the chunks he hurled aside would have broken Drake's back. A gray dust settled over everyone, and helped form complex footprints on the floor. Time screamed by. Another shift in the building's edifice elevated the panic.

Drake rarely prayed, but he threw one out for the people now. A vital wall had weakened. Still, the patients streamed out and away. Still, doctors and nurses and more patients leapt in to help. Smyth came running through with an unconscious older woman in his arms. Lauren deposited a child with a paramedic. At least two doctors were being forced to attend to patients actually inside the lobby that was crumbling all around them. Then, the far side of the lobby collapsed. Debris plumed toward them, a thick cloud. The area had been previously emptied, but that said nothing for where they were now.

Drake scooped up two limping young men and ran them outside, charged back in. A scream brought him around, let him catch a girl before she tumbled onto a jagged pile of plaster. Yorgi bounded and leapt between wreckage, clearing out passages and openings where some imagined they might be safe.

The alarm bells stopped, leaving a torturous, resounding silence in their wake. Then a deep roar and thunder like nothing he'd ever heard sent Drake into overdrive.

The lobby, a later addition to the front of the hospital and not integral, was coming down.

But he'd just seen Dahl plunging back in.

Drake didn't hesitate, just stormed the sagging door that fronted the main body of the hospital, ducking a rain of wreckage. A lone doctor staggered past him, bleeding from the ear and scooped up by Smyth. A nurse, clothing smudged and stained, rested with her head against the door jamb. Drake eased her through and pointed her in the right direction. Few words were spoken as the selfless helped the needy to safety. Drake stopped dead in a frozen heart-rending torment as a handful of doctors and nurses hurried past, carrying and shielding babies between them. Drake felt agony, fury and a stirring sadness. He waited and then moved on, deeper into the hallways.

"Dahl!"

Then it came; the collapse of something, possibly everything. Without chance to gauge how destructive this latest shockwave would be, Drake watched the ceiling slump down to within an inch of his head. Metal fittings swung to and fro, one catching him across the skull.

Drake merely ducked and forged on.

Alicia shouted as she emerged at his back. "What's going on?"

"Dahl," Drake answered as if that explained everything.

It did.

The Mad Swede exploded into view, bellowing for adrenalin and pushing a hospital bed complete with terrified patient at full speed. He took the corner like a pro, ducked under debris and then clapped eyes on Drake.

"Run!" he cried.

Drake turned to Alicia. "Leg it!" he yelled.

Alicia spun to a newly appeared Hayden. "Fuck!" she screamed.

Masses of rubble slammed down all around them. Drake's shin shrieked agony as a brick ricocheted off the bone. Dahl clattered along at his back, jolting through the piles, brute force keeping him straight. A wheel stuck, but then came free, a metal spear parted the sheets between the patient's knees. As Drake turned back he purposely slowed, catching hold of the front of the bed.

Together.

He hauled, Dahl pushed. They hit the lobby and turned, found the front exit blocked by people and rubble. Debris surged down behind them. Hayden leapt for a window, cut and bleeding, leapt out and flapped her hands. Drake heaved on the bed and aimed for it. Alicia grabbed a fallen paramedic and threw him over her shoulder. Dahl pushed with every sinew, every ounce of will, and the last portions of his strength.

Drake stumbled as an entire glass pane fell from the windowed roof and shattered by his left leg. Shards made him wince. Dahl was going too fast. They were going to . . .

From the corner of his eyes, he saw the rest of the team. Kinimaka and Kenzie, Mai and Smyth, Yorgi and Lauren, all still inside and rushing to help. His heart leapt. Together, they heaved the bed and the patient over the last hurdle, and managed to feed everything through the window. Doctors were already at Hayden's side even as wreckage poured over their legs.

Drake turned. The world was going black.

They raced for windows. Without pause they leapt head-first into an unknown fate with sheer hope and the greatest optimism. Drake landed and rolled, scraped and cut by brick and concrete and a dozen other materials. He came back up with eyes to left and right, counting his friends, looking back at the great, fragile edifice.

Kinimaka stood at a window, face staring out. The opening was too small.

Above him the entire building wilted.

CHAPTER FORTY SIX

As fates balanced on a razor's edge, as life's patina slipped between shiny and dull, as a million unfulfilled moments and dreams passed through countless imaginations, the lofty face of the hospital building ceased its gradual slippage. Maybe a load-bearing wall held up, or a critical beam took extra weight, but the destructive process halted.

Already, ten pairs of legs were sprinting toward it.

Dahl was last, exhausted, but Hayden was at the front, stretching every sinew as she reached out for the Hawaiian. Together, they hauled him through a larger gap, Drake and Alicia and Kenzie still peering within to triple-check no one was still inside. In moments they retreated to the parking lot and then a grass bank that rose up around the boundary. Everyone collapsed onto their backs.

"We good?" Drake panted. "Anything serious?"

"Nothing a shower and a bag of painkillers won't cure." Dahl was already sitting up and surveying the chaotic scene. "It looks like a battle zone down there. Surgeons operating between crashed cars." He hung his head. "I do hope we didn't help this occur."

"Not a chance," Drake said. "Webb brought Amari out and with that came the insanity."

Lauren sat up. "And we don't know the outcome of it all."

"Nor will we for some time," Dahl responded.

"On the far worse, unimaginable side of all that, stands another possibility," Hayden said. "That Webb escaped, Amari knows it, and they're now headed for the final showdown. After this—" she looked at the wreckage "—I can't imagine what's next."

The team worked on restoring their depleted reserves as they watched swarms of medics, doctors and nurses arriving to assist.

Police cars motored up and filled the highways. Ambulances sped along and helicopters began to arrive. The spectacle was both uplifting at the sight of human strength and kindness, and depressing that so much effort—if not needed at the whim of a lunatic—could move mountains elsewhere.

Hayden made calls to Argento and DC. Though they knew of the catastrophe they knew little else. Eckernförde, whilst not exactly secluded, was small enough to lack a CCTV network and other security mechanisms. Drake believed Amari would not let it end there. Most likely he'd assume Webb had survived, especially since they were at the end of the quest now. The very last clue led directly to the Philosopher's Stone, the secret of eternal life, invisibility and teleportation. Webb and Amari were both convinced it was real, and that made it real for the SPEAR team. More than anything, it was the individuals they were chasing. The rest of it was just a flame in a hurricane.

Of course, the Arab needed tracking down. Their job was far from over, even if Webb did lie beneath the rubble.

"Amari?" Dahl said.

Hayden dipped her head. "More than anything," she said. "But the penultimate clue was here. Now we don't know anything. I wonder if even he does."

"Bastard has to turn up somewhere," Smyth growled. "We'll grind him to meat."

Drake watched as a policeman broke away from a knot of doctors and started racing toward them. A look of urgency creased the man's face.

"Ey up," he said. "Here comes a cupful of trouble."

"Aww." Alicia seemed back to normal. "Sounds like a description of the Little Sprite."

Mai watched the cop's approach.

Hayden rose to meet him, Dahl too. Drake was close enough to tilt his head up and listen to what the man had to say.

"Somebody down there," he panted, "says they know you. They want to talk."

Drake assumed it was someone they'd helped. "Not necessary. We—"

"The woman is dying."

The team quieted. Drake closed his eyes. "Of course."

"She also said you'd respond quicker if I told you her name. Sabrina Balboni."

Drake felt a catch in his throat. It was their team who had put the Italian master thief in this situation before Beau had betrayed them all. Now . . .

As one, they raced back down the hill on the heels of the cop. Together, they threaded carefully through the throng.

Apart, at least mentally, they surrounded a stretcher where Sabrina lay. The Italian was barely moving and showed no signs of rubble dust. Drake turned to a medic. "How?"

"A knife to the abdomen," the man said heavily. "As if the explosion was not enough."

Drake tried to ignore the twist in his soul and leaned over the stretcher. "Sabrina? Can you hear me, love?"

Eyelids fluttered. The black eyes were filled with pain. He could tell that Sabrina recognized him instantly though.

"Hi."

Her lips quivered. "He . . . he is gone. Beau . . . Beau did this to me."

Drake's fists clenched but he beat down the rising anger and put aside Alicia's terrible muttered curse. He had no right to ask this woman to help them again, but if Webb was loose and the Amari cult in pursuit then nowhere in the world was safe.

"Do you know where?" he asked.

"He has gone . . ." Sabrina broke into a fit of coughing, the wracking gasps making her grimace and starting a fresh blood flow that stained her covering. The medic stepped in. "She needs to go to a hospital."

"How far?" Dahl asked.

The medic shrugged. "Ten minutes."

They couldn't take the risk. Drake leaned so close his lips almost brushed Sabrina's forehead. "I'm sorry," he said. "So sorry, but we need to know everything."

"He has gone . . ." Sabrina said suddenly, voice strong and startling Drake. "To where Saint Germain still lives. It's obvious really. The greatest treasure still resides with him to this very day."

Drake drew away. "Still . . . *still lives?* What the he—?"

Hayden came in from the other side. "Where?" she pressed. "It doesn't matter what Webb believes. Where has he gone?"

"Believes . . . believes he lives in the French Quarter. New Orleans. Germain has a house."

"And the treasure?"

"Says Germain chose . . . French Quarter because of . . . diversity. Ingredients he needs. A peculiar variety, he said."

Sabrina held up a hand and Drake took it.

"Get Beau," she breathed. "Pay him back for me."

Alicia shouldered her way to Sabrina's side. "That will be my job and, girl, I'm gonna earn a commendation for it."

"Than . . . thank you."

"Hey, no need to thank us," Drake said quickly. "We'll come to visit when we're done."

"Grapes." Sabrina tried to crack a smile but all Drake saw was the paramedic's anxious frown. "No. Wine."

"I'll bring an entire rack," Drake said.

"My—" more coughing "—hero."

"We should go." Hayden pulled away.

"One more thing," Sabrina said as the medic rushed to her side. "One more." She clasped Drake's wrist.

"Webb is at his endgame. All finishes now. His life. His vision. Everything for this. He told Beau . . . told him to call in and cash in *all and every resource*. That's what he said."

Drake shared a glance with Hayden. *A sentence with utterly terrible connotations.*

They allowed the medics to take care of Sabrina and gathered together. Hayden made the call.

"We need a fast flight to Louis Armstrong Airport," she said. "And a fully loaded team to meet us there. All threats possible. Just put the damn city on alert."

She headed for a police vehicle. "Finally," she said. "Tyler Webb's finished."

Drake knew most people were at their most vulnerable when approaching victory.

All and every resource?

Wait until he got a taste of what the SPEAR team brought.

CHAPTER FORTY SEVEN

New Orleans smoldered beside the great snake of the Mississippi River, a city rebuilt and rebuilt again and still thriving not the least from the great community spirit. The French Quarter was New Orleans' oldest neighborhood, a tourist hotspot and home to almost every vice, amusement and entertainment a person could imagine. Mostly pronounced *new oar-linz*, and seemingly unaware of compass directions—neighborhoods were uptown, downtown, river or lake—it appeared subject to its own rules and regulations . . . one of the few places in the United States where you could drink liquor outside, where people rode streetcars not trams, and where the dead were always buried above ground in raised mausoleums.

A good place then for procuring odd constituents and mixing old elements, a good place to find the impossible and attempt the incredible. The hard part? Almost nothing is pronounced as it's spelled.

Drake exited the car first as they stepped out onto Bourbon Street, the center of the vibrant hive. The area was busy, noisy and incredibly alive. He felt exposed, atypical, though nobody noticed. The big van was unmarked as were the two that came after, the weapons kept concealed for now. No threats had been issued, no uncommon activity registered. The authorities were subtly heightening their presence and drafting in help. Drake wanted to bag Webb before larger contingents arrived.

But where's the madman? he wondered. *Where do the loonies congregate around the Quarter?*

Their research aboard the plane, whilst not of Karin Blake quality, had yielded some results. The legend was that Saint Germain had reinvented himself some time ago, moved to New Orleans and passed into obscurity. No questions were posited as to why or how, not even the simple ones, but Drake found that was usually the way with legends that endured. Webb himself believed in it and was on the final hunt for the elixir of life right here. The gloves were well and truly off.

The team spread out around and behind him, Alicia at his side. As a bunch, they had been rather subdued since leaving Sabrina, and had received no updates since. Alicia saw that as a good sign. During the long flight they had either slept or feigned it; nobody wanted to deal head-on with the issues Webb had raised.

Drake caught Alicia looking at him and gave her a wink. Then he saw Mai also watching and was reminded of the last time they were together. In bed. The sudden recollection dried his mouth out.

Hayden led the way up onto the sidewalk. "So rather than aimless wandering we do have a plan." She spoke into the comms for benefit of the other teams present. "Do not forget that Amari will be here, and potentially even more of a destructive threat than Webb. Do not forget Webb has bet his whole deviant life on this very day and night. They both have resources—Amari's as far-reaching as Webb's used to be. And Beauregard Alain? Do not underestimate him. Lethal force may be required. I think that's about it. Shall we move out?"

The question was rhetorical, but then a voice spoke out. "Umm, not quite yet."

A new vehicle pulled up. Drake dropped his hand and moved closer to cover. Dahl and Kinimaka stepped to the front; Smyth and Lauren to the back. The doors opened and three serious looking bodyguards stepped out, surveying the area. Black sunglasses and suits spoke of government, and the busy surveillance shouted Secret Service. Drake attempted to keep his jaw stuck together.

Hayden failed. "Is that . . . ? It's a woman. Ah crap. Not now. We can't guarantee her safety."

But there was no stopping Kimberly Crowe. The middle-aged, new Secretary of Defense was a slim, fit woman who clearly worked out. The bones of her cheeks were prominent, the clip of her heels quick and sharp. She approached Hayden, then stopped just a meter away.

"You think this is inappropriate don't you?"

Hayden measured her response. "Is this a flying visit, Madam Secretary?"

"I'm here to help."

Drake saw the determination on Crowe's face. Nobody would say the obvious aloud, so he started to wonder how to phrase a response, but then Alicia stepped in.

"Our track record ain't that good with Secretaries of Defense."

"To safeguard you, Madam, would impact our effectiveness," Hayden amended.

"I have my guards." Crowe swept her hand toward the three men.

Dahl snorted. "You steal 'em from kindergarten?"

"And you might be subjected to some coarseness," Hayden added quickly.

"We can take it. And I can take a back seat." She motioned. "Lead on."

Conscious that Crowe's appearance could mean anything from an inquisitive visit to a brief evaluation, to a full-on appraisal of the team's value to the nation, Hayden turned away. The Secretary knew the risks.

It was time to hunt.

CHAPTER FORTY EIGHT

The plan was simple, and far easier than trawling through thick layers of digital dust and numerical highways. Hayden explained it to the Secretary as they moved out.

"As with all enemies, we usually put aside Webb's beliefs, crazy or not, as they can't help us here. But his life's work? That's key. This man has been leading up to the creation of an alchemical formula called the Philosopher's Stone, a substance also known as the elixir of life. Once the most hunted prize on the planet, it's now Webb's ultimate goal."

"I've heard of it."

"But its history is fascinating. It can be traced back to Adam, who got the knowledge from God. Passed down among biblical patriarchs, it was how they achieved their durability. It involves the Temple of Solomon, and Psalms in the Bible."

"But you put that aside, right?" Crowe said. "As a little kooky."

"Yes and no," Hayden said. "On this occasion it could help. The Internet is vast, and full of lies. Who knows which facts are actual facts anymore? Especially when they relate to a three-hundred-year-old Count. If we had time to research properly, old books, old libraries, museums and such, we could work it out. But we never do. Real life moves too fast to take a breather. Real soldiers and real teams have to think and study on the go."

Crowe followed Hayden between groups of revelers. "Makes sense. But I still don't hear your point."

"All right. Webb believes, through learning the secrets of alchemy, teleportation, invisibility and with advice from the Freemasons handed down from their ultimate founder, he can concoct this Magnum Opus. That's why he embarked upon this quest only after locating Leopold's scroll. To make the liquid, he will now need the right ingredients."

"To make the Philosopher's Stone?" Crowe looked immensely

skeptical. "And you know what they are?"

"We do. I believe it's knowing how they're mixed that changes the outcome. Anyway, during the flight we had the FBI techs tracking local purchases of phosphorous. A certain urine. Special morning dew. Ammonium niter. Magnesium chloride. A few other materials that create sophick; salt, sulfur and mercury. Yes, some of the establishments around here are extremely secretive about what they sell, but others are either complacent or carefully cooperative."

"I understand. So you're telling me we're here to follow a shopping list?"

"Exactly."

Deeper they delved into the French Quarter and beyond. Rundown shops with dirty green shutters and cheap souvenirs boasted the names Church of Voodoo, Leveaux's and Hoodoo Shop. Whether by design or neglect, every establishment labored under an air of disrepair, and several looked downright uninviting. Drake had long ago learned that innocent fronts could often hide dens of terrible iniquity. But tourists wandered in and out of the open doors, snapping pictures, selfies, most laboring under the intense heat.

Hayden stopped. "Blue Voodoo," she said. "Here, apparently, we can find putrefied urine."

Alicia lowered her head across Hayden's shoulders. "Really?"

"Hey, it's not my barbecue."

The team readied and liaised with the local SWAT guys who had also turned up. By now they all wore flak jackets and helmets and carried their weapons exposed. The area was emptying rapidly as people were moved away. Drake took the lead.

"Go." The directive whistled through his comms.

Drake crossed the threshold, gun up, and went left. Dahl went right. Two followed and then Kinimaka went straight down the middle. The counter assistant stared at them in shock.

"Back door?" Drake asked.

But all was empty. If Webb had ever been here, he had moved on. Hayden called out the manager and took him aside.

Drake listened as he quickly answered her question. "Yes, yes, we sold it less than a half hour ago. Odd man with a tall friend. We don't question."

Another store beckoned, this one two blocks away, that sold ammonium niter. Inside, Drake dubiously regarded the plethora of chemicals, urns, mixing bowls and mortar and pestle basins, the vials of hair and teeth and animal remains, the jars of eyeballs, tongues and toenails, the plastic pouches of mandrake, zombie flesh and king's blood. The proprietor looked like he'd ingested all of them.

"Yar, yar," he drawled in a clearly fake English accent. "Man came through just recently. Bought the niter, magnesium, some phosphorous. Said he needed the morning dew." A cackle, a flash of blackened teeth and a whip of dreadlocks. "I said 'you mean the *special* dew?' He said 'yes'. I said 'Don't sell it'. He looked rather miffed."

Hayden fought to take him down a little. "You recommend anywhere?"

"Verily, verily. Magick Lounge. They surely have all kinds of . . . crap. Oh, and why are those chaps dressed like the men in black?"

Drake winced at the references to Secretary Crowe's bodyguards but leaned close to Dahl. "Dude speaks better toff than you."

The Swede sighed. "Spoken like a true northern peasant."

Kimberly Crowe turned to the team. "So what is the special dew? Dare I ask?"

The proprietor sniffed. "Precipitation gathered at dawn off the petals of a deadly, noxious plant. Is it lethal or is it not? Would you try some?"

"Doubtful." Crowe backed away. "Very doubtful."

"Depending on how blasted ya got the night before, eh?" Alicia blurted before remembering who she was speaking to. But then she only shrugged. "Fuckin' true isn't it?"

The entire force moved on, Hayden ticking items off her list. As they paused in a square behind the Magick Lounge, a steaming sun trap that stank of fried chicken, marijuana, cigarettes and jasmine, the leader of the SPEAR team spoke out.

"Only the sophick elements remain after the dew. Be ready."

"We should go straight on to the next," Smyth chaffed. "Looks like we're still ten minutes behind."

"Our luck?" Drake said. "We'd miss him. Beside, cops are looking at the three possible places."

Mai tapped Smyth's shoulder. "And also, what if he's en route? Our presence could tip him off."

Smyth grumped in silence, throwing out a questing glance at Lauren. The New Yorker's face was open, slightly smiling. He smiled back.

Drake followed Dahl into the Magick Lounge. The wide open doors threw them all a little, but once inside, again, there was no sign of Webb. Hayden made the instant decision to move fast on the remaining businesses.

"Split up," she said. "We're at the last chance saloon here."

Nobody balked, nobody lingered. There were instant movements and dozens of pairs of legs raced out of the door. Locations were followed on hand-held GPS devices. Drake and the team arrowed straight toward the nearest. A guess had been put forward that they were less than five minutes behind Webb. The narrow streets between shops and restaurants, some abandoned, some crumbled no doubt from Katrina, although the French Quarter had gotten some extra protection from reinforced levees, were a maze, a boiling warren of coffee smells, piled-up rubbish and stinking corners. Drake sweated hard beneath his helmet. Hayden shouted out that their final destination was a minute away and the team slowed.

But they did not stop.

They cut down an alley so narrow it rubbed their shoulders on both sides, then emerged carefully opposite a shuttered shop that ran two stories and sported three balconies around its height. To Drake, it looked closed but that very fact put him on alert. An American flag hung suspended in no breeze, attached to one of the railings. A row of well-tended plant pots lined another balcony. The odd layout of the streets, from shop to restaurant to private garages to beautifully painted, shuttered homes to rough drinking venue was never more apparent as Drake stared at a row of conflicting images. But the shop?

It sat quiet and sunstruck, its paved sidewalk faded, and its windows secured as if ignoring the world. He moved out into the open and held up a hand, signaling a pause. Two crowds of tourists sauntered to the left, several catching sight of Drake and pausing to stare. The main group came closer.

And then parted.

Webb and Beau emerged slowly at first, looking bored, but then made a beeline for the seemingly closed shop. Maybe they had called ahead, promised more money for privacy? That was how it was done, wasn't it? In wealthy circles?

Drake lowered his HK. "Hey, knobheads!"

Webb broke into a sprint. Beau flung something from a closed fist that cut brick above Drake's skull, showering him with dust. A second projectile followed, confusing the Yorkshireman and then the Frenchman was there, a ninja in black, the persona of shadowy death, and Drake felt the HK twist from his hands.

He struck low, catching Beau in the ribs. Alicia pushed at his back, trying to force him away from the narrow alley, but Beau held him there, striking almost as fast as his mind could work. The assassin hit brick as often as he did Drake, but none of the blows fazed him.

Drake found his only recourse was to fling himself past Beau. That allowed Alicia to come to the fore and made Beau concentrate on her. The man's face, familiar and sometimes smiling, sometimes grim, but part of their team, now bore no signs of recognition, empathy or mercy. He might as well have been a robot, programmed to kill.

Alicia kicked at shins and punched at the stomach and groin. Beau danced beautifully, a master puppeteer. Spins and sweeps put Alicia on her back, then Drake was at his heels, Kinimaka trying to emerge from the alley.

Shit. The big Hawaiian's bloody stuck!

As calamitous as ever, Mano Kinimaka could not move forward as brick walls pinned him in from both sides. Soldiers chaffed behind him, Crowe and her entourage at the back. Drake dived at Beau, striking thighs, and Alicia kicked out, but the

Frenchman buried a pile driver into Kinimaka's stomach that effectively turned him into a gasping, unmoving blockage.

Hayden cried out: "Webb's already inside!"

The barrel of a gun pressed under Kinimaka's armpit, but Beau twirled away before shots could be fired. Kinimaka groaned loudly as Dahl pushed at his back. Flesh nipped and material tore apart. Beau skipped between Drake and Alicia, trying to keep them down.

Drake slammed a fist against the man's thigh, ecstatic to fetch a heavy grunt. So the fucker was human after all! Then Beau somehow managed to jab him below the eye with a finger and kick him in the stomach at the same time. Drake folded, rolling away.

Alicia was up, but Drake saw Beau jumping after Webb now and figured freeing up the rest of the team was the best bet. Not looking the Hawaiian in the face, they grabbed his jacket and tugged whilst Dahl pushed.

Alicia's face was set to impish. "Better hope this works, big man. As a last resort I'm gonna be tweaking those nuts."

With a scream of terror and a whoosh of air out of Mano's mouth he was falling amongst them. Dahl and Hayden immediately hopped out, followed quickly by the rest.

Beau ran into the shop.

Drake cast an eye around the area. Minimal escape routes, large crowds. Kenzie appeared at his shoulder.

"Have you seen a proper sword shop around here yet?"

"Umm, no love, I haven't. You sure have no love for the gun."

"Tool me up properly I'm a firecracker."

Drake coughed. "Right. Cheers. I'll remember that one for sure."

With no sign of Amari and the tourists backing off, Hayden ordered an assault of the shop. As one the team bolted, ranging out in a protective shroud. Drake wrenched at the door. Dahl and Smyth barged in, guns up. Hayden followed, then Drake squeezed in an instant before Kinimaka. Inside, the shop was dim, tricking their eyes for several seconds. Drake saw Webb screaming at a man behind the counter. He saw the madman

The Treasures of Saint Germain

rifling through a crate that the proprietor had placed on the counter; vials, packets and small tubs flying everywhere. He saw Webb turn in triumph, clutching a bright red packet.

"Where's the others?" he said. "The ingredients. Quick now."

Drake leveled his gun. Where was . . . ?

The shadow fell upon them as if from out of the skies. Webb shrieked laughter. Beau landed on two feet from his perch above the door, kicked and punched and sent them against one another. Weapons scattered but jackets broke their falls. Webb snatched up another red packet and screamed.

"You don't have the salt? That's the *easiest* component!"

Webb took hold of the man's shirt and used it to throw him aside. Then he bolted around the counter, heading for the back. Beau kicked out at Mai who had just come through the door, sending her backwards into Kenzie. Then, like living smoke, he was gliding after his boss. Drake reached for his gun, forcing down the frustration. Both he and Dahl managed to squeeze off a shot but they were speculative and aimed high because of the fallen shopkeeper.

"What are you idiots trying to do?" Alicia moaned. "Drop a shelf on the bastard's head?"

The team ran; Drake and Dahl racing around the counter, the others filing after them. A narrow passage led to a back door, thrown open. They were forced to slow in case Beau was waiting with another nasty surprise, but then emerged into a small yard that backed straight onto another shop.

Rear door smashed in.

Another race, turning into a chase as they caught sight of Beau streaking through the curio shop ahead. A different door banged aside and then the open street again, barging through pedestrians and crashing through another door and another store. Bright sunlight and dimmed interiors. Blue skies and flashing, multicolored lights.

The team thinned out, then bunched up, then broke for a minute before reforming inside a costume shop. Through this one and then among a large yard filled with Mardi Gras paraphernalia. Twisting between floats and hanging figures that looked like demons; black goats and gaudy men in top hats swaying as if they were alive.

Another sighting of Beau, and then Webb, but an entire, crowded float fell in their way, making the going more difficult. Drake found himself scrabbling over the head of a green dragon whilst Alicia used its long red tongue to pull herself in his wake. Then they clambered over an enormous crocodile wearing a crown, the entire team at their backs.

"Feels like a fuckin' nightmare," Drake muttered.

"Are you kidding?" Alicia panted back. "Did you see the size of that tongue? More like a dream."

There were broken jesters and windowless streetcars, a woman blowing a trumpet. The float went on and on, even more vexing because they could see the yard's exit just ahead. The final obstacles were evil clowns and provoked more than a few screams from Alicia, Lauren and, of course, Kinimaka.

Drake jumped down, sweating a river. The exit door was flung wide. A shop doorway across the street was broken in half, the bottom panel swinging. He cursed. *If only for a clear shot!* He crossed the road, entered the store and saw an unhappy shopkeeper.

"Which way?"

"Out back."

More running and chasing. A brief glimpse of Webb saw him clutching another packet and grinning more evilly than any possessed clown through the ages.

A sprint down a long dissecting street and Drake began to smell the river much more strongly. Their quarry broke right, barged through another store and knocked over another shopkeeper. The team raced hard in pursuit, their sweat spattering the dusty floors behind them. Only twice did Drake achieve clear line of sight for a shot, but passed on both occasions for fear of hitting bystanders or chancing a ricochet. Only once did they venture past other cops, who immediately tagged along. Kimberly Crowe was at the end of the line, finding it hard to keep up.

"Is Webb heading for the river?" Hayden asked aloud. "Is this purposeful?"

"You sure as hell can't land a chopper around here," Smyth said. "And the roads are narrow."

They gatecrashed two more stores, drifting ever closer to the river. Lauren, at the back, had been swiping at her cell. Now she shouted out, "It's easy onto the river around here. There's a Moonwalk, and something like a dock. A steamboat. It's pretty open."

Kenzie had drifted off one store ago and now returned, face flushed. In her right hand she held a katana, in her left a short Ninja sword, both with scabbards. "Now I'm ready for that sausage man." She grinned. "We'll see how he fights without skin."

And, with a certain amount of ceremony, she proffered the ninja sword to Dahl. The Swede looked like he was going to decline, but then saw the formality and hope in her and held out a hand. Quickly, he strapped it to his back, following Kenzie's example. Crowe didn't have the energy to question any of it.

They came out into a street, to their left a wide, scenic view of the mighty Mississippi River.

"That can't be good," Mai said.

Webb and Beau were approaching the water, close enough to still make out the packets clutched in Webb's hand.

To their right a massive contingent of mercenaries poured out of a church doorway, giving chase. Bullets began to form a latticework in the air.

Amari.

Drake said: "Well at least this packs all the zealot parties together. Won't end well though."

"Nah," Alicia said. "It's gonna end bloody. Very bloody."

Dahl included the whole team with one look. "Stay safe, my friends. And pray we all make it through this one."

Drake ran hard, not liking the sudden, unexpected silence all around.

CHAPTER FORTY NINE

Upon the Moonwalk—the well-lit path that ran along the side of the Mississippi at the edge of the French Quarter, affording great views, questionable odors and steady, romantic strolls—a new version of madness erupted.

Beau shepherded Webb to the railings, then turned and flung several unseen objects that took running mercs in the skull and neck and sent them cartwheeling with the force, straight into their colleagues. Drake noted that every bullet fired at Webb went high, and logically deduced that Amari must now know everything.

The Arab was aware that Webb had cracked every clue, collected every ingredient and was closer than anyone in history to concocting a dose of Magnum Opus—the elixir of life. *Now,* Drake thought. *Amari wants it for himself!*

The theory was moot. Webb leapt high, seemingly straight into the muddy waters. Beau swiveled, revolved and rotated in impossible fashion, taking out several mercs before slipping over the railing, still facing the mercs and with arms outstretched, throwing projectiles even as he fell toward the waters.

Drake and the team closed in on the mercs. Amari saw them and screamed out an order.

"Break!"

Drake soon saw what he meant. The mercs didn't turn and trade fire. What they did was to shift as a group to the right and toward a gap in the railings where a narrow dock stretched like a wooden runway toward the Mississippi. Amari ran among them, plus the people Drake remembered as his six acolytes. The whole gang was here. *Good. That makes it all easier.*

A powerful engine started up as Drake reached the railings. Over the top rail he saw Webb and Beau seated in a bright yellow powerboat, the Frenchman pulling at the throttle and the nose lifting into the air. Spray plumed toward him, leaving him sightless as Webb's transport pulled away.

"Always a plan," Smyth growled. "What next?"

"Where's he going?" Mai worried. "Remember the 'all and every resource' line? We haven't seen anything near that yet."

"But now we know how Amari got here," Dahl said, nodding toward the slipway.

A bobbing mass of boats was moored there, crowded together and tapping at each other's sides. Even now mercenaries were clambering from boat to boat, using them as a walkway to get to their own, starting them up and roaring the engines, readying guns and rifles.

Hayden called the authorities. "Police boats," Drake heard her say. "As many as . . . shit, that ain't enough."

"Choppers!" Alicia cried so loudly Drake almost laughed before realizing what she meant. "Yeah," Hayden shouted as she ran ahead. "Bring all yer choppers too."

They hurried onto the dock, grappling with and throwing off the rearguard of mercs. Shots were fired. One man went down with a thigh wound, another with a smashed shoulder. Smyth took a round to the vest. Yorgi almost broke a thumb, wrestling a rifle away from a much larger man.

In the end, when Kenzie approached the dock and slowly unsheathed her sword, the trailing merc contingent turned tail and ran. Alicia, Mai and Kinimaka nipped at their heels, guessing the right way was to introduce them to the Mississippi, preferably head first.

Weapons disappeared and focus was lost. Nobody died. Drake noted that boats were moored to the left and to the right, and the loss of mercs was clearing space among them.

"Stay with the mission." He tapped open his comms. "We're chasing Webb."

To the right they broke and copied the earlier antics of the mercs; walking from bobbing craft to craft, heading fast for the outer vessels. Each was moored to the next so that when Drake found a useable vessel all he had to do was untie a short length of rope.

They occupied four speedboats, started them up and pulled away from the dock. Drake saw a SWAT team scrambling toward more boats and another ranging along the Moonwalk, shouting at Amari and the mercs as if that might put them off. In an act of uncharacteristic intelligence, the mercs didn't fire upon the running SWAT men and began to pull further out into the center of the river.

Webb was already speeding through the murky, rolling waters, passing by a huge white river boat called the *Delta Queen*. As one, about ten of Amari's boats took off in hot pursuit, engines screaming and water parting around them. The mercs held their guns high or over their shoulders, unmasked and uncaring as the bright, hot sun blazed down.

Drake opened the throttle and held on tight, Alicia gripping the windshield as she fixed eyes on their quarry. Three other boats suddenly surrounded him, blasting along at his side, trying to close the gap. Spray and walls of water gave him the best shower he'd had in days.

Alicia's face dripped. "I hate this bloody boat. It's pink, Drake. Fucking pink!"

The Yorkshireman kept a stoic face. "Didn't notice."

" 'Course you did." Alicia blew water away by flapping her lips. "Probably picked it on purpose."

"Why the hell would I do that?" Drake maneuvered into the center of the waterway, powering hard just ten meters away from the trailing Amari boat.

"I dunno. Does it remind you of Sprite?"

Drake spluttered. "For fu—"

"As usual," Hayden's voice interrupted them, "comms are wide open. Thought you would have learned by now."

Alicia shrugged, shedding a waterfall. "Don't care."

"Maybe you should." Drake bent lower, steadied the wheel with one hand and prepped his gun with the other. It was a Heckler & Koch UMP, the lighter, cheaper successor to the MP5. Embraced by various agencies including Border Patrol, it was the easiest weapon for the traveling SPEAR team to lay their hands on at short notice. Still, it provided more stopping power, larger cartridges and was easier to carry. Disadvantages were less accuracy at range and a slower firing rate, but Drake had thought these less important.

Until he jumped on a speedboat, powered down the wide Mississippi, chasing over a dozen other boats loaded with mercs and lunatics, surrounded by his colleagues in a similar position.

Can't plan for everything.

Webb could be seen ahead, laying on the power; Beau watching the chasing teams. Drake teased every ounce of power out of his pink speedboat, glancing across at Dahl who stood at the helm of a lime green craft.

The corners of the Swede's mouth turned up just a little. "If you're nice to them maybe they'll let you borrow the boat at weekends," he purred over the comms.

"Oh, you're so bloody funny I'm gonna crash." Drake looked past the Swede to the other vessels. Hayden and Mai rode a mostly yellow one and appeared cramped with Crowe and two bodyguards installed. Kinimaka, Smyth, Lauren and Yorgi were packed into an orange boat, the Russian piloting whilst the soldiers made ready with H&Ks. Drake's eyes came to rest on the vision of Kenzie, standing upright in the sleek, bouncing boat, arms crossed, the pommel of her sword jutting up over her shoulders.

"Crap, that can't be good," Alicia's voice jerked him back to reality.

Two of Amari's boats had peeled off and were now arcing back around toward the pursuers. Alicia steadied her rifle and Drake made more of a gap between his boat and Dahl's. The last thing they needed was an evasive maneuver resulting in a crash. The first of Amari's boats headed straight for Drake, mercs already firing. The bullets shot wide or skipped into the Mississippi. Alicia lined up her sights.

Both boats sped toward each other at a combined speed of over 80 mph. Smashing against a heavy swell, both boats took flight, their pilots struggling at the wheels, and came bouncing back up for more.

"Drake . . ." Alicia began.

"They ain't stopping, pal." Dahl's voice.

Drake held steady, breathing deeply through his mouth. "Fuck 'em," he said.

The enemy boat was now a gray wedge blocking out the horizon. It was only when Drake saw the fear in the eyes of the mercs most forward and the determined set of the pilot's visage that he realized what was really happening.

"Kamikaze," he cried to warn the others, then wrenched hard at the wheel. Alicia lurched to the side, smashing her shoulder and her head. The stern veered around, skimming off a waterfall, the prow shuddered and struggled to make headway. Drake goosed the throttle. The enemy boat loomed. In another vital moment, Dahl managed to sight his weapon whilst steering, aim, and take out the pilot. The boat skated off course.

And then exploded.

Drake was already low; Alicia knocked to the footwell. Terrible fragments struck their boat and arrowed overhead or flew straight up into the air. Drake had guessed the pilot was wearing a vest, but the action was still shocking.

Dead man's trigger.

The merc boat lay dead in the water, wreckage still crashing down. Drake jumped up and without ceremony opened the throttle. Again, their battered boat raced down the center of the Mississippi.

Amari's second boat aimed for their third in line, coincidentally the yellow one carrying Hayden, Mai and the Secretary of Defense. It was hard for Drake to envision a United States' official of such stature putting herself so deeply in harm's way but then, when she made the light decision to travel to New Orleans and meet the SPEAR team mid-mission, could she really have foreseen what would happen? Even the chase through the French Quarter didn't set a person up for a powerboat battle along the third biggest watershed in the world.

This time the enemy pilot lived as Mai sent their boat curving wide one way and then back around. Drake could see mercs screaming at the man who held the wheel, then tearing his jacket apart and flinching, shocked to see the dynamite strapped to his chest. Some headed overboard at that point but the pilot blew himself up anyway, sending the shattered boat into the air and then reeling back down.

"Amari has his fanatics with him," Drake said soberly. "That's our warning."

Kinimaka's boat was closing in on Amari's last in line, close enough to exchange fire. The Hawaiian's boat skipped skew-whiff on an errant wave but he managed to manhandle it back into place. Smyth fired carefully, each bullet a pop at timed intervals. Mercs fell, gouting blood. Return fire sent Lauren and Yorgi to the floor, the thief losing his grip on his new Glock. Kinimaka plowed on and Smyth managed to take out the pilot. Mercs fell all around and some plunged overboard as the craft lost momentum.

Kinimaka powered past. They couldn't afford to lose a single second. Webb raced ahead with no obstructions, though Amari in the lead boat might be slowly catching him. The Arabs did this every day back home, it seemed, giving them a slight advantage, though never on a river as mighty as this.

"Still no sign of Webb's resources," Drake muttered.

"No, but ours are on their way," Hayden shouted back over engine and water roar.

Drake looked up and back, saw choppers pounding at the skies and a veritable flotilla of new vessels shooting along behind.

"If Webb thought this was an escape route, it seems the asshole was a little mistaken."

"But Webb's nowhere to be seen." Lauren was using field glasses. "Beau is driving the boat."

Drake squinted. Indeed, only one man could be seen aboard the lead boat. Hayden voiced her opinion. "He's so desperate he's already making the potion," she said. "That's my bet, guys. Whatever he believes it will infuse within him, I don't know, but that's what he's doing."

"Immortality?" Lauren offered. "Invisibility?"

"Ooh, I'd love me some of that." Alicia rubbed the side of her head. "Bloody Sprite wouldn't know what hit her. And Samurai Sheila." She stared at Kenzie, then affected a fake expression of shock. "Oh, shit. Did I say that out loud? Over the comms?"

Mai gave nothing in return. Kenzie glanced over with speculative eyes. "So nothing has changed, eh Alicia? Maybe, just maybe, one day, you will need me to help save your life."

"Unlikely."

"Then . . . we shall see who mocks who."

"I will never—"

Drake shut it down. "On mission," he grated. "We have world security threats to deal with."

Kinimaka's and Dahl's boats were now darting amongst the mercs'. The Swede broadsided one, sending it veering into a third, glass fiber and steel falling away. Kinimaka slammed into the rear third of another, making the front end spin around and sending three mercs flying, akimbo, into the river's hungry belly.

An enemy vessel swung around and came at Dahl hard. Drake was close now, almost touching the Swede's stern. A head-on crash was looking likely. More sacrifices by Amari, though this pilot was clearly a regular merc.

Dahl braced andABkenzie slipped down into her seat. Mercs cried out frantically and Drake slowed. Hayden appeared to the right, running broadside. As the vessels almost came together, Hayden's yellow boat collided with the back of the mercs', physically wrenching it aside. Dahl's boat shot through the clear water and Hayden swung a long right to rejoin the chase, her prow tattered but holding up.

The mercs were dead in the water, capable only of waiting to be picked up.

Drake closed in on the rear of the next boat as Alicia fired her H&K. Smyth let loose his Glock, and Mai picked mercs off one by one. Above, choppers had started to crowd the skies and motor boats pounded the waves in pursuit. Ahead, Amari led the charge after Webb with the set face and shouted threats of a fanatic.

And Webb himself, crouched low, was already mixing together the first component of the alchemical mixture that the Scroll of Leopold and Saint Germain's strict roster of clues revealed was the only true way to prepare the greatest treasure ever imagined—the elixir of life.

CHAPTER FIFTY

The great swell of the Mississippi River had never seen nor heard the like of it. As soldiers, Drake and the SPEAR team stood often at death's door. Most of the time they cheated it. But there were no illusions in Drake's mind. Nobody cheated death forever.

Nobody.

A final chapter was coming, maybe not this year but soon enough, when they would all stand and die together. He did not fear it. A man or woman couldn't live this life forever and he just couldn't see himself willingly resigning. So what was the alternative?

Skipping now from swell to swell, he counted off the boats. Webb's, and then six of Amari's and four of their own. All battered. The waters were vicious and deadly. Amari's mercenaries swept wide every now and then to squeeze off several submachine gun rounds, spiking the air with lead. Kinimaka and Dahl swept with them, picking off the odd body but making very little headway.

The mighty river curved gracefully to the right and then the left, a vast curvature of undulating water bordered by grass banks and levees, docks and busy yards. Its enormous width spanned their horizons, its murk growing only darker as the sun passed its zenith. Drake studied the skylines ahead and to the sides, always conscious that Webb had a plan and potential reinforcements.

How does he intend to escape?

Rotors chopped above and motorboats raced behind, all loaded with different versions of law enforcement. One of the mercs tried lobbing a grenade at Dahl's boat but it fell short and succeeded only in soaking the Swede and the Israeli. Dahl shot the man through the shoulder and nobody tried it again.

"Can't you make this thing go any faster?" Alicia complained.

"We'll be on here all day at this rate."

"Oh sure," Drake said. "I'll just flip the switch on the nitrous."

"I don't even know what that means."

"Shit, one day we're gonna have to get you down for a Fast and Furious fest."

"Isn't that what we do every night? Sometimes twice?"

Drake shook his head slowly. Alicia gripped his shoulder tight. To their right the boat containing Hayden, Mai and the Secretary of Defense skimmed the surface of the Mississippi. Drake saw Kimberly Crowe crouched down low, her two bodyguards around her. Yes, she had somehow managed to insert herself into the midst of all this mess, but he couldn't knock her courage.

"Can you transfer the Secretary out?" he asked Hayden through the comms.

"Maybe," came the reply. "But I'm loathe to start the maneuver when we're blind as to what comes next."

"Send the choppers in," Dahl said. "Blast 'em all out of the water."

Drake saw Hayden nod. "I think it's coming to that."

Another one of Amari's boats broke away, this one bowing to the left and coming right around. It sped hard at Drake's boat, its arrow-shaped prow aiming to cut him in half, but at an order from Hayden one of the SWAT choppers swooped low and opened fire. The boat exploded into detonating fragments, still coasting forward as it shattered. A plume of fire and smoke marked its death.

Drake didn't give it a second glance. Webb was turning.

"Wait. What's he doing?"

Beyond Amari, the lead boat appeared to have left it extremely late to turn, so sharp was the angle Beau made it achieve. The whole vessel canted sideways, the spray curling out from underneath.

The SPEAR team reacted instantaneously, following Beau's maneuver, then Amari began shouting orders across the rolling swells. The movements put Drake's boat alongside one of the mercs'. Alicia fired her gun twice, sending two mercs into the

Mississippi before return fire was made. Bullets slammed into their hull and glanced across the windshield. Drake swerved to the side. Alicia held on and wounded another merc. The boats came together hard, slamming hulls with a crash that left widening cracks and a flood of water.

"We're going down," Drake said.

Alicia stared at the foam filling the boat and her boots. "Now I have wet feet. Fucksake, Drake, get a grip."

The Yorkshireman swore. He was skimming along at full speed as the water poured in, not only into the boat but into the engine too, aiming for a sandbar that bordered the place where Beau was headed. A merc leaned out, handgun raised, but Alicia knocked it aside as they closed up once more, smashing him in the face for good measure. Drake flicked a glance off the horizon and spotted exactly what Beau was speeding toward.

"We need to get ashore anyway, guys. The water is killing the engine."

Kinimaka's voice hit the comms at exactly the same time. "Guys, is that a private airport?"

"Has to be," Smyth growled. "It sure as hell ain't public. Lauren can barely see it on the map."

Makes sense, Drake thought. In a perfect world Webb's short hop over the Mississippi from the French Quarter couldn't have been easier. And then . . . airborne. Private flights meant questionable flight plans and the potential for disappearing completely, depending where you landed.

Alicia fired again. Water covered Drake's boots, and the boat wallowed. He flicked at the throat mic.

"We're about to crash. Or sink. Or both."

Dahl replied. "Stop whining. Just send us a bloody postcard."

Drake wrestled hard with the wheel, steering them straight at the sandbar. The hull struck hard, the momentum sending them airborne. Water streamed off the boat as it cleared the raised finger of sand, many meters higher than the pursuing merc boat. Drake saw a SWAT guy leaning over the skids of his helicopter, sighting on the merc boat, and firing as he flew past. The bullet took out the pilot and sent the boat veering madly. Drake's came down hard.

"Now there's a copper who can use his chopper . . ." Alicia said, then grunted and huffed as the hull grinded and bounced. The boat's momentum sent it skidding into the bank and, as it hit, Drake and Alicia jumped ashore. They tucked and rolled but still landed heavily, bruised and bleeding around the face. Drake rose and looked around.

The speedboats were racing toward a makeshift dock. Beau and Webb were already there, the American jumping ashore and clutching a heavy leather satchel in one hand. Webb looked both haggard and ecstatic, a man reaching the end of a long quest. Coming up to the dock now was Amari and his boats full of mercs and acolytes.

Drake and Alicia ran hard along the muddy bank, trying to cut their enemies off. Two choppers blasted overhead, reconnoitering the airport, but Drake had no link to their comms. The area was screened by a row of trees.

Shots were already being fired. Hopeful attempts to bring down Webb or Beau before they reached their plane. Surely they realized that the game was up. No way would they be allowed to get airborne.

Hayden came over the comms. "I see Webb running through a gate and into some kind of compound at the rear of the airport. Locking it. Amari's closing in. Shooting the lock off. Drake, be careful, you're just a few feet away."

Screened by the treeline, Drake and Alicia crept around the last of the thick reaching branches. He counted roughly twenty mercs and four acolytes, dressed in white, and Amari. The airport's rear security gate had been destroyed and now the mercs were filing through, spreading out into the compound. Drake saw grounded helicopters and the wings of planes and two large hangars. He slipped around the corner.

Hayden called for them to wait then, eight seconds later, pounded up with the entire team. She turned to Kimberly Crowe.

"Please. Wait here."

The Secretary remained still. "Not a problem."

It would have to suffice. The SPEAR team rushed toward the rear gate and the backs of the sprinting mercs. Webb was already crossing the center of the compound toward a large contingent of men. Activity was everywhere ahead of him, men jumping in and out of choppers, ground teams rushing to help, rotors warming up. Even a small jet was roaring its twin engines.

All and every resource.

Drake looked from Webb's army to Amari's mercs, the police and SWAT helicopters hovering overhead, and the firepower all around. To jump right into the center of this madness would be like leaping into an active volcano.

Nevertheless, the SPEAR team did it with gusto.

CHAPTER FIFTY ONE

"If I die today I hope that I do it well. If I survive this day I hope that I see my loved ones once more. If my friends and colleagues stand over my lifeless body at the end of all this I hope that they stand strong. And remember me, my family. Remember my vital heart, my sense of excitement, my glittering eyes. I am now only a memory but still, in you, I live on. I can live forever."

Kinimaka chanted the words softly as they ran toward the great battlefield.

Drake blinked what could only be river water from his eyes. "Seems a bit long for a proverb, mate."

"I wrote it when my mother died," he said. "And think it through whenever our friends have died. Today seems like a good day for great songs."

Before anyone could respond, all hell broke loose. Not one event was limited to a single lifespan though. Through Drake's eyes the amalgamation of violence and intense action was a non-stop, severely lethal rollercoaster ride. Webb ran for his waiting choppers, which were lined up four in a row. His own ranks of mercenaries thundered past, firing into Amari's troops. The Arab dived for cover. SWAT choppers swooped down from above, men hanging out of doors and sending volleys of lead into the pitch battle. Oil cans, vehicles and crates were scattered everywhere, enabling soldiers and mercenaries to scramble for cover.

Drake saw Beau urging Webb toward the first helicopter in line, its rotors already sending out a huge wash. That was fine. When Webb had boarded and it started to lift, Drake shot the pilot.

The black beast crashed back down, landing hard on both skids. Beau dived inside and manhandled Webb out. Drake saw Hayden loose another shot in their direction. A guard went down. The SWAT chopper plunged in again, raking a trail through the mercenaries, but now another contingent were lining up an RPG, forcing the chopper to veer away. Smyth managed to clip the missile launcher before it fired.

Other choppers were also ready to fly, three more at the far side of the airfield and two nearby. The sleek gray jet was taxiing slowly to line up its nose with the runway. Webb could break in any direction, but Drake still couldn't see how he could escape.

Then three more RPGs appeared and the skies were laced with white smoke and death.

Amari's mercs fought hand to hand with Webb's; punched, kicked and knifed in the back. Shots were fired around containers, bullets crisscrossing the compound. Drake, Alicia and Dahl drove into the back of Amari's mercs. Drake bruised a neck and then ribs, spun his enemies around and knocked one unconscious. The other wouldn't give in, produced a knife and looked shocked when it ended up stuck in his own abdomen.

Dahl threw his man against a crate, smashing it to bits and then had to duck fast behind another. Alicia used the bits of sharpened wood he'd just made to fend off her own attacker. Her H&K then whipped left and right, lining up mercs and taking them down. Two she dispatched just as they drew a bead on her and then ducked behind an oil drum, tempting fate no further. Kinimaka was watching Amari as the cult leader scuttled toward the jet plane. Hayden had eyes only for Webb.

"Second bird," she said. "He's on board."

Drake couldn't see the man or Beau, but let loose a salvo that damaged the rotors. Webb emerged shouting a moment later, and pointed at their hiding places. Immediately, two RPGs were trained upon them. Warning shouts came and the team were running by the time the drums and crates erupted in walls of smoke and flame.

Lauren hit the ground, toppled by the shockwave. Yorgi staggered head-first until coming up against Kinimaka's bulk, which stopped him. A SWAT helicopter ventured closer now, its men firing on the RPG launchers. Drake waved for it to retreat but it was already too late. The first missile hit its underside and brought it down, mercifully intact, its occupants shaken but alive.

The chopper bounced and juddered, scraping against the concrete.

Smyth rose and shot the man holding the rocket launcher, then shook his head. "Always another stupid enough to take it up."

"Then shoot 'em all," Kenzie said.

A swell of struggling mercenaries surged into their group. Drake found himself pushing away two fighting men whilst trying to watch Webb and Beau. Dahl and Alicia stayed beside him. Hayden pushed forward, tracking Amari and his acolytes, tailed by Kinimaka, Smyth and Yorgi. A knot of mercs came between the two parties.

Drake shot a merc up close then felled another. One of Webb's and one of Amari's. The third chopper was lifting off, but Drake had already seen it was a ruse. Webb and Beau sprinted amid a crowd, straight for the plane.

The jet itself was closing the gap too, angling for the apex of the runway. Fore and aft doors were wide open, currently filled by two big bulks toting RPGs. SWAT helicopters shied away.

The noise was tremendous. Rotor roar combined with gunfire and the screams of men, punctuated with occasional crashing thunder from the jet and the low grunts of men locked in deadly combat. Drake saw a gap and ran for it, angling for Webb, only thirty meters separating them now. Webb carried his precious satchel. Dahl was there, and Alicia too, running interference to left and right.

Beau, part of the shield around Webb, saw them coming and shouted at his guards. As one, eight men broke off and stood against the three. Drake didn't slow, just hit them head on, firing and taking a round in the chest that sent him sideways. Always fast to recover from injury, taking a bullet to the vest was nevertheless a stunning blow, leaving him on his knees and gasping. Two mercs stood over him, faces grim.

"Do not hesitate!" Beau screamed at them.

They squeezed their triggers but at that moment Kenzie was upon them. The Israeli was a vision of death in artistry, her katana falling and slicing this way and that, and her body rotating twice. When the mercs lay dead she held out a hand.

"Cheers," Drake said.

"Cold-blooded killers deserve a violent end," she said. "And I am happy to oblige."

Mai stood nearby, throwing off another guard. "Are you hurt?"

"Well, my nipples do smart a bit."

"He's fine," Alicia said. "We eat bullets for breakfast."

Before anyone could respond, Dahl threw two mercs toward them. "Stop gibbering and finish these two boys off, would you? I have my hands full." The Swede punched two more, breaking bones, a nose and a kneecap. One huge forearm knocked a man's jaw out of line in a spray of incisors. When they all looked up, Webb was climbing the hastily lowered steps of the plane.

Beau was waiting on the tarmac, staring at the SPEAR team as the plane swallowed his boss and then started to taxi away again.

Hayden was closing in on Amari.

The final RPG-toting man had been taken out and now two more SWAT choppers were swooping toward the bunch of struggling mercs. Angry voices shouted down through loudspeakers, warning the fighters to stand down, instructing them to lower their weapons.

Drake couldn't shake off Kinimaka's words: *If I die today I hope . . .*

CHAPTER FIFTY TWO

Hayden fought in the burning pit.

With the raging sunlight beating down from above, the melting asphalt radiating it from below and the glaring brightness all around, she battled her way close to Amari. The Arab and his remaining four acolytes were weak but crazed, untrained but desperate, which made them as dangerous as their mercs in her eyes. No telling what they might do.

She leapt at a man with a facial scar and goatee beard, fired first and sensed him fall away. Her vision filled with another jacket, another merc, always another. Kinimaka moved between crates and drums to her right and Smyth to her left. Lauren and Yorgi were paces behind. Hayden came around another metal barrel, ducked a blow and fell backwards.

Kinimaka took the merc out as he strode after her. She picked herself up, moved forward. A chopper skimmed low overhead. A bullet zipped right through an oil drum, ricocheting past both her and Smyth before either could blink, spilling out viscous liquid in a thick stream. They reached the end of the barrels and Amari was right before them, facing away, facing the jet that carried Tyler Webb.

"Stop it! Stop that plane!"

His acolytes screamed and surged forward, a cluster of grenades held in their hands.

"The Ascended Master must not be disturbed!"

Four acolytes, four men loyal to Amari and his madness, held the grenades aloft.

"Master of Alchemy! Mystic Adventurer! Masonic Guide! I implore your forgiveness for I have failed you!"

Pins were pulled. One grenade in each man's hand to make eight in total. They would either hurl them or run onto the plane with them. Their dice were cast long ago.

The Treasures of Saint Germain

Smyth was on one knee. "All we need is the front runner."

He breathed, let it escape, and then fired. His bullet took off the top of the lead man's head, sending his body sprawling and his primed grenade bouncing. Anyone close by scattered except for the other acolytes. Their mission was divine . . . and blind.

Two grenades exploded, shrapnel shredding the remaining three acolytes in their steps and sending their own bombs into the air. Then came explosion after explosion, flames gouting and fragments flying. Amari watched it all with an open mouth and a face awash with tears. Whether for his friends or for the Count Saint Germain, Hayden knew not.

Amari turned to her, shrieking.

Hayden trained her weapon and stepped forward.

Amari ripped open the front of his shirt to reveal wires, dynamite, and duct tape.

"No! We can—"

Kinimaka flung his entire bulk over her as Amari detonated both the bomb, and himself.

CHAPTER FIFTY THREE

Hayden felt Kinimaka's body buffeted by shrapnel. She could barely breathe as his full weight pressed down upon her. Not a sliver of that glaring light shone through; she lay in a safe cocoon of darkness amid the mayhem. Time went by, and then the bulk was pulled off her. Hayden looked up into the dying day.

"Mano?"

Lauren fell to her knees. "He's . . . he's . . ."

"I'm okay," came the rumble of his voice. "Battered, but okay."

Hayden swallowed in relief, then sat up. The scene all around them was gory, the crates and oil drums devastated. Liquid leaked along the ground in streams and all manner of objects spilled from the crates. Smyth fell beside Lauren.

"You okay?"

"Yeah, I'm good."

Kinimaka crawled up to Hayden. "Good to be alive."

But then Hayden reached out, grabbed him by the jacket and pulled him close. Their eyes were inches apart, their noses brushing. She could feel the beat of his heart, the warmth of his skin, and the blood that trickled from his wounds straight onto hers.

"Stop saving me, Mano."

"I don't . . . I . . . I . . ."

"Get it through your head. We're done. Stop hovering, following and shielding. It's why I went to Dubai without you. To get some damn space."

"I saved your life. I . . ."

"Maybe. Maybe not." Hayden knew then that there would never be a time as meaningful, as piercing as this. If she wanted clear of the Hawaiian then she would have to use this moment, this event which he'd clearly hoped would reunite their affections, to take it well beyond the point of no return.

The Treasures of Saint Germain

"I don't fuck rule followers, Mano. I only fuck the winners who break 'em."

The Hawaiian stared in shock, in horror. Smyth and Lauren turned quickly away and Yorgi pretended he hadn't heard a thing. Hayden dusted herself off and stood alone. Her eyes, misted with tears, surveyed the battleground.

"Get your asses into gear, guys. We ain't done yet."

CHAPTER FIFTY FOUR

Drake and Dahl struck the remnants of Webb's mercs hard as Alicia, Mai and Kenzie raced past. The jet was moving a little faster now, still trying to taxi to the right position for the runway. Beau hadn't moved, and was clearly the last line of defense as Webb no doubt continued to mix his potions.

So Beau would die for Webb's cause? Drake couldn't comprehend it.

Dahl ducked behind a girder fixed into the ground at the end of a hangar. Bullets ricocheted past, sending sparks into his exposed cheeks. He fired around the girder, blindly. Drake peered out low, almost prone. The angle confused the mercs and he took two out.

"Last one," Dahl said.

Help came from the skies as a chopper descended fast, men firing on the mercs' hiding place. A scream and a thud and someone yelled "all clear" and Drake emerged at pace. The chopper disgorged its SWAT contingent.

Drake saw the women converging on Beau and took only one second to consider the volatile three-way melting pot seething around that confrontation, before noting a change in the jet's engine note.

"Now that can't be good," Dahl muttered.

"Summat's not reet," Drake intoned a little broad Yorkshire.

"The nose is all lined up," Dahl said. "You ready for a sprint?"

"Balls, it feels like I've been sprinting all day."

"You beat me, I'll teach you how to drive a boat!"

"Hey—"

But Dahl was already off, running directly for the plane as it taxied away. Drake accelerated as best he could, chest still throbbing from the bullet's impact. A couple of the SWAT guys joined them and the chopper pilot decided they might need a little backup, especially if the plane got away. He lifted his skids and glided along at their side, now the pace vehicle of their race or a goal to reach.

Drake and Dahl came up to the plane fast, running alongside, but within seconds it had started to pull away.

Both doors were latched shut, but then the one just behind the wings cracked open and a tattooed hand appeared, holding a gun. Bullets flew haphazardly, not aimed but intentionally causing concern among the runners. Drake tried to aim his rifle then his handgun, but the jogging destroyed his aim.

"Fuselage," Dahl suggested. "Cockpit."

Engines roared.

"No time!"

Drake knew he needed to get closer. Without hesitation he leapt for the wings, seeing the open door and the unseeing arm as a way inside. The only way. His jump was timed just right. As he landed on the rounded edge of the wing and grappled for the flaps to pull his body up, the plane accelerated again, leaving Dahl's jump two feet too short. The Swede hit the asphalt hard.

Drake worked his fingers into the flap, praying it wouldn't close, and heaved his body upward. First chest, then hips, then knees; he wriggled and hoisted his bulk onto the smooth wing. Rushing air battered him like a living thing, like an enemy. Loose clothing flapped and tried to throw him clear, and at this speed falling onto the runway would be a killing blow.

Drake crouched and looked back, saw Dahl picking himself up and signaling the chopper. Then he stared at the door. The huge arm was still there, popping off shots at random. Steadily, he crab-walked up the wing toward the plane, careful to keep his footing and lean into the tearing wind.

Dahl's voice crackled through the comms. "Problem, mate. They're not going to let the plane take off. They're gonna destroy it rather than risk Webb escaping. You have only a little time to get clear."

Drake cursed. The decision had been made only when the plane hit a certain speed. There was now a real chance it could achieve a clean take-off and the next step was fighter jets shooting it down in the air—which nobody wanted to risk. Drake clambered forward another three steps.

"Is it your bird alongside?"

"Yeah. We have missiles."

The Swede sounded happy at that. Drake cursed.

"Mate," Dahl said. "You have less than two minutes and then we destroy the plane."

Alicia came to a deliberate slow halt as she approached Beau. There was no recognition on the Frenchman's face, no glow of guilt nor flicker of regret. She knew he would likely kill her, but didn't falter for a second.

It was ironic then when the two people she found backing her up were Mai Kitano and Kenzie. Of all her colleagues around the world these were the two she least trusted and had most contention with. She backed away from Beau a little if only to catch their eyes.

"You're kidding me here, right?"

"This man can only be beaten by a team," Mai said. "Acting together. Today, that is us."

"No enemies here," Kenzie said. "For today then."

Alicia felt a rush of pride, of companionship. Together, they would prevail against the unbeatable. She met the dead eyes of the Frenchman.

"Better go fetch your armor, motherfucker. You're gonna need it."

They burst into motion. Mai took Beau head on, her Ninja skills as lightning fast as his own. Alicia came in from the left, striking suddenly and as hard as steel. Kenzie jostled to the right, swirling her katana in a blur as much to distract Beau as to assail him.

If they were hoping Beau would fold quickly or have a bad moment they were disappointed. The slim body weaved and slid among them, smoke in motion once more, and sent out finger strikes like knife blades and punches as hard as boulders.

Mai deflected a throwing star that Alicia didn't even see until it hit the ground. Kenzie struck downwards with her katana but then held it, shuddering, in mid-air as Beau somehow managed to push Mai's arm into its arc. The freeze motion left her open to a triple strike, sending her to her knees, gasping and groaning, the sword lying on the floor.

Beau skipped around her, using her shoulders to shift a straight run into a pivot and spin, landing both feet on Alicia's stomach and sending her tumbling. Mai faced him then, jabbing and striking and dealing out kicks that would fell a lion. Beau took them and gave back even more, bruising Mai's ribcage and thigh bones, making the recently healed scar across her face burn brightly.

Another shuriken saw light, whipped underhand and embedding its razor-sharp blades into Mai's wrist as she flung a hand before her face. The Japanese woman left it there and flung herself at him, striking with the wounded arm, Beau's own shuriken blade slamming down into his skull. The blades bit and blood flowed. Beau staggered away.

"First blood," Mai said. "To me." For now the shuriken had closed its own wound.

With Beau falling back, Kenzie rose and came forward with the katana. A feint to the left, a double spin of the blade to the right and then she struck hard and fast, straight at the man's nose.

Beau held up an arm to ward the deadly blade off.

Kenzie brought it down grimly, sparing him no mercy. Her mouth fell open in shock when the katana struck Beau's arm, but instead of severing the limb, it only glanced away. For the first time Beau gave her a tiny smirk.

"You are no match for—"

Alicia was having none of it. She blitzed her former lover, hitting every part of his body she could reach, bloodying his nose and breaking a finger. He twisted an ankle as he fell to one knee, then thrust with an uppercut that left her jaw shaking and brought blood from her gums. Alicia spat the red into his face. Beau punched her so hard she fell to the ground. Her own previously shed blood smeared her face.

Mai hit out at Beau twice more, the embedded shuriken

tearing the flesh from his cheek right down to the bone. Then Kenzie struck fast, the katana slices sending him stumbling away and, finally, looking worried.

Alicia crawled after him, snagging an ankle as he tried to skip away. Her outstretched arm tripped him. Mai came down knees first onto his solar plexus, a finger jab simultaneously smashing his exposed throat so hard he wouldn't speak for a week. Then Kenzie struck third and with perfect timing, the katana unsteady in her bruised hands and the pommel catching him squarely on the forehead.

Beauregard Alain lay beaten, defeated. Alicia tried to stand but her legs were jelly. Mai swayed in place. Kenzie looked over at both of them.

"What . . . what do we do now?"

"Tie the idiot up," Alicia panted. "They'll want to know why he defected. Twice."

"And you?"

Alicia made a face. "The old me would like to see his French onions sliced. But *new* me? She says put the asshole behind bars."

"With what?" Kenzie said quickly. "I don't carry cuffs, do you?"

"Nah, only for pleasure." Alicia rested on her knees.

The defeated Beau came for them again. Rising up, he dismounted Mai, then undulated himself like a snake across the ground, finishing with a kick that took skin from Alicia's cheek and whipped her head to the side. Scissor-kicking his body upright, he landed on two feet and faced a shocked Kenzie.

Plucked the sword from her hands.

Alicia stared up at the indomitable figure. "Beau," she said. "Why?"

He paused then, blood coating his face and the gleam of bone showing through, his brow matted with sweat. "Ask Michael Crouch," he said. "He is the key."

Alicia stared. Crouch was Drake's old boss and her new one; the well-loved, well-respected, ex-leader of the British Ninth Division. No man stood higher in her opinion. "What does that mean?"

The Treasures of Saint Germain

Beau didn't answer. He threw Kenzie's katana twirling into the air and caught its pommel on the way down. Then he struck left and right at her, diagonal slashes that almost shaved the hairs from her arms. Alicia jumped up with a surge of adrenalin.

Mai screamed as she ripped the shuriken from her wrist. Blood spurted forth in fountains, splashing the ground. But she ran for Beau then, ducked under his katana thrust, and buried the metal star through the meat of his throat. Beau dropped the sword and then all three women fell too; exhausted, bloodied and beaten.

But winners.

Alicia's eyes finally refocused and found the final battle. "What the fuck is that? Hey girls, there's a movie title right there."

Kenzie shielded her eyes. "What?"

"Drake's on a plane."

CHAPTER FIFTY FIVE

Drake inched his way steadily toward the hull, feet slipping beneath him. He was down to one minute thirty left. The jet rushed along at breakneck speed. Drake held onto the window mountings, then envisioned sliding down the wind to grab hold of the door. A tricky maneuver when the plane was stationary, let alone zooming toward take-off speed.

"Fifty seconds." Dahl's voice.

"Crap, I need more time."

A face moved in the window, catching sight of him, and the arm moved around the door, pointing the gun in his direction. The window face belonged to Tyler Webb and was huge and grinning. The red satchel appeared, held up like a trophy. A steaming goblet came into view, smoke trailing from the rim. Webb opened his mouth into the widest of crazy grins. Drake read the flapping lips.

"I told you! I told you I would kill one of you today!"

The gun discharged. The bullet whipped past.

"To me and my everlasting future!" Webb quaffed the mixture.

Drake flung his body backwards. A second shot flew overhead.

"Blow it!" Drake cried. "Blow the goddamn plane. We can't let this maniac get free again."

Dahl came back: "On three. But what about you?"

"Just bring me that bloody chopper."

The helicopter spun a quarter circle in mid-air. The jet thundered down the runway, its wheels pounding the ground and its engines roaring like trapped monsters. The shooter fired again. Drake ran hell for leather along the wing of the plane.

He had no intention of stopping.

The helicopter fired its arsenal, three missiles together screaming into the front of the plane. The area of impact disintegrated in less than a second, replaced by fire. A flaming plume of red and black billowed down the length of the plane, smashing out windows and melting the substructure, obliterating everything in its path. The entire body was engulfed, many parts flying and fragmenting off.

Drake's headlong sprint came to an end as the plane blew up. Metal drooped beneath him as the wing collapsed. A split instant past the very last moment he leapt high, the flames chasing his back. The lowest part of the chopper was its skid. Drake's hands wrapped around the smooth metal, gripping hard and arresting the momentum in his body. Fire chased him—flickering tongues of flame licking his back, setting his jacket alight and singeing the back of his head. Drake screamed as the fire caressed his skin. The pilot swing the chopper away from the blast but it was already receding, its energy spent. Drake hung on grimly, eyes closed against the agony, fingers holding on until they could clasp no longer.

Then he fell. Hit the ground and folded. The devastated airplane drifted to the right, off the runway, a shattered shell engulfed in fire. Webb was inside that and forever gone now, his twisted schemes all destroyed with him. Drake tried to look up as footsteps pounded toward him.

Dahl.

"You fucking knobhead! What were you thinking? Hey, you're still on bloody fire!"

Something flapped at his back. Drake felt the heat subside but the agony lived on. Was he drifting away? Was it all too much? Truth be told, it didn't matter. He trusted his team, his family, more than he had ever trusted any soul in the world. They would take the best care of him.

More bodies surrounded him and he heard the voices of Alicia and Mai, strangely difficult to tear them apart. He felt deep hope that Kinimaka wouldn't stumble over him. He heard Dahl's voice again.

"Get up, dickhead. The vest saved you. It's just the hair on your thick skull that got a little scorched. Drake?"

Touched by the clear concern hidden beneath the usual

insensitive veneer, Drake pushed his hands underneath his body and pushed hard. Reality set back in. He lay at the center of a circle, shielded by his team, choppers landing all around and cops and medics rushing up. Everyone had injuries. Mai dripped blood in streams but still stood shoulder to shoulder with Alicia, being supported by the Englishwoman and Kenzie. Drake wished that it could always be so.

Today. Not tomorrow.

The whole team were together. Webb had not fulfilled his own prophecy after all. He thought again of Kinimaka's song.

I see my loved ones again. All of them. Drake felt truly blessed.

He turned to Dahl. "Are we done?"

Hayden answered for the Swede. "There's just one more bit of intrigue and mystery we have to solve. Then, we all get a day off."

"And where's that?"

"The house of Saint Germain."

CHAPTER FIFTY SIX

Rested, re-clothed to some degree and recuperated to another, the SPEAR team headed back to New Orleans' French Quarter. With all the unfriendly parties either leaderless or captured, the resistance had been stamped out. The cultists were gone forever; the surviving mercenaries in custody. Another threat removed from the world. The entire team had been patched and bandaged, fed painkillers and even stitched. And, on an uplifting note, they had learned that Sabrina Balboni had survived her operations and would make a full recovery, given time.

Everyone moved gingerly as they walked up the middle of Bourbon Street, giving groups of tourists a wide berth.

Hayden looked tired. "A reverse trace of Webb's movements through New Orleans showed him first visiting this area," she said. "And in particular—that house."

Drake stared at an unassuming structure, two-story with white shutters and a small parking garage nearby. Plant pots lined the windows. Even the door locks shone like new. Alicia tapped Hayden's shoulder.

"Why are we here?"

"Webb came to this house for a reason. Don't you want to know what it was?"

Lauren stepped forward. "We know from our research that the fanatics thought Saint Germain was still alive and living in New Orleans. Are you saying this is his house?"

"Again—" Hayden smiled "—why else would Webb come here?"

"The final clue," Mai said.

"From Germain himself?" Drake laughed.

"If not the man," Hayden spread her hands, "then maybe from the place he lived." She shrugged. "There is often a nugget of truth in legend. If Germain did come here then maybe he left a clue behind."

They searched high and low; they ransacked the modern, pristine furniture and the unmarked walls and pictures. They checked for hidden passages and false walls, a basement and an attic. If Tyler Webb had indeed visited these premises then he'd done so with the utmost respect, another oddity. They gathered as a team in the sitting room.

"Nothing," Smyth grumbled.

"A shame," Hayden said. "And a surprise. You know—Amari became obsessed with the legend of Saint Germain whilst being privately educated around Europe. Took the fixation home with him and fanned it until it turned into something horrible. Now, that's all gone. Whatever he knew—lost. "

"And why the quest?" Smyth asked. "Why not skip to the end of that friggin' scroll and come straight to New Orleans?"

"The treasures along the way *pointed* the way," Hayden said. "You can't achieve one without achieving the other. Linguistics helped translate the later-found composition. Alchemy helped mix the potion. Freemasonry opened more doors. From one you beget the next."

"So the mystery of Saint Germain lives on?" Lauren asked.

"Some legends never die. Many will outlive every one of us."

Drake winced in pain. Mai touched her cheek and Alicia hobbled over to a sofa. "That won't be too hard."

"Weirdly though," Lauren said. "This house is actually over two hundred years old."

"Where? Every fitting looks new." Hayden looked stumped.

"And even more interestingly it was built around 1780; the same period history tells us Germain was negotiating truces and helping to install new kings. Many of the buildings around here were built around that time."

"You trying to spook me out?" Smyth smiled. " 'Cause it ain't working."

"Do you realize something?" Dahl said. "The reign of the Pythians is finally over. They're all gone and Webb is dead. Can I get a high five?" He searched for a raised hand among his injured friends and saw none. "Maybe later."

"We've neutralized most of the known threats now," Drake

said. "Maybe we'll grab some downtime."

"Whatever you do," Dahl put in. "Do not go on vacation."

Laughter broke out, followed by groans. Kenzie held her ribs. Hayden looked around at the little group.

"Back to reality."

Drake felt uncertainty creep back in. Nothing was resolved for them personally. Alicia and Mai had issues; as did Hayden and Kinimaka. Smyth and Lauren were battling over the prisoner, Nicholas Bell. Even Drake thought the New Yorker had a soft spot for the terrorist. Kenzie loved Dahl.

He grinned. *I can work with that.* They talked briefly of the new Secretary and her ballsy attitude, of how she had faded rightly to the background when the battle elevated to new heights, of the secret base and the new location. They wondered if anything would change. Kinimaka said nothing—it was almost as if he was already gone.

Change was coming.

Drake looked up and saw something that resembled a face staring at them from the top of the stairs. White and middle-aged, he knew that face. His heart pounded. It was the janitor from the German hospital. He started to cry out a warning and then the face was gone, merged into the background.

Had he ever seen it? No. Of course not. Just a trick of the light. Somehow he'd subconsciously crossed the spooky disappearing janitor with Lauren's story of the old house and started seeing ghosts. He grinned at himself.

"Drake?" Alicia saw his concern.

"Weird," he said. "I just want to check upstairs." The hairs on the back of his neck still stood on end. At least, those that remained.

"Why?"

"Nah, don't worry—"

The house rumbled. The street shook. The team stared at each other in surprise as a small earthquake shook the city. After a moment the reverberations stopped but it was long enough for Drake to change his mind.

No need to check upstairs. Stupid, frazzled brain playing

tricks. He was now certain all he'd seen was a patch of light, a play of color.

"Hayden," he said. "Let's get the hell out of Louisiana."

"There is one last item to discuss," she said.

"Oh aye? Spit it out then, love."

"Webb ranted a lot. He was clearly a special case headed for the nuthouse. But he was also a stalker, a watcher, and a gatherer of information. He said things about us that may or may not be true. But guys, whatever it is, and true or not, a nasty little stockpile exists somewhere and really needs to be found."

Drake understood her fears. Webb had taped and recorded everyone except Mai and Dahl, he thought. In compromising ways or not, it all had to be unearthed and destroyed.

"We'll get it done, Hayden."

"And the things he said about us . . ."

"Sound like our own crosses to bear," Drake said. "But if anyone wants to share I for one will not back away."

"And me," Dahl said. "Anything."

The team voiced their support, their agreement and their warmth. Drake wished it could always be like this as, he imagined, so did every mother, father, brother and sister at the perfect, content family moment.

But life changed everything.

"So," he said. "Shall we see what tomorrow brings?"

THE END

Please read on for more information on the future of the Matt Drake world:

The Treasures of Saint Germain

I hope you enjoyed reading this book as much as I enjoyed writing it. Drake's story will continue soon with the release of part 15. Next up will be Alicia 3 in the very near future. The Gold Team have been quiet for a while and I'm looking forward to getting them into lots of trouble in what might be their final outing. If you want more Gold Team after Alicia 3, please drop me a message on Facebook or through email to let me know. I'd love to write a part 4.

If you don't already receive my emails and would like to sign up to my new Mailing List please follow this link:
http://eepurl.com/b-xWeT

First hand, release-related news, updates and giveaways can be found on my Facebook page—
https://www.facebook.com/davidleadbeaternovels/

And remember:
Reviews are everything to an author and essential to the future of the Matt Drake, Alicia Myles and other series. Please consider leaving even a few lines at Amazon, it will make all the difference.

Other Books by David Leadbeater:

The Matt Drake Series
The Bones of Odin (Matt Drake #1)
The Blood King Conspiracy (Matt Drake #2)
The Gates of hell (Matt Drake 3)
The Tomb of the Gods (Matt Drake #4)
Brothers in Arms (Matt Drake #5)
The Swords of Babylon (Matt Drake #6)
Blood Vengeance (Matt Drake #7)
Last Man Standing (Matt Drake #8)
The Plagues of Pandora (Matt Drake #9)
The Lost Kingdom (Matt Drake #10)
The Ghost Ships of Arizona (Matt Drake #11)
The Last Bazaar (Matt Drake #12)

The Alicia Myles Series
Aztec Gold (Alicia Myles #1)
Crusader's Gold (Alicia Myles #2)

The Torsten Dahl Thriller Series
Stand Your Ground (Dahl Thriller #1)

The Disavowed Series:
The Razor's Edge (Disavowed #1)
In Harm's Way (Disavowed #2)
Threat Level: Red (Disavowed #3)

The Chosen Few Series
Chosen (The Chosen Trilogy #1)
Guardians (The Chosen Tribology #2)

The Treasures of Saint Germain

Short Stories
Walking with Ghosts (A short story)
A Whispering of Ghosts (A short story)

Connect with the author on Twitter: @dleadbeater2011
Visit the author's website: **www.davidleadbeater.com**

All helpful, genuine comments are welcome. I would love to hear from you.
davidleadbeater2011@hotmail.co.uk

Printed in Poland
by Amazon Fulfillment
Poland Sp. z o.o., Wrocław